THE BEST SHORT STORIES

OF

Jack London

THE BEST SHORT STORIES
OF
Jack London

With an introduction by
EUGENE BURDICK

FAWCETT PREMIER • NEW YORK

Introduction

Once, years ago, I visited with a German on his tiny island in the Southern Solomons. He had come here long before, had married a coal-black Melanesian princess and, through her, he owned the island. He had once been a sailor, but had jumped a sailing ship because of harsh treatment. He was a tough and wiry man. He ran his island like a ship . . . and a taut one. It was every bit as taut as his ship. He lived a life which was thin by modern standards, but rich in one thing: independence.

He had two possessions he valued greatly. One was an old and rust-stained sextant; the second was an old yellowed photograph. The picture had four people in it, but their features were blurred by time and the pitiless quiet assault of the tropics. Even so the faces were vaguely familiar.

"That is me, that is my wife, that is Jack London, and that is his wife, Charmian," the German said. "They were here on a boat called the Snark. He said he was a writer. We piloted them to Lord Howe Reefs."

"He was a writer," I said. "A very famous one."

"No, he was a sailor," the German said with a heavy finality. "Maybe he wrote, but he was a sailor first. He held the pen like a marlinespike."

The German was partly right, but he missed a great deal. London did, indeed, often write with the power of the marlinespike, but he could also write with the delicacy of a whaler doing scrimshaw on a whale's tooth.

London was a marvelous instrument of experience. He was possessed of an uncanny perception of the ordinary as well as the bizarre. Most of what he experienced led him to "write with a marlinespike."

First, he was a man of the Pacific. All of the stories in this collection take place either upon the vast waters of the Pacific or on the lands that border it. In the North it was bitterly cold. Indeed, the cold becomes a presence in London's stories . . . a thing that pursues every man, penalizes him brutally for his mistakes, is cunning and utterly impartial.

In the eerie story, "To Build a Fire," the reader at first seems to be viewing only a man and a dog moving across a snow-covered landscape. But then the cold begins to work: tobacco juice hardens into amber crystal on the man's chin, one finger after another loses sensation, matches begin to take on a mystical importance . . . and then the man makes his first tiny mistake. It takes him time to realize that the mistake is irrevocable, that the string of his personal guillotine has been cut and the blade is sliding slowly towards him. In the end he holds the mass of matches between his frozen hands, smells them burning his flesh . . . and loses.

When the story is over, the reader understands about cold. Not just everyday cold, the kind which modern arctic clothing and Primus stoves and alcohol pellets can overcome. This is a cold so ominous and relentless that it takes on a personality.

In the South Seas, where the water is warm and the islands are lush, the Pacific was no more kind. The waters were uncharted, sharks were everywhere, passages had to be shot using sail only, typhoons loomed up suddenly and without warning. Even today, when the Pacific has been largely tamed by radar and fathometers and planes and engines, it is a deadly place. In London's time Pacific sailors suffered casualties as regularly as soldiers in a fighting platoon. The reefs of Rarotonga, Noumea, the thousands of little islands of the Molaccas and Borneo were studded with the wrecks of unlucky or unskillful sailors. No one instituted a search for a missing vessel . . . everyone knew its fate. In any case the reaches were too vast to search.

In the superb "The Pearls of Parlay," London writes of a typhoon, that most difficult of things to describe. Most writers skirt the subject if they can. A typhoon is one of the most awesome things known to man. All the atomic bombs so far exploded do not equal the energy which a season's typhoons expend against atolls, high islands, reefs and ships. London's description is masterful, an exercise in economy and the glancing insight. The barometer begins to fall, the sea falls flat, there is the sudden approach of a film of quiet black water, and suddenly a whole lagoon full of vessels is in mortal danger. In the end London does the impossible: he makes the wind visible, gives it palpable character.

The men who roamed London's Pacific were a strange, savage and remorseless type. They were the wolves of their time, the men who took great risks, asked no quarter, gave none. The whole theme of "The Heathen" rests upon the surprising fact that one man would risk his existence to save another. When it occurred, the two men were locked together for the rest of their lives. When the end comes and Otoo goes under the water, blood gushing from the shark-severed stubs of both hands, London has said more than a hundred books could say on the character of the men who lived in the old days on the Pacific.

There are few women in these stories. This is not because London disliked women. Quite the contrary. In his own person he was enormously attractive to women and he reciprocated. Some of his affairs enraged the Puritanical morals of his time. But in London's Pacific there were, in simple fact, very few women. Whether they were the whores of Woomooloo or the "demis" of Tahiti or a Parisian ballerina, they are "off-stage" because the Pacific was a masculine place. "The Wit of Porportuk" is an exception, and there the beautiful fawn-like girl El-Soo is made to pay a price as grim and brutal as that suffered by any man.

This is not a world which lends itself to delicate writing. It is a world in which a fist is blunt and an instrument, hunger is a fearful gripe in the bowels, the whisky is eye-watering. But despite the subject matter, London could and did write with a touch that was almost exquisite. In "Lost Face" there are, for example, all of the elements of cruelty and implacability which London knew so well. But there is much more. There is an aching nostalgia for things that might have been, the calculation of a fragile balance between life and death. In "A Piece of Steak," London depicts a battered pug with a softness of detail and an eye for the human condition which is very rare indeed.

In a way the German was right. London did write with a marlinespike, but he could also catch the tiny fragment of authenticity which passes so quickly it is almost lost. In their sum, however, they make London much more than a ham-fisted writer.

London's world will never exist again. The web of law is too tightly drawn, science has made us too invulnerable to the way of nature. But it is precisely for this reason that London's stature as a writer has grown. He can take that lost and savage world and make it live and move for a modern reader. For this reason, if no other, he will not soon be forgotten. It is the mark of the master writer.

—EUGENE BURDICK
University of California

Contents

THE BEST SHORT STORIES

OF

Jack London

To Build a Fire

DAY HAD BROKEN cold and gray, exceedingly cold and gray, when the man turned aside from the main Yukon trail and climbed the high earth-bank, where a dim and little-travelled trail led eastward through the fat spruce timberland. It was a steep bank, and he paused for breath at the top, excusing the act to himself by looking at his watch. It was nine o'clock. There was no sun nor hint of sun, though there was not a cloud in the sky. It was a clear day, and yet there seemed an intangible pall over the face of things, a subtle gloom that made the day dark, and that was due to the absence of sun. This fact did not worry the man. He was used to the lack of sun. It had been days since he had seen the sun, and he knew that a few more days must pass before that cheerful orb, due south, would just peep above the sky line and dip immediately from view.

The man flung a look back along the way he had come. The Yukon lay a mile wide and hidden under three feet of ice. On top of this ice were as many feet of snow. It was all pure white, rolling in gentle undulations where the ice jams of the freeze-up had formed. North and south, as far as his eye could see, it was unbroken white, save for a dark hairline that curved and twisted from around the spruce-covered island to the south, and that curved and twisted away into the north, where it disappeared behind another spruce-covered island. This dark hairline was the trail—the main trail—that led south five hundred miles to the Chilcoot Pass, Dyea, and salt water; and that led north seventy miles to Dawson, and still on to the north a thousand miles to Nulato, and finally to St. Michael, on Bering Sea, a thousand miles and half a thousand more.

But all this—the mysterious, far-reaching hairline trail, the absence of sun from the sky, the tremendous cold, and the strangeness and weirdness of it all—made no impression on

the man. It was not because he was long used to it. He was a
newcomer in the land, a *chechaquo*, and this was his first
winter. The trouble with him was that he was without im-
agination. He was quick and alert in the things of life, but
only in the things, and not in the significances. Fifty degrees below zero meant eighty-odd degrees of frost. Such
fact impressed him as being cold and uncomfortable, and
that was all. It did not lead him to meditate upon his frailty
as a creature of temperature, and upon man's frailty in
general, able only to live within certain narrow limits of heat
and cold; and from there on it did not lead him to the con-
jectural field of immortality and man's place in the universe.
Fifty degrees below zero stood for a bite of frost that hurt
and that must be guarded against by the use of mittens, ear
flaps, warm moccasins, and thick socks. Fifty degrees below
zero was to him just precisely fifty degrees below zero. That
there should be anything more to it than that was a thought
that never entered his head.

As he turned to go on, he spat speculatively. There was a
sharp, explosive crackle that startled him. He spat again. And
again, in the air, before it could fall to the snow, the spittle
crackled. He knew that at fifty below spittle crackled on the
snow, but this spittle had crackled in the air. Undoubtedly
it was colder than fifty below—how much colder he did not
know. But the temperature did not matter. He was bound for
the old claim on the left fork of Henderson Creek, where
the boys were already. They had come over across the divide
from the Indian Creek country, while he had come the round-
about way to take a look at the possibilities of getting out
logs in the spring from the islands in the Yukon. He would
be in to camp by six o'clock; a bit after dark, it was true,
but the boys would be there, a fire would be going, and a hot
supper would be ready. As for lunch, he pressed his hand
against the protruding bundle under his jacket. It was also
under his shirt, wrapped up in a handkerchief and lying
against the naked skin. It was the only way to keep the
biscuits from freezing. He smiled agreeably to himself as
he thought of those biscuits, each cut open and sopped in
bacon grease, and each enclosing a generous slice of fried
bacon.

He plunged in among the big spruce trees. The trail was
faint. A foot of snow had fallen since the last sled had passed
over, and he was glad he was without a sled, travelling light.

In fact, he carried nothing but the lunch wrapped in the handkerchief. He was surprised, however, at the cold. It certainly was cold, he concluded, as he rubbed his numb nose and cheekbones with his mittened hand. He was a warm-whiskered man, but the hair on his face did not protect the high cheekbones and the eager nose that thrust itself aggressively into the frosty air.

At the man's heels trotted a dog, a big native husky, the proper wolf dog, gray-coated and without any visible or temperamental difference from its brother, the wild wolf. The animal was depressed by the tremendous cold. It knew that it was no time for travelling. Its instinct told it a truer tale than was told to the man by the man's judgment. In reality, it was not merely colder than fifty below zero; it was colder than sixty below, than seventy below. It was seventy-five below zero. Since the freezing point is thirty-two above zero, it meant that one hundred and seven degrees of frost obtained. The dog did not know anything about thermometers. Possibly in its brain there was no sharp consciousness of a condition of very cold such as was in the man's brain. But the brute had its instinct. It experienced a vague but menacing apprehension that subdued it and made it slink along at the man's heels, and that made it question eagerly every unwonted movement of the man as if expecting him to go into camp or to seek shelter somewhere and build a fire. The dog had learned fire, and it wanted fire, or else to burrow under the snow and cuddle its warmth away from the air.

The frozen moisture of its breathing had settled on its fur in a fine powder of frost, and especially were its jowls, muzzle, and eyelashes whitened by its crystalled breath. The man's red beard and mustache were likewise frosted, but more solidly, the deposit taking the form of ice and increasing with every warm, moist breath he exhaled. Also, the man was chewing tobacco, and the muzzle of ice held his lips so rigidly that he was unable to clear his chin when he expelled the juice. The result was that a crystal beard of the color and solidity of amber was increasing its length on his chin. If he fell down it would shatter itself, like glass, into brittle fragments. But he did not mind the appendage. It was the penalty all tobacco chewers paid in that country, and he had been out before in two cold snaps. They had not been so cold as this, he knew, but by the spirit thermometer

at Sixty Mile he knew they had been registered at fifty below
and at fifty-five.

He held on through the level stretch of woods for several
miles, crossed a wide flat of nigger heads, and dropped
down a bank to the frozen bed of a small stream. This was
Henderson Creek, and he knew he was ten miles from the
forks. He looked at his watch. It was ten o'clock. He was
making four miles an hour, and he calculated that he would
arrive at the forks at half-past twelve. He decided to cele-
brate that event by eating his lunch there.

The dog dropped in again at his heels, with a tail drooping
discouragement, as the man swung along the creek bed. The
furrow of the old sled trail was plainly visible, but a dozen
inches of snow covered the marks of the last runners. In a
month no man had come up or down that silent creek. The
man held steadily on. He was not much given to thinking, and just then particularly he had nothing to think about
save that he would eat lunch at the forks and that at six
o'clock he would be in camp with the boys. There was nobody to talk to; and, had there been, speech would have
been impossible because of the ice muzzle on his mouth. So
he continued monotonously to chew tobacco and to increase
the length of his amber beard.

Once in a while the thought reiterated itself that it was
very cold and that he had never experienced such cold. As
he walked along he rubbed his cheekbones and nose with
the back of his mittened hand. He did this automatically,
now and again changing hands. But, rub as he would, the
instant he stopped his cheekbones went numb, and the following instant the end of his nose went numb. He was sure
to frost his cheeks; he knew that, and experienced a pang of
regret that he had not devised a nose strap of the sort Bud
wore in cold snaps. Such a strap passed across the cheeks, as
well, and saved them. But it didn't matter much, after all.
What were frosted cheeks? A bit painful, that was all; they
were never serious.

Empty as the man's mind was of thoughts, he was keenly
observant, and he noticed the changes in the creek, the
curves and bends and timber jams, and always he sharply
noted where he placed his feet. Once, coming around a
bend, he shied abruptly, like a startled horse, curved away
from the place where he had been walking, and retreated
several paces back along the trail. The creek he knew was

frozen clear to the bottom—no creek could contain water in that arctic winter—but he knew also that there were springs that bubbled out from the hillsides and ran along under the snow and on top the ice of the creek. He knew that the coldest snaps never froze these springs, and he knew likewise their danger. They were traps. They hid pools of water under the snow that might be three inches deep, or three feet. Sometimes a skin of ice half an inch thick covered them, and in turn was covered by the snow. Sometimes there were alternate layers of water and ice skin, so that when one broke through he kept on breaking through for a while, sometimes wetting himself to the waist.

That was why he had shied in such panic. He had felt the give under his feet and heard the crackle of a snow-hidden ice skin. And to get his feet wet in such a temperature meant trouble and danger. At the very least it meant delay, for he would be forced to stop and build a fire, and under its protection to bare his feet while he dried his socks and moccasins. He stood and studied the creek bed and its banks, and decided that the flow of water came from the right. He reflected awhile, rubbing his nose and cheeks, then skirted to the left, stepping gingerly and testing the footing for each step. Once clear of the danger, he took a fresh chew of tobacco and swung along at his four-mile gait.

In the course of the next two hours he came upon several similar traps. Usually the snow above the hidden pools had a sunken, candied appearance that advertised the danger. Once again, however, he had a close call; and once, suspecting danger, he compelled the dog to go on in front. The dog did not want to go. It hung back until the man shoved it forward, and then it went quickly across the white, unbroken surface. Suddenly it broke through, floundered to one side, and got away to firmer footing. It had wet its forefeet and legs, and almost immediately the water that clung to it turned to ice. It made quick efforts to lick the ice off its legs, then dropped down in the snow and began to bite out the ice that had formed between the toes. This was matter of instinct. To permit the ice to remain would mean sore feet. It did not know this. It merely obeyed the mysterious prompting that arose from the deep crypts of its being. But the man knew, having achieved a judgment on the subject, and he removed the mitten from his right hand and helped tear out the ice particles. He did not expose his fingers more than a minute, and was astonished at the swift numbness that smote them. It certainly was cold. He pulled on the mitten hastily, and beat the hand savagely across his chest.

At twelve o'clock the day was at its brightest. Yet the sun was too far south on its winter journey to clear the horizon. The bulge of the earth intervened between it and Henderson Creek, where the man walked under a clear sky at noon and cast no shadow. At half-past twelve, to the minute, he arrived at the forks of the creek. He was pleased at the speed he had made. If he kept it up, he would certainly be with the boys by six. He unbuttoned his jacket and shirt and drew forth his lunch. The action consumed no more than a quarter of a minute, yet in that brief moment the numbness laid hold of the exposed fingers. He did not put the mitten on, but, instead, struck the fingers a dozen sharp smashes against his leg. Then he sat down on a snow-covered log to eat. The sting that followed upon the striking of his fingers against his leg ceased so quickly that he was startled. He had had no chance to take a bit of biscuit. He struck the fingers repeatedly and returned them to the mitten, baring the other hand for the purpose of eating. He tried to take a mouthful, but the ice muzzle prevented. He had forgotten to build a fire and thaw out. He chuckled at his foolishness, and as he chuckled he noted the numbness creeping into the exposed fingers. Also, he noted that the stinging which had first come to his toes when he sat down was already passing away. He wondered whether the toes were warm or numb. He moved them inside the moccasins and decided that they were numb.

He pulled the mitten on hurriedly and stood up. He was a bit frightened. He stamped up and down until the stinging returned into the feet. It certainly was cold, was his thought. That man from Sulphur Creek had spoken the truth when telling how cold it sometimes got in the country. And he had laughed at him at the time! That showed one must not be too sure of things. There was no mistake about it, it was cold. He strode up and down, stamping his feet and threshing his arms, until reassured by the returning warmth. Then he got out matches and proceeded to make a fire. From the undergrowth, where high water of the previous spring had lodged a supply of seasoned twigs, he got his firewood. Working carefully from a small beginning, he soon had a roaring fire, over which he thawed the ice from his face and in the protection of which he ate his biscuits. For the moment the cold of space was outwitted. The dog took satisfaction in the fire, stretching out close enough for warmth and far enough away to escape being singed.

When the man had finished, he filled his pipe and took his comfortable time over a smoke. Then he pulled on his mittens, settled the ear flaps of his cap firmly about his ears, and took the creek trail up the left fork. The dog was disappointed and yearned back toward the fire. This man did not know cold. Possibly all the generations of his ancestry had been ignorant of cold, of real cold, of cold one hundred and seven degrees below freezing point. But the dog knew; all its ancestry knew, and it had inherited the knowledge. And it knew that it was not good to walk abroad in such fearful cold. It was the time to lie snug in a hole in the snow and wait for a curtain of cloud to be drawn across the face of outer space whence this cold came. On the other hand, there was no keen intimacy between the dog and the man. The one was the toil slave of the other, and the only caresses it had ever received were the caresses of the whip lash and of harsh and menacing throat sounds that threatened the whip lash. So the dog made no effort to communicate its apprehension to the man. It was not concerned in the welfare of the man; it was for its own sake that it yearned back toward the fire. But the man whistled, and spoke to it with the sound of whip lashes, and the dog swung in at the man's heels and followed after.

The man took a chew of tobacco and proceeded to start a new amber beard. Also, his moist breath quickly powdered with white his mustache, eyebrows, and lashes. There did not seem to be so many springs on the left fork of the Henderson, and for half an hour the man saw no signs of any. And then it happened. At a place where there were no signs, where the soft, unbroken snow seemed to advertise solidity beneath, the man broke through. It was not deep. He wet himself halfway to the knees before he floundered out to the firm crust.

He was angry, and cursed his luck aloud. He had hoped to get into camp with the boys at six o'clock, and this would delay him an hour, for he would have to build a fire and dry out his footgear. This was imperative at that low temperature—he knew that much; and he turned aside to the bank, which he climbed. On top, tangled in the underbrush about the trunks of several small spruce trees, was a highwater deposit of dry firewood—sticks and twigs, principally, but also larger portions of seasoned branches and fine, dry, last year's grasses. He threw down several large pieces on top of the snow. This served for a foundation and prevented the young flame from drowning itself in the snow it otherwise would melt. The flame he got by touching a match to a small shred of birch bark that he took from his pocket. This burned even more readily than paper. Placing it on the foundation, he fed the young flame with wisps of dry grass and with the tiniest dry twigs.

He worked slowly and carefully, keenly aware of his danger. Gradually, as the flame grew stronger, he increased the size of the twigs with which he fed it. He squatted in the snow, pulling the twigs out from their entanglement in the brush and feeding directly to the flame. He knew there must be no failure. When it is seventy-five below zero, a man must not fail in his first attempt to build a fire—that is, if his feet are wet. If his feet are dry, and he fails, he can run along the trail for half a mile and restore his circulation. But the circulation of wet and freezing feet cannot be restored by running when it is seventy-five below. No matter how fast he runs, the wet feet will freeze the harder.

All this the man knew. The old-timer on Sulphur Creek had told him about it the previous fall, and now he was appreciating the advice. Already all sensation had gone out of his feet. To build the fire he had been forced to remove his mittens, and the fingers had quickly gone numb. His pace of four miles an hour had kept his heart pumping blood to the surface of his body and to all the extremities. But the instant he stopped, the action of the pump eased down. The cold of space smote the unprotected tip of the planet, and he, being on that unprotected tip, received the full force of the blow. The blood of his body recoiled before it. The blood was alive, like the dog, and like the dog it wanted to hide away and cover itself up from the fearful cold. So long as he walked four miles an hour, he pumped that blood, willy-nilly, to the surface; but now it ebbed away and sank down into the recesses of his body. The extremities were the first to feel its absence. His wet feet froze the faster, and his exposed fingers numbed the faster, though they had not yet begun to freeze. Nose and cheeks were already freezing, while the skin of all his body chilled as it lost its blood.

But he was safe. Toes and nose and cheeks would be only touched by the frost, for the fire was beginning to burn with strength. He was feeding it with twigs the size of his finger. In another minute he would be able to feed it with branches the size of his wrist, and then he could remove his wet footgear, and, while it dried, he could keep his naked feet warm by the fire, rubbing them at first, of course, with snow. The fire was a success. He was safe. He remembered the advice of the old-timer on Sulphur Creek, and smiled. The old-timer had been very serious in laying down the law that no man must travel alone in the Klondike after fifty below. Well, here he was; he had had the accident; he was alone; and he had saved himself. Those old-timers were rather womanish, some of them, he thought. All a man had to do was to keep his head, and he was all right. Any man who was a man could travel alone. But it was surprising, the rapidity with which his cheeks and nose were freezing. And he had not thought his fingers could go lifeless in so short a time. Lifeless they were, for he could scarcely make them move together to grip a twig, and they seemed remote from his body and from him. When he touched a twig, he had to look and see whether or not he had hold of it. The wires were pretty well down between him and his finger ends.

All of which counted for little. There was the fire, snapping and crackling and promising life with every dancing flame. He started to untie his moccasins. They were coated with ice; the thick German socks were like sheaths of iron halfway to the knees; and the moccasion strings were like rods of steel all twisted and knotted as by some conflagration. For a moment he tugged with his numb fingers, then, realizing the folly of it, he drew his sheath knife.

But before he could cut the strings, it happened. It was his own fault or, rather, his mistake. He should not have built the fire under the spruce tree. He should have built it in the open. But it had been easier to pull the twigs from the brush and drop them directly on the fire. Now the tree under which he had done this carried a weight of snow on its boughs. No wind had blown for weeks, and each bough was fully freighted. Each time he had pulled a twig he had communicated a slight agitation to the tree—an imperceptible agitation, so far as he was concerned, but an agitation sufficient to bring about the disaster. High up in the tree one bough capsized its load of snow. This fell on the boughs beneath, capsizing them. This process continued, spreading out and involving the whole tree. It grew like an avalanche, and it descended without warning upon the man and the fire, and the fire was blotted out! Where it had burned was a mantle of fresh and disordered snow.

The man was shocked. It was as though he had just heard his own sentence of death. For a moment he sat and stared at the spot where the fire had been. Then he grew very calm. Perhaps the old-timer on Sulphur Creek was right. If he had only had a trail mate he would have been in no danger now. The trail mate could have built the fire. Well, it was up to him to build the fire over again, and this second time there must be no failure. Even if he succeeded, he would most likely lose some toes. His feet must be badly frozen by now, and there would be some time before the second fire was ready.

Such were his thoughts, but he did not sit and think them. He was busy all the time they were passing through his mind. He made a new foundation for a fire, this time in the open, where no treacherous tree could blot it out. Next he gathered dry grasses and tiny twigs from the high-water flotsam. He could not bring his fingers together to pull them out, but he was able to gather them by the handful. In this way he got many rotten twigs and bits of green moss that were undesirable, but it was the best he could do. He worked methodically, even collecting an armful of the larger branches to be used later when the fire gathered strength. And all the while the dog sat and watched him, a certain yearning wistfulness in its eyes, for it looked upon him as the fire provider, and the fire was slow in coming.

When all was ready, the man reached in his pocket for a second piece of birch bark. He knew the bark was there, and, though he could not feel it with his fingers, he could hear its crisp rustling as he fumbled for it. Try as he would, he could not clutch hold of it. And all the time, in his consciousness, was the knowledge that each instant his feet were freezing. This thought tended to put him in a panic, but he fought against it and kept calm. He pulled on his mittens with his teeth, and threshed his arms back and forth, beating his hands with all his might against his sides.

He did this sitting down, and he stood up to do it; and all the while the dog sat in the snow, its wolf brush of a tail curled around warmly over its forefeet, its sharp wolf ears pricked forward intently as it watched the man. And the man, as he beat and threshed with his arms and hands, felt a great surge of envy as he regarded the creature that was warm and secure in its natural covering.

After a time he was aware of the first faraway signals of sensation in his beaten fingers. The faint tingling grew stronger till it evolved into a stinging ache that was excruciating, but which the man hailed with satisfaction. He stripped the mitten from his right hand and fetched forth the birch bark. The exposed fingers were quickly going numb again. Next he brought out his bunch of sulphur matches. But the tremendous cold had already driven the life out of his fingers. In his effort to separate one match from the others, the whole bunch fell in the snow. He tried to pick it out of the snow, but failed. The dead fingers could neither touch nor clutch. He was very careful. He drove the thought of his freezing feet, and nose, and cheeks, out of his mind, devoting his whole soul to the matches. He watched, using the sense of vision in place of that of touch, and when he saw his fingers on each side the bunch, he closed them—that is, he willed to close them, for the wires were down, and the fingers did not obey. He pulled the mitten on the right hand, and beat it fiercely against his knee. Then, with both mittened hands, he scooped the bunch of matches, along with much snow, into his lap. Yet he was no better off.

After some manipulation he managed to get the bunch between the heels of his mittened hands. In this fashion he carried it to his mouth. The ice crackled and snapped when by a violent effort he opened his mouth. He drew the lower jaw in, curled the upper lip out of the way, and scraped the bunch with his upper teeth in order to separate a match. He succeeded in getting one, which he dropped on his lap. He was no better off. He could not pick it up. Then he devised a way. He picked it up in his teeth and scratched it on his leg. Twenty times he scratched before he succeeded in lighting it. As it flamed he held it with his teeth to the birch bark. But the burning brimstone went up his nostrils and into his lungs, causing him to cough spasmodically. The match fell into the snow and went out.

The old-timer on Sulphur Creek was right, he thought in the moment of controlled despair that ensued: after fifty below, a man should travel with a partner. He beat his hands, but failed in exciting any sensation. Suddenly he bared both hands, removing the mittens with his teeth. He caught the whole bunch between the heels of his hands. His arm muscles not being frozen enabled him to press the hand heels tightly against the matches. Then he scratched the bunch along his leg. It flared into flame, seventy sulphur matches at once! There was no wind to blow them out. He kept his head to one side to escape the strangling fumes, and held the blazing bunch to the birch bark. As he so held it, he became aware of sensation in his hand. His flesh was burning. He could smell it. Deep down below the surface he could feel it. The sensation developed into pain that grew acute. And still he endured it, holding the flame of the matches clumsily to the bark that would not light readily because his own burning hands were in the way, absorbing most of the flame.

At last, when he could endure no more, he jerked his hands apart. The blazing matches fell sizzling into the snow, but the birch bark was alight. He began laying dry grasses and the tiniest twigs on the flame. He could not pick and choose, for he had to lift the fuel between the heels of his hands. Small pieces of rotten wood and green moss clung to the twigs, and he bit them off as well as he could with his teeth. He cherished the flame carefully and awkwardly. It meant life, and it must not perish. The withdrawal of blood from the surface of his body now made him begin to shiver, and he grew more awkward. A large piece of green moss fell squarely on the little fire. He tried to poke it out with his fingers, but his shivering frame made him poke too far, and he disrupted the nucleus of the little fire, the burning grasses and tiny twigs separating and scattering. He tried to poke them together again, but in spite of the tenseness of the effort, his shivering got away with him, and the twigs were hopelessly scattered. Each twig gushed a puff of smoke and went out. The fire provider had failed. As he looked apathetically about him, his eyes chanced on the dog, sitting across the ruins of the fire from him, in the snow, making restless, hunching movements, slightly lifting one forefoot and then the other, shifting its weight back and forth on them with wistful eagerness.

The sight of the dog put a wild idea into his head. He remembered the tale of the man, caught in a blizzard, who killed a steer and crawled inside the carcass, and so was saved. He would kill the dog and bury his hands in the warm body until the numbness went out of them. Then he could build another fire. He spoke to the dog, calling it to him; but in his voice was a strange note of fear that frightened the animal, who had never known the man to speak in such way before. Something was the matter, and its suspicious nature sensed danger—it knew not what danger, but somewhere, somehow, in its brain arose an apprehension of the man. It flattened its ears down at the sound of the man's voice, and its restless, hunching movements and the liftings and shiftings of its forefeet became more pronounced; but it would not come to the man. He got on his hands and knees and crawled toward the dog. This unusual posture again excited suspicion, and the animal sidled mincingly away.

The man sat up in the snow for a moment and struggled for calmness. Then he pulled on his mittens, by means of his teeth, and got upon his feet. He glanced down at first in order to assure himself that he was really standing up, for the absence of sensation in his feet left him unrelated to the earth. His erect position in itself started to drive the webs of suspicion from the dog's mind; and when he spoke peremptorily, with the sound of whip lashes in his voice, the dog rendered its customary allegiance and came to him. As it came within reaching distance, the man lost his control. His arms flashed out to the dog, and he experienced genuine surprise when he discovered that his hands could not clutch, that there was neither bend nor feeling in the fingers. He had forgotten for the moment that they were frozen and that they were freezing more and more. All this happened quickly, and before the animal could get away, he encircled its body with his arms. He sat down in the snow, and in this fashion held the dog, while it snarled and whined and struggled.

But it was all he could do, hold its body encircled in his arms and sit there. He realized that he could not kill the dog. There was no way to do it. With his helpless hands he could neither draw nor hold his sheath knife nor

throttle the animal. He released it, and it plunged wildly
away, with tail between its legs, and still snarling. It halted
forty feet away and surveyed him curiously, with ears sharply pricked forward.

The man looked down at his hands in order to locate
them, and found them hanging on the ends of his arms.
It struck him as curious that one should have to use his
eyes in order to find out where his hands were. He began
threshing his arms back and forth, beating the mittened
hands against his sides. He did this for five minutes, violently, and his heart pumped enough blood up to the surface to put a stop to his shivering. But no sensation was
aroused in the hands. He had an impression that they hung
like weights on the ends of his arms, but when he tried
to run the impression down, he could not find it.

A certain fear of death, dull and oppressive, came to him.
This fear quickly became poignant as he realized that it
was no longer a mere matter of freezing his fingers and
toes, or of losing his hands and feet, but that it was a
matter of life and death with the chances against him. This
threw him into a panic, and he turned and ran up the
creek bed along the old, dim trail. The dog joined in behind and kept up with him. He ran blindly, without intention, in fear such as he had never known in his life. Slowly,
as he plowed and floundered through the snow, he began
to see things again—the banks of the creek, the old timber
jams, the leafless aspens, and the sky. The running made
him feel better. He did not shiver. Maybe, if he ran on,
his feet would thaw out; and, anyway, if he ran far enough,
he would reach camp and the boys. Without doubt he
would lose some fingers and toes and some of his face; but
the boys would take care of him, and save the rest of him
when he got there. And at the same time there was another
thought in his mind that said he would never get to the
camp and the boys; that it was too many miles away, that
the freezing had too great a start on him, and that he
would soon be stiff and dead. This thought he kept in the
background and refused to consider. Sometimes it pushed
itself forward and demanded to be heard, but he thrust it
back and strove to think of other things.

It struck him as curious that he could run at all on feet
so frozen that he could not feel them when they struck
the earth and took the weight of his body. He seemed to

himself to skim along above the surface, and to have no connection with the earth. Somewhere he had once seen a winged Mercury, and he wondered if Mercury felt as he felt when skimming over the earth.

His theory of running until he reached camp and the boys had one flaw in it: he lacked the endurance. Several times he stumbled, and finally he tottered, crumpled up, and fell. When he tried to rise, he failed. He must sit and rest, he decided, and next time he would merely walk and keep on going. As he sat and regained his breath, he noted that he was feeling quite warm and comfortable. He was not shivering, and it even seemed that a warm glow had come to his chest and trunk. And yet, when he touched his nose or cheeks, there was no sensation. Running would not thaw them out. Nor would it thaw out his hands and feet. Then the thought came to him that the frozen portions of his body must be extending. He tried to keep this thought down, to forget it, to think of something else; he was aware of the panicky feeling that it caused, and he was afraid of the panic. But the thought asserted itself, and persisted, until it produced a vision of his body totally frozen. This was too much, and he made another wild run along the trail. Once he slowed down to a walk, but the thought of the freezing extending itself made him run again.

And all the time the dog ran with him, at his heels. When he fell down a second time, it curled its tail over its forefeet and sat in front of him, facing him, curiously eager and intent. The warmth and security of the animal angered him, and he cursed it till it flattened down its ears appeasingly. This time the shivering came more quickly upon the man. He was losing in his battle with the frost. It was creeping into his body from all sides. The thought of it drove him on, but he ran no more than a hundred feet, when he staggered and pitched headlong. It was his last panic. When he had recovered his breath and control, he sat up and entertained in his mind the conception of meeting death with dignity. However, the conception did not come to him in such terms. His idea of it was that he had been making a fool of himself, running around like a chicken with its head cut off—such was the simile that occurred to him. Well, he was bound to freeze anyway, and he might as well take it decently. With this new-found peace of mind came the first glimmerings of drowsiness. A good idea, he thought, to sleep off to death. It was like taking an anesthetic. Freezing was not so bad as people thought. There were lots worse ways to die.

He pictured the boys finding his body next day. Suddenly he found himself with them, coming along the trail and looking for himself. And, still with them, he came around a turn in the trail and found himself lying in the snow. He did not belong with himself any more, for even then he was out of himself, standing with the boys and looking at himself in the snow. It certainly was cold, was his thought. When he got back to the States he could tell the folks what real cold was. He drifted on from this to a vision of the old-timer on Sulphur Creek. He could see him quite clearly, warm and comfortable, and smoking a pipe.

"You were right, old hoss; you were right," the man mumbled to the old-timer of Sulphur Creek.

Then the man drowsed off into what seemed to him the most comfortable and satisfying sleep he had ever known. The dog sat facing him and waiting. The brief day drew to a close in a long, slow twilight. There were no signs of a fire to be made, and, besides, never in the dog's experience had it known a man to sit like that in the snow and make no fire. As the twilight drew on, its eager yearning for the fire mastered it, and with a great lifting and shifting of forefeet, it whined softly, then flattened its ears down in anticipation of being chidden by the man. But the man remained silent. Later the dog whined loudly. And still later it crept close to the man and caught the scent of death. This made the animal bristle and back away. A little longer it delayed, howling under the stars that leaped and danced and shone brightly in the cold sky. Then it turned and trotted up the trail in the direction of the camp it knew, where were the other food providers and fire providers.

An Odyssey of the North

THE SLEDS were singing their eternal lament to the creaking of the harnesses and the tinkling bells of the leaders; but the men and dogs were tired and made no sound. The trail was heavy with new-fallen snow, and they had come far, and the runners, burdened with flintlike quarters of frozen moose, clung tenaciously to the unpacked surface and held back with a stubbornness almost human. Darkness was coming on, but there was no camp to pitch that night. The snow fell gently through the pulseless air, not in flakes, but in tiny frost crystals of delicate design. It was very warm—barely ten below zero—and the men did not mind. Meyers and Bettles had raised their ear flaps, while Malemute Kid had even taken off his mittens.

The dogs had been fagged out early in the afternoon, but they now began to show new vigor. Among the more astute there was a certain restlessness—an impatience at the restraint of the traces, an indecisive quickness of movement, a sniffing of snouts and pricking of ears. These became incensed at their more phlegmatic brothers, urging them on with numerous sly nips on their hinder quarters. Those, thus chidden, also contracted and helped spread the contagion. At last the leader of the foremost sled uttered a sharp whine of satisfaction, crouching lower in the snow and throwing himself against the collar. The rest followed suit. There was an ingathering of back bands, a tightening of traces; the sleds leaped forward, and the men clung to the gee poles, violently accelerating the uplift of their feet that they might escape going under the runners. The weariness of the day fell from them, and they whooped encouragement to the dogs. The animals responded with joyous yelps. They were swinging through the gathering darkness at a rattling gallop.

"Gee! Gee!" the men cried, each in turn, as their sleds

abruptly left the main trail, heeling over on single runners
like luggers on the wind.

Then came a hundred yards' dash to the lighted parch-
ment window, which told its own story of the home cabin,
the roaring Yukon stove, and the steaming pots of tea. But
the home cabin had been invaded. Threescore huskies cho-
rused defiance, and as many furry forms precipitated themselves upon the dogs which drew the first sled. The door
was flung open, and a man, clad in the scarlet tunic of
the Northwest Police, waded knee-deep among the furious
brutes, calmly and impartially dispensing soothing justice
with the butt end of a dog whip. After that the men shook
hands; and in this wise was Malemute Kid welcomed to
his own cabin by a stranger.

Stanley Prince, who should have welcomed him, and who
was responsible for the Yukon stove and hot tea afore-
mentioned, was busy with his guests. There were a dozen
or so of them, as nondescript a crowd as ever served the
Queen in the enforcement of her laws or the delivery of
her mails. They were of many breeds, but their common
life had formed of them a certain type—a lean and wiry
type, with trail-hardened muscles, and sun-browned faces,
and untroubled souls which gazed frankly forth, clear-eyed
and steady. They drove the dogs of the Queen, wrought
fear in the hearts of her enemies, ate of her meager fare,
and were happy. They had seen life, and done deeds, and
lived romances; but they did not know it.

And they were very much at home. Two of them were
sprawled upon Malemute Kid's bunk, singing chansons
which their French forebears sang in the days when first
they entered the Northwest land and mated with its Indian women. Bettles' bunk had suffered a similar invasion,
and three or four lusty voyageurs worked their toes among
its blankets as they listened to the tale of one who had
served on the boat brigade with Wolseley when he fought
his way to Khartoum. And when he tired, a cowboy told
of courts and kings and lords and ladies he had seen when
Buffalo Bill toured the capitals of Europe. In a corner two
half-breeds, ancient comrades in a lost campaign, mended
harnesses and talked of the days when the Northwest flamed
with insurrection and Louis Riel was king.

Rough jests and rougher jokes went up and down, and
great hazards by trail and river were spoken of in the light

of commonplaces, only to be recalled by virtue of some grain of humor or ludicrous happening. Prince was led away by these uncrowned heroes who had seen history made, who regarded the great and the romantic as but the ordinary and the incidental in the routine of life. He passed his precious tobacco among them with lavish disregard, and rusty chains of reminiscence were loosened, and forgotten odysseys resurrected for his especial benefit.

When conversation dropped and the travelers filled the last pipes and unlashed their tight-rolled sleeping furs, Prince fell back upon his comrade for further information.

"Well, you know what the cowboy is," Malemute Kid answered, beginning to unlace his moccasins; "and it's not hard to guess the British blood in his bed partner. As for the rest, they're all children of the *coureurs du bois,* mingled with God knows how many other bloods. The two turning in by the door are the regulation 'breeds' or *Boisbrûles.* That lad with the worsted breech scarf—notice his eyebrows and the turn of his jaw—shows a Scotchman wept in his mother's smoky tepee. And that handsome-looking fellow putting the capote under his head is a French half-breed—you heard him talking; he doesn't like the two Indians turning in next to him. You see, when the 'breeds' rose under Riel the full-bloods kept the peace, and they've not lost much love for one another since."

"But I say, what's that glum-looking fellow by the stove? I'll swear he can't talk English. He hasn't opened his mouth all night."

"You're wrong. He knows English well enough. Did you follow his eyes when he listened? I did. But he's neither kith nor kin to the others. When they talked their own patois you could see he didn't understand. I've been wondering myself what he is. Let's find out."

"Fire a couple of sticks into the stove!" Malemute Kid commanded, raising his voice and looking squarely at the man in question.

He obeyed at once.

"Had discipline knocked into him somewhere," Prince commented in a low tone.

Malemute Kid nodded, took off his socks, and picked his way among recumbent men to the stove. There he hung his damp footgear among a score or so of mates.

"When do you expect to get to Dawson?" he asked tentatively.

The man studied him a moment before replying. "They say seventy-five mile. So? Maybe two days."

The very slightest accent was perceptible, while there was no awkward hesitancy or groping for words.

"Been in the country before?"

"No."

"Northwest Territory?"

"Yes."

"Born there?"

"No."

"Well, where the devil were you born? You're none of these." Malemute Kid swept his hand over the dog drivers, even including the two policemen who had turned into Prince's bunk. "Where did you come from? I've seen faces like yours before, though I can't remember just where."

"I know you," he irrelevantly replied, at once turning the drift of Malemute Kid's questions.

"Where? Ever see me?"

"No; your partner, him priest, Pastilik, long time ago. Him ask me if I see you, Malemute Kid. Him give me grub. I no stop long. You hear him speak 'bout me?"

"Oh! you're the fellow that traded the otter skins for the dogs?"

The man nodded, knocked out his pipe, and signified his disinclination for conversation by rolling up in his furs. Malemute Kid blew out the slush lamp and crawled under the blankets with Prince.

"Well, what is he?"

"Don't know—turned me off, somehow, and then shut up like a clam. But he's a fellow to whet your curiosity. I've heard of him. All the coast wondered about him eight years ago. Sort of mysterious, you know. He came down out of the North, in the dead of winter, many a thousand miles from here, skirting Bering Sea and traveling as though the devil were after him. No one ever learned where he came from, but he must have come far. He was badly travel-worn when he got food from the Swedish missionary on Golovin Bay and asked the way south. We heard of this afterward. Then he abandoned the shore line, heading right across Norton Sound. Terrible weather, snowstorms and high winds, but he pulled through where a thousand other men would have died, missing St. Michael's and making the land at Pastilik. He'd lost all but two dogs, and was nearly gone with starvation.

"He was so anxious to go on that Father Roubeau fitted him out with grub; but he couldn't let him have any dogs, for he was only waiting my arrival to go on a trip himself. Mr. Ulysses knew too much to start on without animals, and fretted around for several days. He had on his sled a bunch of beautifully cured otter skins, sea otters, you know, worth their weight in gold. There was also at Pastilik an old Shylock of a Russian trader, who had dogs to kill. Well, they didn't dicker very long, but when the Strange One headed south again, it was in the rear of a spanking dog team. Mr. Shylock, by the way, had the otter skins. I saw them, and they were magnificent. We figured it up and found the dogs brought him at least five hundred apiece. And it wasn't as if the Strange One didn't know the value of sea otter; he was an Indian of some sort, and what little he talked showed he'd been among white men.

"After the ice passed out of the sea, word came up from Nunivak Island that he'd gone in there for grub. Then he dropped from sight, and this is the first heard of him in eight years. Now where did he come from? and what was he doing there? and why did he come from there? He's Indian, he's been nobody knows where, and he's had discipline, which is unusual for an Indian. Another mystery of the North for you to solve, Prince."

"Thanks awfully, but I've got too many on hand as it is," he replied.

Malemute Kid was already breathing heavily; but the young mining engineer gazed straight up through the thick darkness, waiting for the strange orgasm which stirred his blood to die away. And when he did sleep, his brain worked on, and for the nonce he, too, wandered through the white unknown, struggled with the dogs on endless trails, and saw men live, and toil, and die like men.

The next morning, hours before daylight, the dog drivers and policemen pulled out for Dawson. But the powers that saw to Her Majesty's interests and ruled the destinies of her lesser creatures gave the mailmen little rest, for a week later they appeared at Stuart River, heavily burdened with letters for Salt Water. However, their dogs had been replaced by fresh ones; but, then, they were dogs.

The men had expected some sort of a layover in which to rest up; besides, this Klondike was a new section of the Northland, and they had wished to see a little something of the Golden City where dust flowed like water and dance halls rang with never-ending revelry. But they dried their socks and smoked their evening pipes with much the same gusto as on their former visit, though one or two bold spirits speculated on desertion and the possibility of crossing the unexplored Rockies to the east, and thence, by the Mackenzie Valley, of gaining their old stamping grounds in the Chippewyan country. Two or three even decided to return to their homes by that route when their terms of service had expired, and they began to lay plans forthwith, looking forward to the hazardous undertaking in much the same way a city-bred man would to a day's holiday in the woods.

He of the Otter Skins seemed very restless, though he took little interest in the discussion, and at last he drew Malemute Kid to one side and talked for some time in low tones. Prince cast curious eyes in their direction, and the mystery deepened when they put on caps and mittens and went outside. When they returned, Malemute Kid placed his gold scales on the table, weighed out the matter of sixty ounces, and transferred them to the Strange One's sack. Then the chief of the dog drivers joined the conclave, and certain business was transacted with him. The next day the gang went on upriver, but He of the Otter Skins took several pounds of grub and turned his steps back toward Dawson.

"Didn't know what to make of it," said Malemute Kid in response to Prince's queries; "but the poor beggar wanted to be quit of the service for some reason or other—at least it seemed a most important one to him, though he wouldn't let on what. You see, it's just like the army: he signed for two years, and the only way to get free was to buy himself out. He couldn't desert and then stay here, and he was just wild to remain in the country. Made up his mind when he got to Dawson, he said; but no one knew him, hadn't a cent, and I was the only one he'd spoken two words with. So he talked it over with the lieutenant-governor, and made arrangements in case he could

get the money from me—loan, you know. Said he'd pay
back in the year, and, if I wanted, would put me onto
something rich. Never'd seen it, but knew it was rich.

"And talk! why, when he got me outside he was ready
to weep. Begged and pleaded; got down in the snow to me
till I hauled him out of it. Palavered around like a crazy
man. Swore he's worked to this very end for years and years,
and couldn't bear to be disappointed now. Asked him what
end, but he wouldn't say. Said they might keep him on
the other half of the trail and he wouldn't get to Dawson
in two years, and then it would be too late. Never saw a
man take on so in my life. And when I said I'd let him
have it, had to yank him out of the snow again. Told him
to consider it in the light of a grubstake. Think he'd have
it? No sir! Swore he'd give me all he found, make me
rich beyond the dreams of avarice, and all such stuff. Now
a man who puts his life and time against a grubstake
ordinarily finds it hard enough to turn over half of what he
finds. Something behind all this, Prince; just you make a
note of it. We'll hear of him if he stays in the country——"

"And if he doesn't?"

"Then my good nature gets a shock, and I'm sixty some
odd ounces out."

The cold weather had come on with the long nights,
and the sun had begun to play his ancient game of peeka-
boo along the southern snow line ere aught was heard of
Malemute Kid's grubstake. And then, one bleak morning in
early January, a heavily laden dog train pulled into his
cabin below Stuart River. He of the Otter Skins was there,
and with him walked a man such as the gods have almost
forgotten how to fashion. Men never talked of luck and
pluck and five-hundred-dollar dirt without bringing in the
name of Axel Gunderson; nor could tales of nerve or
strength or daring pass up and down the campfire without
the summoning of his presence. And when the conversation
flagged, it blazed anew at mention of the woman who
shared his fortunes.

As has been noted, in the making of Axel Gunderson
the gods had remembered their old-time cunning and cast
him after the manner of men who were born when the
world was young. Full seven feet he towered in his picturesque costume which marked a king of Eldorado. His chest,

neck, and limbs were those of a giant. To bear his three hundred pounds of bone and muscle, his snowshoes were greater by a generous yard than those of other men. Rough-hewn, with rugged brow and massive jaw and unflinching eyes of palest blue, his face told the tale of one who knew but the law of might. Of the yellow of ripe corn silk, his frost-incrusted hair swept like day across the night and fell far down his coat of bearskin. A vague tradition of the sea seemed to cling about him as he swung down the narrow trail in advance of the dogs; and he brought the butt of his dog whip against Malemute Kid's door as a Norse sea rover, on southern foray, might thunder for admittance at the castle gate.

Prince bared his womanly arms and kneaded sour-dough bread, casting, as he did so, many a glance at the three guests—three guests the like of which might never come under a man's roof in a lifetime. The Strange One, whom Malemute Kid had surnamed Ulysses, still fascinated him; but his interest chiefly gravitated between Axel Gunderson and Axel Gunderson's wife. She felt the day's journey, for she had softened in comfortable cabins during the many days since her husband mastered the wealth of frozen pay streaks, and she was tired. She rested against his great breast like a slender flower against a wall, replying lazily to Male-mute Kid's good-natured banter, and stirring Prince's blood strangely with an occasional sweep of her deep, dark eyes. For Prince was a man, and healthy, and had seen few women in many months. And she was older than he, and an Indian besides. But she was different from all native wives he had met: she had traveled—had been in his country among others, he gathered from the conversation; and she knew most of the things the women of his own race knew, and much more that it was not in the nature of things for them to know. She could make a meal of sun-dried fish or a bed in the snow; yet she teased them with tantalizing details of many-course dinners, and caused strange internal dissensions to arise at the mention of various quondam dishes which they had well-nigh forgotten. She knew the ways of the moose, the bear, and the little blue fox, and of the wild amphibians of the Northern seas; she was skilled in the lore of the woods and the streams, and the tale writ by man and bird and beast upon the delicate snow crust was to her an open book; yet Prince caught

the appreciative twinkle in her eye as she read the Rules
of the Camp. These rules had been fathered by the unquenchable Bettles at a time when his blood ran high, and
were remarkable for the terse simplicity of their humor.
Prince always turned them to the wall before the arrival
of ladies; but who could suspect that this native wife——
Well, it was too late now.

This, then, was the wife of Axel Gunderson, a woman
whose name and fame had traveled with her husband's,
hand in hand, through all the Northland. At table, Malemute Kid baited her with the assurance of an old friend,
and Prince shook off the shyness of first acquaintance and
joined in. But she held her own in the unequal contest,
while her husband, slower in wit, ventured naught but applause. And he was very proud of her; his every look and
action revealed the magnitude of the place she occupied in
his life. He of the Otter Skins ate in silence, forgotten in
the merry battle; and long ere the others were done he
pushed back from the table and went out among the dogs.
Yet all too soon his fellow travelers drew on their mittens
and parkas and followed him.

There had been no snow for many days, and the sleds
slipped along the hard-packed Yukon trail as easily as if it
had been glare ice. Ulysses led the first sled; with the second came Prince and Axel Gunderson's wife; while Malemute Kid and the yellow-haired giant brought up the third.

"It's only a hunch, Kid," he said, "but I think it's
straight. He's never been there, but he tells a good story,
and shows a map I heard of when I was in the Kootenay
country years ago. I'd like to have you go along; but he's
a strange one, and swore point-blank to throw it up if
anyone was brought in. But when I come back you'll get
first tip, and I'll stake you next to me, and give you a half
share in the town site besides.

"No! no!" he cried, as the other strove to interrupt. "I'm
running this, and before I'm done it'll need two heads. If
it's all right, why, it'll be a second Cripple Creek, man; do
you hear?—a second Cripple Creek! It's quartz, you know,
not placer; and if we work it right we'll corral the whole
thing—millions upon millions. I've heard of the place before, and so have you. We'll build a town—thousands of
workmen—good waterways—steamship lines—big carrying
trade—light-draught steamers for head reaches—survey a

railroad, perhaps—sawmills—electric-light plant—do our own
banking—commercial company—syndicate—— Say! just you
hold your hush till I get back!"

The sleds came to a halt where the trail crossed the
mouth of Stuart River. An unbroken sea of frost, its wide
expanse stretched away into the unknown east. The snowshoes were withdrawn from the lashings of the sleds. Axel
Gunderson shook hands and stepped to the fore, his great
webbed shoes sinking a fair half yard into the feathery surface and packing the snow so the dogs should not wallow.
His wife fell in behind the last sled, betraying long practice
in the art of handling the awkward footgear. The stillness
was broken with cheery farewells; the dogs whined; and
He of the Otter Skins talked with his whip to a recalci-
trant wheeler.

An hour later the train had taken on the likeness of a
black pencil crawling in a long, straight line across a mighty
sheet of foolscap.

II

One night, many weeks later, Malemute Kid and Prince
fell to solving chess problems from the torn page of an
ancient magazine. The Kid had just returned from his Bonanza properties and was resting up preparatory to a long
moose hunt. Prince, too, had been on creek and trail nearly
all winter, and had grown hungry for a blissful week of
cabin life.

"Interpose the black knight, and force the king. No, that
won't do. See, the next move——"

"Why advance the pawn two squares? Bound to take it
in transit, and with the bishop out of the way——"

"But hold on! That leaves a hole, and——"

"No; it's protected. Go ahead! You'll see it works."

It was very interesting. Somebody knocked at the door
a second time before Malemute Kid said, "Come in." The
door swung open. Something staggered in. Prince caught
one square look and sprang to his feet. The horror in his
eyes caused Malemute Kid to whirl about; and he, too,
was startled, though he had seen bad things before. The
thing tottered blindly toward them. Prince edged away till
he reached the nail from which hung his Smith & Wesson.

"My God! what is it?" he whispered to Malemute Kid.

"Don't know. Looks like a case of freezing and no grub," replied the Kid, sliding away in the opposite direction. "Watch out! It may be mad," he warned, coming back from closing the door.

The thing advanced to the table. The bright flame of the slush lamp caught its eye. It was amused, and gave voice to eldritch cackles which betokened mirth. Then, suddenly, he—for it was a man—swayed back, with a hitch to his skin trousers, and began to sing a chantey, such as men lift when they swing around the capstan circle and the sea snorts in their ears:

> "Yan-kee ship come down de ri-ib-er,
>   Pull! my bully boys! Pull!
> D'yeh want—to know de captain ru-uns her?
>   Pull! my bully boys! Pull!
> Jon-a-than Jones ob South Caho-li-in-a,
>   Pull! my bully—"

He broke off abruptly, tottered with a wolfish snarl to the meat shelf, and before they could intercept was tearing with his teeth at a chunk of raw bacon. The struggle was fierce between him and Malemute Kid; but his mad strength left him as suddenly as it had come, and he weakly surrendered the spoil. Between them they got him upon a stool, where he sprawled with half his body across the table. A small dose of whiskey strengthened him, so that he could dip a spoon into the sugar caddy which Malemute Kid placed before him. After his appetite had been somewhat cloyed, Prince, shuddering as he did so, passed him a mug of weak beef tea.

The creature's eyes were alight with a somber frenzy, which blazed and waned with every mouthful. There was very little skin to the face. The face, for that matter, sunken and emaciated, bore little likeness to human countenance. Frost after frost had bitten deeply, each depositing its stratum of scab upon the half-healed scar that went before. This dry, hard surface was of a bloody-black color, serrated by grievous cracks wherein the raw red flesh peeped forth. His skin garments were dirty and in tatters, and the fur of one side was singed and burned away, showing where he had lain upon his fire.

Malemute Kid pointed to where the sun-tanned hide had been cut away, strip by strip—the grim signature of famine.

"Who—are—you?" slowly and distinctly enunciated the Kid.

The man paid no heed.

"Where do you come from?"

"Yan-kee ship come down de ri-ib-er," was the quavering response.

"Don't doubt the beggar came down the river," the Kid said, shaking him in an endeavor to start a more lucid flow of talk.

But the man shrieked at the contact, clapping a hand to his side in evident pain. He rose slowly to his feet, half leaning on the table.

"She laughed at me—so—with the hate in her eye; and she—would—not—come."

His voice died away, and he was sinking back when Malemute Kid gripped him by the wrist and shouted, "Who? Who would not come?"

"She, Unga. She laughed, and struck at me, so, and so. And then——"

"Yes?"

"And then——"

"And then what?"

"And then he lay very still in the snow a long time. He is—still in—the—snow."

The two men looked at each other helplessly.

"Who is in the snow?"

"She, Unga. She looked at me with the hate in her eye, and then——"

"Yes, yes."

"And then she took the knife, so; and once, twice—she was weak. I traveled very slow. And there is much gold in that place, very much gold."

"Where is Unga?" For all Malemute Kid knew, she might be dying a mile away. He shook the man savagely, repeating again and again, "Where is Unga? Who is Unga?"

"She—is—in—the—snow."

"Go on!" The Kid was pressing his wrist cruelly.

"So—I—would—be—in—the—snow—but—I—had—a—debt—to—pay. It—was—heavy—I—had—a—debt—to—pay—a—debt—to—pay—I—had——" The faltering monosyllables ceased as he fumbled in his pouch and drew forth a buckskin sack. "A—debt—to—pay—five—pounds—of—gold—grub—stake—Mal—e—mute—Kid—I——" The exhausted head dropped upon the table; nor could Malemute Kid rouse it again.

"It's Ulysses," he said quietly, tossing the bag of dust on the table. "Guess it's all day with Axel Gunderson and the woman. Come on, let's get him between the blankets. He's Indian; he'll pull through and tell a tale besides."

As they cut his garments from him, near his right breast could be seen two unhealed, hard-lipped knife thrusts.

III

"I will talk of the things which were in my own way; but you will understand. I will begin at the beginning, and tell of myself and the woman, and, after that, of the man."

He of the Otter Skins drew over to the stove as do men who have been deprived of fire and are afraid the Promethean gift may vanish at any moment. Malemute Kid picked up the slush lamp and placed it so its light might fall upon the face of the narrator. Prince slid his body over the edge of the bunk and joined them.

"I am Naass, a chief, and the son of a chief, born between a sunset and a rising, on the dark seas, in my father's oomiak. All of a night the men toiled at the paddles, and the women cast out the waves which threw in upon us, and we fought with the storm. The salt spray froze upon my mother's breast till her breath passed with the passing of the tide. But I—I raised my voice with the wind and the storm, and lived.

"We dwelt in Akatan——"

"Where?" asked Malemute Kid.

"Akatan, which is in the Aleutians; Akatan, beyond Chignik, beyond Kardalak, beyond Unimak. As I say, we dwelt in Akatan, which lies in the midst of the sea on the edge of the world. We farmed the salt seas for the fish, the seal, and the otter; and our homes shouldered about one another on the rocky strip between the rim of the forest and the yellow beach where our kayaks lay. We were not many, and the world was very small. There were strange lands to the east—islands like Akatan; so we thought all the world was islands and did not mind.

"I was different from my people. In the sands of the beach were the crooked timbers and wave-warped planks of a boat such as my people never built; and I remember on the point of the island which overlooked the ocean three ways there stood a pine tree which never grew there, smooth and straight and tall. It is said the two men came to that spot, turn about, through many days, and watched with the passing of the light. These two men came from out of the sea in the boat which lay in pieces on the beach. And they were white like you, and weak as the little children when the seal have gone away and the hunters come home empty. I know of these things from the old men and the old women, who got them from their fathers and mothers before them. These strange white men did not take kindly to our ways at first, but they grew strong, what of the fish and the oil, and fierce. And they built them each his own house, and took the pick of our women, and in time children came. Thus he was born who was to become the father of my father's father.

"As I said, I was different from my people, for I carried the strong, strange blood of this white man who came out of the sea. It is said we had other laws in the days before these men; but they were fierce and quarrelsome, and fought with our men till there were no more left who dared to fight. Then they made themselves chiefs, and took away our old laws and gave us new ones, insomuch that the man was the son of his father, and not his mother, as our way had been. They also ruled that the son, first-born, should have all things which were his father's before him, and that the brothers and sisters should shift for themselves. And they gave us other laws. They showed us new ways in the catching of fish and the killing of bear which were thick in the woods; and they taught us to lay by bigger stores for the time of famine. And these things were good.

"But when they had become chiefs, and there were no more men to face their anger, they fought, these strange white men, each with the other. And the one whose blood I carry drove his seal spear the length of an arm through the other's body. Their children took up the fight, and their children's children; and there was great hatred between them, and black doings, even to my time, so that in each family but one lived to pass down the blood of them that went before. Of my blood I was alone; of the other man's there was but a girl. Unga, who lived with her mother. Her father and my father did not come back from the fishing one night; but afterward they washed up to the beach on the big tides, and they held very close to each other.

"The people wondered, because of the hatred between the houses, and the old men shook their heads and said the fight would go on when children were born to her and children to me. They told me this as a boy, till I came to believe, and to look upon Unga as a foe, who was to be the mother of children which were to fight with mine. I thought of these things day by day, and when I grew to a stripling I came to ask why this should be so. And they answered, 'We do not know, but that in such way your fathers did.' And I marveled that those which were to come should fight the battles of those that were gone, and in it I could see no right. But the people said it must be, and I was only a stripling.

"And they said I must hurry, that my blood might be the older and grow strong before hers. This was easy, for I was head man, and the people looked up to me because of the deeds and the laws of my fathers, and the wealth which was mine. Any maiden would come to me, but I found none to my liking. And the old men and the mothers of maidens told me to hurry, for even then were the hunters bidding high to the mother of Unga; and should her children grow strong before mine, mine would surely die.

"Nor did I find a maiden till one night coming back from the fishing. The sunlight was lying, so, low and full in the eyes, the wind free, and the kayaks racing with the white seas. Of a sudden the kayak of Unga came driving past me, and she looked upon me, so, with her black hair flying like a cloud of night and the spray wet on her cheek. As I say, the sunlight was full in the eyes, and I was a stripling; but somehow it was all clear, and I knew it to be the call of kind to kind. As she whipped ahead she looked back within the space of two strokes—looked as only the woman Unga could look—and again I knew it as the call of kind. The people shouted as we ripped past the lazy oomiaks and left them far behind. But she was quick at the paddle, and my heart was like the belly of a sail, and I did not gain. The wind freshened, the sea whitened, and, leaping like the seals on the windward breech, we roared down the golden pathway of the sun."

Naass was crouched half out of his stool, in the attitude

of one driving a paddle, as he ran the race anew. Somewhere across the stove he beheld the tossing kayak and the flying hair of Unga. The voice of the wind was in his ears, and its salt beat fresh upon his nostrils.

"But she made the shore, and ran up the sand, laughing, to the house of her mother. And a great thought came to me that night—a thought worthy of him that was chief over all the people of Akatan. So, when the moon was up, I went down to the house of her mother, and looked upon the goods of Yash-Noosh, which were piled by the door—the goods of Yash-Noosh, a strong hunter who had it in mind to be the father of the children of Unga. Other young men had piled their goods there and taken them away again; and each young man had made a pile greater than the one before.

"And I laughed to the moon and the stars, and went to my own house where my wealth was stored. And many trips I made, till my pile was greater by the fingers of one hand than the pile of Yash-Noosh. There were fish, dried in the sun and smoked; and forty hides of the hair seal, and half as many of the fur, and each hide was tied at the mouth and big bellied with oil; and ten skins of bear which I killed in the woods when they came out in the spring. And there were beads and blankets and scarlet clothes, such as I got in trade from the people who lived to the east, and who got them in trade from the people who lived still beyond in the east. And I looked upon the pile of Yash-Noosh and laughed, for I was head man in Akatan, and my wealth was greater than the wealth of all my young men, and my fathers had done deeds, and given laws, and put their names for all time in the mouths of the people.

"So, when the morning came, I went down to the beach, casting out of the corner of my eye at the house of the mother of Unga. My offer yet stood untouched. And the women smiled, and said sly things one to the other. I wondered, for never had such a price been offered; and that night I added more to the pile, and put beside it a kayak of well-tanned skins which never yet had swam in the sea. But in the day it was yet there, open to the laughter of all men. The mother of Unga was crafty, and I grew angry at the shame in which I stood before my people. So that night I added till it became a great pile, and I hauled up my oomiak, which was of the value of twenty kayaks. And in the morning there was no pile.

"Then made I preparation for the wedding, and the people that lived even to the east came for the food of the feast and the potlatch token. Unga was older than I by the age of four suns in the way we reckoned the years. I was only a stripling; but then I was a chief, and the son of a chief, and it did not matter.

"But a ship shoved her sails above the floor of the ocean, and grew larger with the breath of the wind. From her scuppers she ran clear water, and the men were in haste and worked hard at the pumps. On the bow stood a mighty man, watching the depth of the water and giving commands with a voice of thunder. His eyes were of the pale blue of the deep waters, and his head was maned like that of a sea lion. And his hair was yellow, like the straw of a southern harvest or the manila rope yarns which sailormen plait.

"Of late years we had seen ships from afar, but this was the first to come to the beach of Akatan. The feast was broken, and the women and children fled to the houses, while we men strung our bows and waited with spears in hand. But when the ship's forefoot smelled the beach the strange men took no notice of us, being busy with their own work. With the falling of the tide they careened the schooner and patched a great hole in her bottom. So the women crept back, and the feast went on.

"When the tide rose, the sea wanderers kedged the schooner to deep water and then came among us. They bore presents and were friendly; so I made room for them, and out of the largeness of my heart gave them tokens such as I gave all the guests, for it was my wedding day, and I was head man in Akatan. And he with the mane of the sea lion was there, so tall and strong that one looked to see the earth shake with the fall of his feet. He looked much and straight at Unga, with his arms folded, so, and stayed till the sun went away and the stars came out. Then he went down to his ship. After that I took Unga by the hand and led her to my own house. And there was singing and great laughter, and the women said sly things, after the manner of women at such times. But we did not care. Then the people left us alone and went home.

"The last noise had not died away when the chief of the sea wanderers came in by the door. And he had with him black bottles, from which we drank and made merry. You see, I was only a stripling, and had lived all my days on the

edge of the world. So my blood became as fire, and my heart
as light as the froth that flies from the surf to the cliff. Unga
sat silent among the skins in the corner, her eyes wide, for
she seemed to fear. And he with the mane of the sea lion
looked upon her straight and long. Then his men came in
with bundles of goods, and he piled before me wealth such
as was not in all Akatan. There were guns, both large and
small, and powder and shot and shell, and bright axes and
knives of steel, and cunning tools, and strange things the
like of which I had never seen. When he showed me by sign
that it was all mine, I thought him a great man to be so free;
but he showed me also that Unga was to go away with him
in his ship. Do you understand?—that Unga was to go away
with him in his ship. The blood of my fathers flamed hot on
the sudden, and I made to drive him through with my spear.
But the spirit of the bottles had stolen the life from my arm,
and he took me by the neck, so, and knocked my head against
the wall of the house. And I was made weak like a newborn
child, and my legs would no more stand under me. Unga
screamed, and she laid hold of the things of the house with
her hands, till they fell all about us as he dragged her to
the door. Then he took her in his great arms, and when she
tore at his yellow hair laughed with a sound like that of the
big bull seal in the rut.

"I crawled to the beach and called upon my people, but
they were afraid. Only Yash-Noosh was a man, and they
struck him on the head with an oar, till he lay with his face
in the sand and did not move. And they raised the sails to
the sound of their songs, and the ship went away on the
wind.

"The people said it was good, for there would be no more
war of the bloods in Akatan; but I said never a word, waiting
till the time of the full moon, when I put fish and oil in my
kayak and went away to the east. I saw many islands and
many people, and I, who had lived on the edge, saw that
the world was very large. I talked by signs; but they had not
seen a schooner nor a man with the mane of a sea lion, and
they pointed always to the east. And I slept in queer places,
and ate odd things, and met strange faces. Many laughed, for
they thought me light of head; but sometimes old men
turned my face to the light and blessed me, and the eyes of
the young women grew soft as they asked me of the strange
ship, and Unga, and the men of the sea.

"And in this manner, through rough seas and great storms, I came to Unalaska. There were two schooners there, but neither was the one I sought. So I passed on to the east, with the world growing ever larger, and in the island of Unamok there was no word of the ship, nor in Kadiak, nor in Atognak. And so I came one day to a rocky land, where men dug great holes in the mountain. And there was a schooner, but not my schooner, and men loaded upon it the rocks which they dug. This I thought childish, for all the world was made of rocks; but they gave me food and set me to work. When the schooner was deep in the water, the captain gave me money and told me to go; but I asked which way he went, and he pointed south. I made signs that I would go with him, and he laughed at first, but then, being short of men, took me to help work the ship. So I came to talk after their manner, and to heave on ropes, and to reef the stiff sails in sudden squalls, and to take my turn at the wheel. But it was not strange, for the blood of my fathers was the blood of the men of the sea.

"I had thought it an easy task to find him I sought, once I got among his own people; and when we raised the land one day, and passed between a gateway of the sea to a port, I looked for perhaps as many schooners as there were fingers to my hands. But the ships lay against the wharves for miles, packed like so many little fish; and when I went among them to ask for a man with the mane of a sea lion, they laughed, and answered me in the tongues of many peoples. And I found that they hailed from the uttermost parts of the earth.

"And I went into the city to look upon the face of every man. But they were like the cod when they run thick on the banks, and I could not count them. And the noise smote upon me till I could not hear, and my head was dizzy with much movement. So I went on and on, through the lands which sang in the warm sunshine; where the harvests lay rich on the plains; and where great cities were fat with men that lived like women, with false words in their mouths and their hearts black with the lust of gold. And all the while my people of Akatan hunted and fished, and were happy in the thought that the world was small.

"But the look in the eyes of Unga coming home from the fishing was with me always, and I knew I would find her when the time was met. She walked down quiet lanes in the dusk of the evening, or led me chases across the thick fields wet with the morning dew, and there was a promise in her eyes such as only the woman Unga could give.

"So I wandered through a thousand cities. Some were gentle and gave me food, and others laughed, and still others cursed; but I kept my tongue between my teeth, and went strange ways and saw strange sights. Sometimes I, who was a chief and the son of a chief, toiled for men—men rough of speech and hard as iron, who wrung gold from the sweat and sorrow of their fellow men. Yet no word did I get of my quest till I came back to the sea like a homing seal to the rookeries. But this was at another port, in another country which lay to the north. And there I heard dim tales of the yellow-haired sea wanderer, and I learned that he was a hunter of seals, and that even then he was abroad on the ocean.

"So I shipped on a seal schooner with the lazy Siwashes, and followed his trackless trail to the north where the hunt was then warm. And we were away weary months, and spoke many of the fleet, and heard much of the wild doings of him I sought; but never once did we raise him above the sea. We went north, even to the Pribilofs, and killed the seals in herds on the beach, and brought their warm bodies aboard till our scuppers ran grease and blood and no man could stand upon the deck. Then were we chased by a ship of slow steam, which fired upon us with great guns. But we put on sail till the sea was over our decks and washed them clean, and lost ourselves in a fog.

"It is said, at this time, while we fled with fear at our hearts, that the yellow-haired sea wanderer put in to the Pribilofs, right to the factory, and while the part of his men held the servants of the company, the rest loaded ten thousand green skins from the salt houses. I say it is said, but I believe; for in the voyages I made on the coast with never a meeting the northern seas rang with his wildness and daring, till the three nations which have lands there sought him with their ships. And I heard of Unga, for the captains sang loud in her praise, and she was always with him. She had learned the ways of his people, they said, and was happy. But I knew better—knew that her heart harked back to her own people by the yellow beach of Akatan.

"So, after a long time, I went back to the port which is by a gateway of the sea, and there I learned that he had gone across the girth of the great ocean to hunt for the seal to the east of the warm land which runs south from the Russian Seas. And I, who was become a sailorman, shipped with men of his own race, and went after him in the hunt of the seal. And there were few ships off that new land; but we hung on the flank of the seal pack and harried it north through all the spring of the year. And when the cows were heavy with pup and crossed the Russian line, our men grumbled and were afraid. For there was much fog, and every day men were lost in the boats. They would not work, so the captain turned the ship back toward the way it came. But I knew the yellow-haired sea wanderer was unafraid, and would hang by the pack, even to the Russian Isles, where few men go. So I took a boat, in the black of night, when the lookout dozed on the fo'c'slehead, and went alone to the warm, long land. And I journeyed south to meet the men by Yeddo Bay, who are wild and unafraid. And the Yoshiwara girls were small, and bright like steel, and good to look upon; but I could not stop, for I knew that Unga rolled on the tossing floor by the rookeries of the north.

"The men by Yeddo Bay had met from the ends of the earth, and had neither gods nor homes, sailing under the flag of the Japanese. And with them I went to the rich beaches of Copper Island, where our salt piles became high with skins. And in that silent sea we saw no man till we were ready to come away. Then one day the fog lifted on the edge of a heavy wind, and there jammed down upon us a schooner, with close in her wake the cloudy funnels of a Russian man-of-war. We fled away on the beam of the wind, with the schooner jamming still closer and plunging ahead three feet to our two. And upon her poop was the man with the mane of the sea lion, pressing the rails under with the canvas and laughing in his strength of life. And Unga was there—I knew her on the moment—but he sent her below when the cannons began to talk across the sea. As I say, with three feet to our two, till we saw the rudder lift green at every jump—and I swinging on to the wheel and cursing, with my back to the Russian shot. For we knew he had it in mind to run before us, that he might get away while we were caught. And they knocked our masts out of us till we dragged into the wind like a wounded gull; but he went on over the edge of the sky line—he and Unga.

"What could we? The fresh hides spoke for themselves.

So they took us to a Russian port, and after that to a lone country, where they set us to work in the mines to dig salt. And some died, and—and some did not die."

Naass swept the blanket from his shoulders, disclosing the gnarled and twisted flesh, marked with the unmistakable striations of the knout. Prince hastily covered him, for it was not nice to look upon.

"We were there a weary time and sometimes men got away to the south, but they always came back. So, when we who hailed from Yeddo Bay rose in the night and took the guns from the guards, we went to the north. And the land was very large, with plains, soggy with water, and great forests. And the cold came, with much snow on the ground, and no man knew the way. Weary months we journeyed through the endless forest—I do not remember, now, for there was little food and often we lay down to die. But at last we came to the cold sea, and but three were left to look upon it. One had shipped from Yeddo as captain, and he knew in his head the lay of the great lands, and of the place where men may cross from one to the other on the ice. And he led us—I do not know, it was so long—till there were but two. When we came to that place we found five of the strange people which live in that country, and they had dogs and skins, and we were very poor. We fought in the snow till they died, and the captain died, and the dogs and skins were mine. Then I crossed on the ice, which was broken, and once I drifted till a gale from the west put me upon the shore. And after that, Golovin Bay, Pastilik, and the priest. Then south, south, to the warm sunlands where first I wandered.

"But the sea was no longer fruitful, and those who went upon it after the seal went to little profit and great risk. The fleets scattered and the captains and the men had no word of those I sought. So I turned away from the ocean which never rests, and went among the lands, where the trees, the houses, and the mountains sit always in one place and do not move. I journeyed far, and came to learn many things, even to the way of reading and writing from books. It was well I should do this, for it came upon me that Unga must know these things, and that someday, when the time was met—we—you understand, when the time was met.

"So I drifted, like those little fish which raise a sail to the wind but cannot steer. But my eyes and my ears were open always, and I went among men who traveled much, for I knew they had but to see those I sought to remember. At last there came a man, fresh from the mountains, with pieces of rock in which the free gold stood to the size of peas, and he had heard, he had met, he knew them. They were rich, he said, and lived in the place where they drew the gold from the ground.

"It was in a wild country, and very far away; but in time I came to the camp, hidden between the mountains, where men worked night and day, out of the sight of the sun. Yet the time was not come. I listened to the talk of the people. He had gone away—they had gone away—to England, it was said, in the matter of bringing men with much money together to form companies. I saw the house they had lived in; more like a palace, such as one sees in the old countries. In the nighttime I crept in through a window that I might see in what manner he treated her. I went from room to room, and in such way thought kings and queens must live, it was all so very good. And they all said he treated her like a queen, and many marveled as to what breed of woman she was for there was other blood in her veins, and she was different from the women of Akatan, and no one knew her for what she was. Aye, she was a queen; but I was a chief, and the son of a chief, and I had paid for her an untold price of skin and boat and bead.

"But why so many words? I was a sailorman, and knew the way of the ships on the seas. I followed to England, and then to other countries. Sometimes I heard of them by word of mouth, sometimes I read of them in the papers; yet never once could I come by them, for they had much money, and traveled fast, while I was a poor man. Then came trouble upon them, and their wealth slipped away one day like a curl of smoke. The papers were full of it at the time; but after that nothing was said, and I knew they had gone back where more gold could be got from the ground.

"They had dropped out of the world, being now poor, and so I wandered from camp to camp, even north to the Kootenay country, where I picked up the cold scent. They had come and gone, some said this way, and some that, and still others that they had gone to the country of the Yukon. And I went this way, and I went that, ever journeying from place to place, till it seemed I must grow weary of the world which was so large. But in the Kootenay I traveled a bad

trail, and a long trail, with a breed of the Northwest, who saw
fit to die when the famine pinched. He had been to the
Yukon by an unknown way over the mountains, and when
he knew his time was near gave me the map and the secret
of a place where he swore by his gods there was much gold.

"After that all the world began to flock into the north. I
was a poor man; I sold myself to be a driver of dogs. The
rest you know. I met him and her in Dawson. She did not
know me, for I was only a stripling, and her life had been
large, so she had no time to remember the one who had paid
for her an untold price.

"So? You bought me from my term of service. I went back
to bring things about in my own way, for I had waited long,
and now that I had my hand upon him was in no hurry. As
I say, I had it in mind to do my own way, for I read
back in my life, through all I had seen and suffered, and remembered the cold and hunger of the endless forest by the
Russian Seas. As you know, I led him into the east—him
and Unga—into the east where many have gone and few
returned. I led them to the spot where the bones and the
curses of men lie with the gold which they may not have.

"The way was long and the trail unpacked. Our dogs were
many and ate much; nor could our sleds carry till the break
of spring. We must come back before the river ran free. So
here and there we cached grub, that our sleds might be light-
ened and there be no chance of famine on the back trip.
At the McQuestion there were three men, and near them we
built a cache, as also did we at the Mayo, where was a hunting camp of a dozen Pellys which had crossed the divide from
the south. After that, as we went on into the east, we saw no
men; only the sleeping river, the moveless forest, and the
White Silence of the North. As I say, the way was long and
the trail unpacked. Sometimes, in a day's toil, we made no
more than eight miles, or ten, and at night we slept like
dead men. And never once did they dream that I was Naass,
head man of Akatan, the righter of wrongs.

"We now made smaller caches, and in the nighttime it
was a small matter to go back on the trail we had broken
and change them in such way that one might deem the
wolverines the thieves. Again there be places where there is
a fall to the river, and the water is unruly, and the ice makes
above and is eaten away beneath. In such a spot the sled
I drove broke through, and the dogs; and to him and Unga

it was ill luck, but no more. And there was much grub on that sled, and the dogs the strongest. But he laughed, for he was strong of life, and gave the dogs that were left little grub till we cut them from the harnesses one by one and fed them to their mates. We would go home light, he said, traveling and eating from cache to cache, with neither dogs nor sleds; which was true, for our grub was very short, and the last dog died in the traces the night we came to the gold and the bones and the curses of men.

"To reach that place—and the map spoke true—in the heart of the great mountains, we cut ice steps against the wall of a divide. One looked for a valley beyond, but there was no valley; the snow spread away, level as the great harvest plains, and here and there about us mighty mountains shoved their white heads among the stars. And midway on that strange plain which should have been a valley the earth and the snow fell away, straight down toward the heart of the world. Had we not been sailormen our heads would have swung round with the sight, but we stood on the dizzy edge that we might see a way to get down. And on one side, and one side only, the wall had fallen away till it was like the slope of the decks in a topsail breeze. I do not know why this thing should be so, but it was so. 'It is the mouth of hell,' he said; 'let us go down.' And we went down.

"And on the bottom there was a cabin, built by some man, of logs which he had cast down from above. It was a very old cabin, for men had died there alone at different times, and on pieces of birch bark which were there we read their last words and their curses. One had died of scurvy; another's partner had robbed him of his last grub and powder and stolen away; a third had been mauled by a bald-face grizzly; a fourth had hunted for game and starved—and so it went, and they had been loath to leave the gold, and had died by the side of it in one way or another. And the worthless gold they had gathered yellowed the floor of the cabin like in a dream.

"But his soul was steady, and his head clear, this man I had led thus far. 'We have nothing to eat,' he said, 'and we will only look upon this gold, and see whence it comes and how much there be. Then we will go away quick, before it gets into our eyes and steals away our judgment. And in this way we may return in the end, with more grub, and possess it all.' So we looked upon the great vein, which cut the wall of the pit as a true vein should, and we measured it, and traced it from above and below, and drove the stakes of the claims and blazed the trees in token of our rights. Then, our knees shaking with lack of food, and a sickness in our bellies, and our hearts chugging close to our mouths, we climbed the mighty wall for the last time and turned our faces to the back trip.

"The last stretch we dragged Unga between us, and we fell often, but in the end we made the cache. And lo, there was no grub. It was well done, for he thought it the wolverines, and damned them and his gods in the one breath. But Unga was brave, and smiled, and put her hand in his, till I turned away that I might hold myself. 'We will rest by the fire,' she said, 'till morning, and we will gather strength from our moccasins.' So we cut the tops of our moccasins in strips, and boiled them half of the night, that we might chew them and swallow them. And in the morning we talked of our chance. The next cache was five days' journey; we could not make it. We must find game.

" 'We will go forth and hunt,' he said.

" 'Yes,' said I, 'we will go forth and hunt.'

"And he ruled that Unga stay by the fire and save her strength. And we went forth, he in quest of the moose and I to the cache I had changed. But I ate little, so they might not see in me much strength. And in the night he fell many times as he drew into camp. And I, too, made to suffer great weakness, stumbling over my snowshoes as though each step might be my last. And we gathered strength from our moccasins.

"He was a great man. His soul lifted his body to the last; nor did he cry aloud, save for the sake of Unga. On the second day I followed him, that I might not miss the end. And he lay down to rest often. That night he was near gone; but in the morning he swore weakly and went forth again. He was like a drunken man, and I looked many times for him to give up, but his was the strength of the strong, and his soul the soul of a giant, for he lifted his body through all the weary day. And he shot two ptarmigan, but would not eat them. He needed no fire; they meant life; but his thought was for Unga, and he turned toward camp. He no longer walked, but crawled on hand and knee through the snow. I came to him, and read death in his eyes. Even then it was not too late to eat of the ptarmigan. He cast away his rifle and carried the birds in his mouth like a dog. I walked by

his side, upright. And he looked at me during the moments
he rested, and wondered that I was so strong. I could see
it, though he no longer spoke; and when his lips moved,
they moved without sound. As I say, he was a great man,
and my heart spoke for softness; but I read back in my life,
and remembered the cold and hunger of the endless forest
by the Russian Seas. Besides, Unga was mine, and I had
paid for her an untold price of skin and boat and bead.

"And in this manner we came through the white forest,
with the silence heavy upon us like a damp sea mist. And the
ghosts of the past were in the air and all about us; and I saw
the yellow beach of Akatan, and the kayaks racing home from
the fishing, and the houses on the rim of the forest. And the
men who had made themselves chiefs were there, the law-
givers whose blood I bore and whose blood I had wedded in
Unga. Aye, and Yash-Noosh walked with me, the wet sand in
his hair, and his war spear, broken as he fell upon it, still in
his hand. And I knew the time was met, and saw in the eyes
of Unga the promise.

"As I say, we came thus through the forest, till the smell
of the camp smoke was in our nostrils. And I bent above
him, and tore the ptarmigan from his teeth. He turned on
his side and rested, the wonder mounting in his eyes, and the
hand which was under slipping slow toward the knife at his
hip. But I took it from him, smiling close in his face. Even
then he did not understand. So I made to drink from black
bottles, and to build high upon the snow a pile of goods,
and to live again the things which happened on the night of
my marriage. I spoke no word, but he understood. Yet was
he unafraid. There was a sneer to his lips, and cold anger,
and he gathered new strength with the knowledge. It was
not far, but the snow was deep, and he dragged himself very
slow. Once he lay so long I turned him over and gazed into
his eyes. And sometimes he looked forth, and sometimes
death. And when I loosed him he struggled on again. In this
way we came to the fire. Unga was at his side on the instant.
His lips moved without sound; then he pointed at me, that
Unga might understand. And after that he lay in the snow,
very still, for a long while. Even now is he there in the
snow.

"I said no word till I had cooked the ptarmigan. Then I
spoke to her, in her own tongue, which she had not heard in
many years. She straightened herself, so, and her eyes were

wonder-wide, and she asked who I was, and where I had learned that speech.

" 'I am Naass,' I said.

" 'You?' she said. 'You?' And she crept close that she might look upon me.

" 'Yes,' I answered; 'I am Naass, head man of Akatan, the last of the blood, as you are the last of the blood.'

"And she laughed. By all the things I have seen and the deeds I have done may I never hear such a laugh again It put the chill to my soul, sitting there in the White Silence, alone with death and this woman who laughed.

" 'Come!' I said, for I thought she wandered. 'Eat of the food and let us be gone. It is a far fetch from here to Akatan.'

"But she shoved her face in his yellow mane, and laughed till it seemed the heavens must fall about our ears. I had thought she would be overjoyed at the sight of me, and eager to go back to the memory of old times, but this seemed a strange form to take.

" 'Come!' I cried, taking her strong by the hand. 'The way is long and dark. Let us hurry!'

" 'Where?' she asked, sitting up, and ceasing from her strange mirth.

" 'To Akatan,' I answered, intent on the light to grow on her face at the thought. But it became like his, with a sneer to the lips, and cold anger.

" 'Yes,' she said; 'we will go, hand in hand, to Akatan, you and I. And we will live in the dirty huts, and eat of the fish and oil, and bring forth a spawn—a spawn to be proud of all the days of our life. We will forget the world and be happy, very happy. It is good, most good. Come! Let us hurry. Let us go back to Akatan.'

"And she ran her hand through his yellow hair, and smiled in a way which was not good. And there was no promise in her eyes.

"I sat silent, and marveled at the strangeness of woman. I went back to the night when he dragged her from me and she screamed and tore at his hair—at his hair which now she played with and would not leave. Then I remembered the price and the long years of waiting; and I gripped her close, and dragged her away as he had done. And she held back, even as on that night, and fought like a she-cat for its whelp. And when the fire was between us and the man, I loosed her, and she sat and listened. And I told her of all that lay between, of all that had happened to me on strange seas, of all that I had done in strange lands; of my weary quest, and the hungry years, and the promise which had been mine from the first. Aye, I told all, even to what had passed that day between the man and me, and in the days yet young. And as I spoke I saw the promise grow in her eyes, full and large like the break of dawn. And I read pity there, the tenderness of woman, the love, the heart and the soul of Unga. And I was a stripling again, for the look was the look of Unga as she ran up the beach, laughing, to the home of her mother. The stern unrest was gone, and the hunger, and the weary waiting. The time was met. I felt the call of her breast, and it seemed there I must pillow my head and forget. She opened her arms to me, and I came against her. Then, sudden, the hate flamed in her eye, her hand was at my hip. And once, twice, she passed the knife.

" 'Dog!' she sneered, as she flung me into the snow. 'Swine!' And then she laughed till the silence cracked, and went back to her dead.

"As I say, once she passed the knife, and twice; but she was weak with hunger, and it was not meant that I should die. Yet was I minded to stay in that place, and to close my eyes in the last long sleep with those whose lives had crossed with mine and led my feet on unknown trails. But there lay a debt upon me which would not let me rest.

"And the way was long, the cold bitter, and there was little grub. The Pellys had found no moose, and had robbed my cache. And so had the three white men, but they lay thin and dead in their cabin as I passed. After that I do not remember, till I came here, and found food and fire—much fire."

As he finished, he crouched closely, even jealously, over the stove. For a long while the slush-lamp shadows played tragedies upon the wall.

"But Unga!" cried Prince, the vision still strong upon him.

"Unga? She would not eat of the ptarmigan. She lay with her arms about his neck, her face deep in his yellow hair. I drew the fire close, that she might not feel the frost, but she crept to the other side. And I built a fire there; yet it was little good, for she would not eat. And in this manner they still lie up there in the snow."

"And you?" asked Malemute Kid.

"I do not know; but Akatan is small, and I have little wish to go back and live on the edge of the world. Yet is there small use in life. I can go to Constantine, and he will put irons upon me, and one day they will tie a piece of rope, so, and I will sleep good. Yet—no; I do not know."

"But, Kid," protested Prince, "this is murder!"

"Hush!" commanded Malemute Kid. "There be things greater than our wisdom, beyond our justice. The right and the wrong of this we cannot say, and it is not for us to judge."

Naass drew yet closer to the fire. There was a great silence, and in each man's eyes many pictures came and went.

Lost Face

It was the end. Subienkow had traveled a long trail of bitterness and horror, homing like a dove for the capitals of Europe, and here, farther away than ever, in Russian America, the trail ceased. He sat in the snow, arms tied behind him, waiting the torture. He stared curiously before him at a huge Cossack, prone in the snow, moaning in his pain. The men had finished handling the giant and turned him over to the women. That they had exceeded the fiendishness of the men the man's cries attested.

Subienkow looked on and shuddered. He was not afraid to die. He had carried his life too long in his hands, on that weary trail from Warsaw to Nulato, to shudder at mere dying. But he objected to the torture. It offended his soul. And this offense, in turn, was not due to the mere pain he must endure, but to the sorry spectacle the pain would make of him. He knew that he would pray, and beg, and entreat, even as Big Ivan and the others that had gone before. This would not be nice. To pass out bravely and cleanly, with a smile and a jest—ah, that would have been the way. But to lose control, to have his soul upset by the pangs of the flesh, to screech and gibber like an ape, to become the veriest beast—ah, that was what was so terrible.

There had been no chance to escape. From the beginning, when he dreamed the fiery dream of Poland's independence, he had become a puppet in the hands of fate. From the beginning, at Warsaw, at St. Petersburg, in the Siberian mines, in Kamchatka, on the crazy boats of the fur thieves, fate had been driving him to this end. Without doubt, in the foundations of the world was graved this end for him—for him, who was so fine and sensitive, whose nerves scarcely sheltered under his skin, who was a dreamer and a poet and an artist. Before he was dreamed of, it had been determined that the quivering bundle of sensitiveness that constituted him should

59

be doomed to live in raw and howling savagery, and to die in this far land of night, in this dark place beyond the last boundaries of the world.

He sighed. So that thing before him was Big Ivan—Big Ivan the giant, the man without nerves, the man of iron, the Cossack turned freebooter of the seas, who was as phlegmatic as an ox, with a nervous system so low that what was pain to ordinary men was scarcely a tickle to him. Well, well, trust these Nulato Indians to find Big Ivan's nerves and trace them to the roots of his quivering soul. They were certainly doing it. It was inconceivable that a man could suffer so much and yet live. Big Ivan was paying for his low order of nerves. Already he had lasted twice as long as any of the others.

Subienkow felt that he could not stand the Cossack's sufferings much longer. Why didn't Ivan die? He would go mad if that screaming did not cease. But when it did cease, his turn would come. And there was Yakaga awaiting him, too, grinning at him even now in anticipation—Yakaga, whom only last week he had kicked out of the fort, and upon whose face he had laid the lash of his dog whip. Yakaga would attend to him. Doubtlessly Yakaga was saving for him more refined tortures, more exquisite nerve-racking. Ah! That must have been a good one, from the way Ivan screamed. The squaws bending over him stepped back with laughter and clapping of hands. Subienkow saw the monstrous thing that had been perpetrated, and began to laugh hysterically. The Indians looked at him in wonderment that he should laugh. But Subienkow could not stop.

This would never do. He controlled himself, the spasmodic twitchings slowly dying away. He strove to think of other things, and began reading back in his own life. He remembered his mother and his father, and the little spotted pony, and the French tutor who had taught him dancing and sneaked him an old worn copy of Voltaire. Once more he saw Paris, and dreary London, and gay Vienna, and Rome. And once more he saw that wild group of youths who had dreamed, even as he, the dream of an independent Poland with a king of Poland on the throne at Warsaw. Ah, there it was that the long trail began. Well, he had lasted longest. One by one, beginning with the two executed at St. Petersburg, he took up the count of the passing of those brave spirits. Here one had been beaten to death by a jailer, and

there, on that bloodstained highway of the exiles, where they
had marched for endless months, beaten and maltreated by
their Cossack guards, another had dropped by the way. Always it had been savagery—brutal, bestial savagery. They had
died—of fever, in the mines, under the knout. The last two
had died after the escape, in the battle with the Cossacks,
and he alone had won to Kamchatka with the stolen papers
and the money of a traveler he had left lying in the snow.

It had been nothing but savagery. All the years, with his
heart in studios and theaters and courts, he had been hemmed
in by savagery. He had purchased his life with blood. Everybody had killed. He had killed that traveler for his passports.
He had proved that he was a man of parts by dueling with
two Russian officers on a single day. He had had to prove
himself in order to win to a place among the fur thieves. He
had had to win to that place. Behind him lay the thousand-
years-long road across all Siberia and Russia. He could not
escape that way. The only way was ahead, across the dark
and icy sea of Bering to Alaska. The way had led from savagery to deeper savagery. On the scurvy-rotten ships of the
fur thieves, out of food and out of water, buffeted by the
interminable storms of that stormy sea, men had become
animals. Thrice he had sailed east from Kamchatka. And
thrice, after all manner of hardship and suffering, the survivors had come back to Kamchatka. There had been no out-
let for escape, and he could not go back the way he had come,
for the mines and the knout awaited him.

Again, the fourth and last time, he had sailed east. He had
been with those who first found the fabled Seal Islands; but
he had not returned with them to share the wealth of furs
in the mad orgies of Kamchatka. He had sworn never to go
back. He knew that to win to those dear capitals of Europe
he must go on. So he had changed ships and remained in the
dark new land. His comrades were Slavonian hunters and
Russian adventurers, Mongols and Tatars and Siberian abo-
rigines; and through the savages of the New World they had
cut a path of blood. They had massacred whole villages
that refused to furnish the fur tribute; and they in turn had
been massacred by ships' companies. He, with one Finn, had
been the sole survivors of such a company. They had spent a
winter of solitude and starvation on a lonely Aleutian isle,
and their rescue in the spring by another fur ship had been
one chance in a thousand.

But always the terrible savagery had hemmed him in.
Passing from ship to ship, and ever refusing to return, he had
come to the ship that explored south. All down the Alaskan
coast they had encountered nothing but hosts of savages.
Every anchorage among the beetling island or under the
frowning cliffs of the mainland had meant a battle or a
storm. Either the gales blew, threatening destruction, or the
war canoes came off, manned by howling natives with the
war paint on their faces, who came to learn the bloody virtues
of the sea rovers' gunpowder. South, south they had coasted,
clear to the myth land of California. Here, it was said, were
Spanish adventurers who had fought their way up from Mexico. He had had hopes of those Spanish adventurers. Es-
caping to them, the rest would have been easy—a year or
two, what did it matter more or less?—and he would win to
Mexico, then a ship, and Europe would be his. But they had
met no Spaniards. Only had they encountered the same im-
pregnable wall of savagery. The denizens of the confines of the
world, painted for war, had driven them back from the shores.
At last, when one boat was cut off and every man killed, the
commander had abandoned the quest and sailed back to the
North.

The years had passed. He had served under Tebenkoff
when Michaelovski Redoubt was built. He had spent two
years in the Kuskokwim country. Two summers, in the
month of June, he had managed to be at the head of
Kotzebue Sound. Here, at this time, the tribes assembled
for barter; here were to be found spotted deerskins from
Siberia, ivory from the Diomedes, walrus skins from the
shores of the Arctic, strange stone lamps, passing in trade
from tribe to tribe, no one knew whence, and, once, a hunting knife of English make; and here, Subienkow knew, was
the school in which to learn geography. For he met Eskimos
from Norton Sound, from King Island and St. Lawrence
Island, from Cape Prince of Wales, and Point Barrow. Such
places had other names, and their distances were measured
in days.

It was a vast region these trading savages came from, and a
vaster region from which, by repeated trade, their stone
lamps and that steel knife had come. Subienkow bullied and
cajoled and bribed. Every far journeyer or strange tribesman
was brought before him. Perils unaccountable and unthink-
able were mentioned, as well as wild beasts, hostile tribes,

impenetrable forests, and mighty mountain ranges; but always from beyond came the rumor and the tale of white-skinned men, blue of eye and fair of hair, who fought like devils and who sought always for furs. They were to the east —far, far to the east. No one had seen them. It was the word that had been passed along.

It was a hard school. One could not learn geography very well through the medium of strange dialects, from dark minds that mingled fact and fable and that measured distances by "sleeps" that varied according to the difficulty of the going. But at last came the whisper that gave Subienkow courage. In the east lay a great river where were these blue-eyed men. The river was called the Yukon. South of Michaelovski Redoubt emptied another great river which the Russians knew as the Kwikpak. These two rivers were one, ran the whisper.

Subienkow returned to Michaelovski. For a year he urged an expedition up the Kwikpak. Then aorse Malakoff, the Russian half-breed, to lead the wildest and most ferocious of the hell's broth of mongrel adventurers who had crossed from Kamchatka. Subienkow was his lieutenant. They threaded the mazes of the great delta of the Kwikpak, picked up the first low hills on the northern bank, and for half a thousand miles, in skin canoes loaded to the gunwales with trade goods and ammunition, fought their way against the five-knot current of a river that ran from two to ten miles wide in a channel many fathoms deep. Malakoff decided to build the fort at Nulato. Subienkow urged to go farther. But he quickly reconciled himself to Nulato. The long winter was coming on. It would be better to wait. Early the following summer, when the ice was gone, he would disappear up the Kwikpak and work his way to the Hudson's Bay Company's posts. Malakoff had never heard the whisper that the Kwikpak was the Yukon, and Subienkow did not tell him.

Came the building of the fort. It was enforced labor. The tiered walls of logs arose to the sighs and groans of the Nulato Indians. The lash was laid upon their backs, and it was the iron hand of the freebooters of the sea that laid on the lash. There were Indians that ran away, and when they were caught they were brought back and spread-eagled before the fort, where they and their tribe learned the efficacy of the knout. Two died under it; others were injured for life; and the rest took the lesson to heart and ran away no more. The snow was flying ere the fort was finished, and then it was the time for furs. A heavy tribute was laid upon the tribe. Blows and lashings continued, and that the tribute should be paid, the women and children were held as hostages and treated with the barbarity that only the fur thieves knew.

Well, it had been a sowing of blood, and now was come the harvest. The fort was gone. In the light of its burning, half the fur thieves had been cut down. The other half had passed under the torture. Only Subienkow remained, or Subienkow and Big Ivan, if that whimpering, moaning thing in the snow could be called Big Ivan. Subienkow caught Yakaga grinning at him. There was no gainsaying Yakaga. The mark of the lash was still on his face. After all, Subienkow could not blame him, but he disliked the thought of what Yakaga would do to him. He thought of appealing to Makamuk, the head chief; but his judgment told him that such appeal was useless. Then, too, he thought of bursting his bonds and dying fighting. Such an end would be quick. But he could not break his bonds. Caribou thongs were stronger than he. Still devising, another thought came to him. He signed for Makamuk, and that an interpreter who knew the coast dialect should be brought.

"Oh, Makamuk," he said, "I am not minded to die. I am a great man, and it were foolishness for me to die. In truth, I shall not die. I am not like these other carrion."

He looked at the moaning thing that had once been Big Ivan, and stirred it contemptuously with his toe.

"I am too wise to die. Behold, I have a great medicine. I alone know this medicine. Since I am not going to die, I shall exchange this medicine with you."

"What is this medicine?" Makamuk demanded.

"It is a strange medicine."

Subienkow debated with himself for a moment, as if loath to part with the secret.

"I will tell you. A little bit of this medicine rubbed on the skin makes the skin hard like a rock, hard like iron, so that no cutting weapon can cut it. The strongest blow of a cutting weapon is a vain thing against it. A bone knife becomes like a piece of mud; and it will turn the edge of the iron knives we have brought among you. What will you give me for the secret of the medicine?"

"I will give you your life," Makamuk made answer through the interpreter.

Subienkow laughed scornfully.

"And you shall be a slave in my house until you die."

The Pole laughed more scornfully.

"Untie my hands and feet and let us talk," he said.

The chief made the sign; and when he was loosed Subienkow rolled a cigarette and lighted it.

"This is foolish talk," said Makamuk. "There is no such medicine. It cannot be. A cutting edge is stronger than any medicine."

The chief was incredulous, and yet he wavered. He had seen too many deviltries of fur thieves that worked. He could not wholly doubt.

"I will give you your life; but you shall not be a slave," he announced.

"More than that."

Subienkow played his game as coolly as if he were bartering for a fox skin.

"It is a very great medicine. It has saved my life many times. I want a sled and dogs, and six of your hunters to travel with me down the river and give me safety to one day's sleep from Michaelovski Redoubt."

"You must live here, and teach us all of your deviltries," was the reply.

Subienkow shrugged his shoulders and remained silent. He blew cigarette smoke out on the icy air, and curiously regarded what remained of the big Cossack.

"That scar!" Makamuk said suddenly, pointing to the Pole's neck, where a livid mark advertised the slash of a knife in a Kamchatkan brawl. "The medicine is not good. The cutting edge was stronger than the medicine."

"It was a strong man that drove the stroke." (Subienkow considered.) "Stronger than you, stronger than your strongest hunter, stronger than he."

Again, with the toe of his moccasin, he touched the Cossack—a grisly spectacle, no longer conscious—yet in whose dismembered body the pain-racked life clung and was loath to go.

"Also the medicine was weak. For at that place there were no berries of a certain kind, of which I see you have plenty in this country. The medicine here will be strong."

"I will let you go downriver," said Makamuk; "and the sled and the dogs and the six hunters to give you safety shall be yours."

"You are slow," was the cool rejoinder. "You have committed an offense against my medicine in that you did not at once accept my terms. Behold, I now demand more. I want one hundred beaver skins." (Makamuk sneered.) "I want one hundred pounds of dried fish." (Makamuk nodded, for fish were plentiful and cheap.) "I want two sleds—one for me and one for my furs and fish. And my rifle must be returned to me. If you do not like the price, in a little while the price will grow."

Yakaga whispered to the chief.

"But how can I know your medicine is true medicine?" Makamuk asked.

"It is very easy. First, I shall go into the woods——"

Again Yakaga whispered to Makamuk, who made a suspicious dissent.

"You can send twenty hunters with me," Subienkow went on. "You see, I must get the berries and the roots with which to make the medicine. Then, when you have brought the two sleds and loaded on them the fish and the beaver skins and the rifle, and when you have told off the six hunters who will go with me—then, when all is ready, I will rub the medicine on my neck, so, and lay my neck there on that log. Then can your strongest hunter take the ax and strike three times on my neck. You yourself can strike the three times."

Makamuk stood with gaping mouth, drinking in this latest and most wonderful magic of the fur thieves.

"But first," the Pole added hastily, "between each blow I must put on fresh medicine. The ax is heavy and sharp, and I want no mistakes."

"All that you have asked shall be yours," Makamuk cried in a rush of acceptance. "Proceed to make your medicine."

Subienkow concealed his elation. He was playing a desperate game, and there must be no slips. He spoke arrogantly.

"You have been slow. My medicine is offended. To make the offense clean you must give me your daughter."

He pointed to the girl, an unwholesome creature, with a cast in one eye and a bristling wolf tooth. Makamuk was angry, but the Pole remained imperturbable, rolling and lighting another cigarette.

"Make haste," he threatened. "If you are not quick, I shall demand yet more."

In the silence that followed, the dreary Northland scene faded from before him, and he saw once more his native land, and France, and once, as he glanced at the wolf-toothed girl, he remembered another girl, a singer and a dancer, whom he had known when first as a youth he came to Paris.

"What do you want with the girl?" Makamuk asked.

"To go down the river with me." Sibuenkow glanced her over critically. "She will make a good wife, and it is an honor worthy of my medicine to be married to your blood."

Again he remembered the singer and dancer and hummed aloud a song she had taught him. He lived the old life over, but in a detached, impersonal sort of way, looking at the memory pictures of his own life as if they were pictures in a book of anybody's life. The chief's voice, abruptly breaking the silence, startled him.

"It shall be done," said Makamuk. "The girl shall go down the river with you. But be it understood that I myself strike the three blows with the ax on your neck."

"But each time I shall put on the medicine," Subienkow answered, with a show of ill-concealed anxiety.

"You shall put the medicine on between each blow. Here are the hunters who shall see you do not escape. Go into the forest and gather your medicine."

Makamuk had been convinced of the worth of the medicine by the Pole's rapacity. Surely nothing less than the greatest of medicines could enable a man in the shadow of death to stand up and drive an old woman's bargain.

"Besides," whispered Yakaga, when the Pole, with his guard, had disappeared among the spruce trees, "when you have learned the medicine you can easily destroy him."

"But how can I destroy him?" Makamuk argued. "His medicine will not let me destroy him."

"There will be some part where he has not rubbed the medicine," was Yakaga's reply. "We will destroy him through that part. It may be his ears. Very well; we will thrust a spear in one ear and out the other. Or it may be his eyes. Surely the medicine will be much too strong to rub on his eyes."

The chief nodded. "You are wise, Yakaga. If he possesses no other devil things, we will then destroy him."

Subienkow did not waste time in gathering the ingredients for his medicine. He selected whatsoever came to hand such as spruce needles, the inner bark of the willow, a strip of birch bark, and a quantity of mossberries, which he made the hunters dig up for him from beneath the snow. A few frozen roots completed his supply, and he led the way back to camp.

Makamuk and Yakaga crouched beside him, noting the quantities and kinds of the ingredients he dropped into the pot of boiling water.

"You must be careful that the mossberries go in first," he explained.

"And—oh yes, one other thing—the finger of a man. Here, Yakaga, let me cut off your finger."

But Yakaga put his hands behind him and scowled.

"Just a small finger," Subienkow pleaded.

"Yakaga, give him your finger," Makamuk commanded.

"There be plenty of fingers lying around," Yakaga grunted, indicating the human wreckage in the snow of the score of persons who had been tortured to death.

"It must be the finger of a live man," the Pole objected.

"Then shall you have the finger of a live man." Yakaga strode over to the Cossack and sliced off a finger.

"He is not yet dead," he announced, flinging the bloody trophy in the snow at the Pole's feet. "Also, it is a good finger, because it is large."

Subienkow dropped it into the fire under the pot and began to sing. It was a French love song that with great solemnity he sang into the brew.

"Without these words I utter into it the medicine is worthless," he explained. "The words are the chiefest strength of it. Behold, it is ready."

"Name the words slowly, that I may know them," Makamuk commanded.

"Not until after the test. When the ax flies back three times from my neck, then will I give you the secret of the words."

"But if the medicine is not good medicine?" Makamuk queried anxioulsy.

Subienkow turned upon him wrathfully.

"My medicine is always good. However, if it is not good, then do by me as you have done to the others. Cut me up a bit at a time, even as you have cut him up." He pointed to the Cossack. "The medicine is now cool. Thus I rub it on my neck, saying this further medicine."

With great gravity he slowly intoned a line of the "Marseillaise," at the same time rubbing the villainous brew thoroughly into his neck.

An outcry interrupted his play acting. The giant Cossack, with a last resurgence of his tremendous vitality, had arisen to his knees. Laughter and cries of surprise and applause arose from the Nulatos, as Big Ivan began flinging himself about in the snow with mighty spasms.

Subienkow was made sick by the sight, but he mastered his qualms and made believe to be angry.

"This will not do," he said. "Finish him, and then we will make the test. Here, you, Yakaga, see that his noise ceases."

While this was being done, Subienkow turned to Makamuk.

"And remember, you are to strike hard. This is not baby work. Here, take the ax and strike the log, so that I can see you strike like a man."

Makamuk obeyed, striking twice, precisely and with vigor, cutting out a large chip.

"It is well." Subienkow looked about him at the circle of savage faces that somehow seemed to symbolize the wall of savagery that had hemmed him about ever since the Czar's police had first arrested him in Warsaw. "Take your ax, Makamuk, and stand so. I shall lie down. When I raise my hand, strike, and strike with all your might. And be careful that no one stands behind you. The medicine is good, and the ax may bounce from off my neck and right out of your hands."

He looked at the two sleds, with the dogs in harness, loaded with furs and fish. His rifle lay on top of the beaver skins. The six hunters who were to act as his guard stood by the sleds.

"Where is the girl?" the Pole demanded. "Bring her up to the sleds before the test goes on."

When this had been carried out, Subienkow lay down in the snow, resting his head on the log like a tired child about to sleep. He had lived so many dreary years that he was indeed tired.

"I laugh at you and your strength, O Makamuk," he said. "Strike, and strike hard."

He lifted his hand. Makamuk swung the ax, broadax for the squaring of logs. The bright steel flashed through the frosty air, poised for a perceptible instant above Makamuk's head, then descended upon Subienkow's bare neck. Clear through flesh and bone it cut its way, biting deeply into the log beneath. The amazed savages saw the head bounce a yard away from the blood-spouting trunk.

There was a great bewilderment and silence, while slowly it began to dawn in their minds that there had been no medicine. The fur thief had outwitted them. Alone, of all their prisoners, he had escaped the torture. That had been the stake for which he played. A great roar of laughter went up. Makamuk bowed his head in shame. The fur thief had fooled him. He had lost face before all his people. Still they continued to roar out their laughter. Makamuk turned, and with bowed head stalked away. He knew that thenceforth he would be no longer known as Makamuk. He would be Lost Face; the record of his shame would be with him until he died; and whenever the tribes gathered in the spring for the salmon, or in the summer for the trading, the story would pass back and forth across the campfires of how the fur chief died peaceably, at a single stroke, by the hand of Lost Face.

"Who was Lost Face?" he could hear, in anticipation, some insolent young buck demand. "Oh, Lost Face," would be the answer, "he who once was Makamuk in the days before he cut off the fur thief's head."

A Piece of Steak

WITH THE LAST MORSEL of bread Tom King wiped his plate clean of the last particle of flour gravy and chewed the resulting mouthful in a slow and meditative way. When he arose from the table, he was oppressed by the feeling that he was distinctly hungry. Yet he alone had eaten. The two children in the other room had been sent early to bed in order that in sleep they might forget they had gone supperless. His wife had touched nothing, and had sat silently and watched him with solicitous eyes. She was a thin, worn woman of the working class, though signs of an earlier prettiness were not wanting in her face. The flour for the gravy she had borrowed from the neighbor across the hall. The last two ha'pennies had gone to buy the bread.

He sat down by the window on a rickety chair that protested under his weight, and quite mechanically he put his pipe in his mouth and dipped into the side pocket of his coat. The absence of any tobacco made him aware of his action, and with a scowl for his forgetfulness he put the pipe away. His movements were slow, almost hulking, as though he were burdened by the heavy weight of his muscles. He was a solid-bodied, stolid-looking man, and his appearance did not suffer from being overprepossessing. His rough clothes were old and slouchy. The uppers of his shoes were too weak to carry the heavy resoling that was itself of no recent date. And his cotton shirt, a cheap, two-shilling affair, showed a frayed collar and ineradicable paint stains.

But it was Tom King's face that advertised him unmistakably for what he was. It was the face of a typical prize fighter; of one who had put in long years of service in the squared ring and, by that means, developed and emphasized all the marks of the fighting beast. It was distinctly a lowering countenance, and, that no feature of it might escape notice, it was clean-shaven. The lips were shapeless and constituted

a mouth harsh to excess, that was like a gash in his face. The
jaw was aggressive, brutal, heavy. The eyes, slow of movement
and heavy-lidded, were almost expressionless under the
shaggy, indrawn brows. Sheer animal that he was, the eyes
were the most animallike feature about him. They were
sleepy, lionlike—the eyes of a fighting animal. The forehead
slanted quickly back to the hair, which, clipped close, showed
every bump of a villainous-looking head. A nose, twice
broken and molded variously by countless blows, and a cauli-
flower ear, permanently swollen and distorted to twice its
size, completed his adornment, while the beard, fresh-shaven
as it was, sprouted in the skin and gave the face a blue-black
stain.

Altogether, it was the face of a man to be afraid of in a
dark alley or lonely place. And yet Tom King was not a
criminal, nor had he ever done anything criminal. Outside of brawls, common to his walk in life, he had harmed
no one. Nor had he ever been known to pick a quarrel. He
was a professional, and all the fighting brutishness of him was
reserved for his professional appearances. Outside the ring he
was slow-going, easy-natured, and, in his younger days, when
money was flush, too openhanded for his own good. He
bore no grudges and had few enemies. Fighting was a business with him. In the ring he struck to hurt, struck to maim,
struck to destroy; but there was no animus in it. It was a
plain business proposition. Audiences assembled and paid for
the spectacle of men knocking each other out. The winner
took the big end of the purse. When Tom King faced the
Woolloomoolloo Gouger, twenty years before, he knew that
the Gouger's jaw was only four months healed after having
been broken in a Newcastle bout. And he had played for that
jaw and broken it again in the ninth round, not because he
bore the Gouger any ill will, but because that was the surest
way to put the Gouger out and win the big end of the purse.
Nor had the Gouger borne him any ill will for it. It was
the game, and both knew the game and played it.

Tom King had never been a talker, and he sat by the window, morosely silent, staring at his hands. The veins stood
out on the backs of the hands, large and swollen; and the
knuckles, smashed and battered and malformed, testified to
the use to which they had been put. He had never heard
that a man's life was the life of his arteries, but well he knew
the meaning of those big, upstanding veins. His heart had

pumped too much blood through them at top pressure. They no longer did the work. He had stretched the elasticity out of them, and with their distention had passed his endurance. He tired easily now. No longer could he do a fast twenty rounds, hammer and tongs, fight, fight, fight, from gong to gong, with fierce rally on top of fierce rally, beaten to the ropes and in turn beating his opponent to the ropes, and rallying fiercest and fastest of all in that last, twentieth round, with the house on its feet and yelling, himself rushing, striking, ducking, raining showers of blows upon showers of blows and receiving showers of blows in return, and all the time the heart faithfully pumping the surging blood through the adequate veins. The veins, swollen at the time, had always shrunk down again, though not quite—each time, imperceptibly at first, remaining just a trifle larger than before. He stared at them and at his battered knuckles, and, for the moment, caught a vision of the youthful excellence of those hands before the first knuckle had been smashed on the head of Benny Jones, otherwise known as the Welsh Terror.

The impression of his hunger came back on him.

"Blimey, but couldn't I go a piece of steak!" he muttered aloud, clenching his huge fists and spitting out a smothered oath.

"I tried both Burke's an' Sawley's," his wife said half apologetically.

"An' they wouldn't?" he demanded.

"Not a ha'penny. Burke said——" She faltered.

"G'wan! Wot'd he say?"

"As how 'e was thinkin' Sandel 'ud do ye tonight, an' as how yer score was comfortable big as it was."

Tom King grunted but did not reply. He was busy thinking of the bull terrier he had kept in his younger days to which he had fed steaks without end. Burke would have given him credit for a thousand steaks—then. But times had changed. Tom King was getting old; and old men, fighting before second-rate clubs, couldn't expect to run bills of any size with the tradesmen.

He had got up in the morning with a longing for a piece of steak, and the longing had not abated. He had not had a fair training for this fight. It was a drought year in Australia, times were hard, and even the most irregular work was difficult to find. He had had no sparring partner, and his food had not been of the best nor always sufficient. He had done

a few days' navvy work when he could get it, and he had
run around the Domain in the early mornings to get his
legs in shape. But it was hard, training without a partner
and with a wife and two kiddies that must be fed. Credit
with the tradesmen had undergone very slight expansion
when he was matched with Sandel. The secretary of the Gayety Club had advanced him three pounds—the loser's end of
the purse—and beyond that had refused to go. Now and
again he had managed to borrow a few shillings from old pals,
who would have lent more only that it was a drought year
and they were hard put themselves. No—and there was no
use in disguising the fact—his training had not been satis-
factory. He should have had better food and no worries. Besides, when a man is forty, it is harder to get into condition
than when he is twenty.

"What time is it, Lizzie?" he asked.

His wife went across the hall to inquire, and came back.

"Quarter before eight."

"They'll be startin' the first bout in a few minutes," he
said. "Only a tryout. Then there's a four-round spar 'tween
Dealer Wells an' Gridley, an' a ten-round go 'tween Star-
light an' some sailor bloke. I don't come on for over an
hour."

At the end of another silent ten minutes he rose to his
feet.

"Truth is, Lizzie, I ain't had proper trainin'."

He reached for his hat and started for the door. He did
not offer to kiss her—he never did on going out—but on this
night she dared to kiss him, throwing her arms around him
and compelling him to bend down to her face. She looked
quite small against the massive bulk of the man.

"Good luck, Tom," she said. "You gotter do 'im."

"Ay, I gotter do 'im," he repeated. "That's all there is to it.
I jus' gotter do 'im."

He laughed with an attempt at heartiness, while she
pressed more closely against him. Across her shoulders he
looked around the bare room. It was all he had in the world,
with the rent overdue, and her and the kiddies. And he was
leaving it to go out into the night to get meat for his mate
and cubs—not like a modern workingman going to his ma-
chine grind, but in the old, primitive, royal, animal way, by
fighting for it.

"I gotter do 'im," he repeated, this time a hint of desperation in his voice. "If it's a win, it's thirty quid—an' I can pay all that's owin', with a lump o' money left over. If it's a lose, I get naught—not even a penny for me to ride home on the tram. The secretary's give all that's comin' from a loser's end. Good-by, old woman. I'll come straight home if it's a win."

"An' I'll be waitin' up," she called to him along the hall.

It was full two miles to the Gayety, and as he walked along he remembered how in his palmy days—he had once been the heavyweight champion of New South Wales—he would have ridden in a cab to the fight, and how, most likely, some heavy backer would have paid for the cab and ridden with him. There were Tommy Burns and that Yankee, Jack Johnson—they rode about in motorcars. And he walked! And, as any man knew, a hard two miles was not the best preliminary to a fight. He was an old un, and the world did not wag well with old uns. He was good for nothing now except navvy work, and his broken nose and swollen ear were against him even in that. He found himself wishing that he had learned a trade. It would have been better in the long run. But no one had told him, and he knew, deep down in his heart, that he would not have listened if they had. It had been so easy. Big money—sharp, glorious fights—periods of rest and loafing in between—a following of eager flatterers, the slaps on the back, the shakes of the hand, the toffs glad to buy him a drink for the privilege of five minutes' talk —and the glory of it, the yelling houses, the whirlwind finish, the referee's "King wins!" and his name in the sporting columns next day.

Those had been times! But he realized now, in his slow, ruminating way, that it was the old uns he had been putting away. He was Youth, rising; and they were Age, sinking. No wonder it had been easy—they with their swollen veins and battered knuckles and weary in the bones of them from the long battles they had already fought. He remembered the time he put out old Stowsher Bill, at Rush-Cutters Bay, in the eighteenth round, and how old Bill had cried afterward in the dressing room like a baby. Perhaps old Bill's rent had been overdue. Perhaps he'd had at home a missus an' a couple of kiddies. And perhaps Bill, that very day of the fight, had had a hungering for a piece of steak. Bill had fought game and taken incredible punishment. He could see now, after he had gone through the mill himself, that

Stowsher Bill had fought for a bigger stake, that night twenty years ago, than had young Tom King, who had fought for glory and easy money. No wonder Stowsher Bill had cried afterward in the dressing room.

Well, a man had only so many fights in him, to begin with. It was the iron law of the game. One man might have a hundred hard fights in him, another man only twenty; each, according to the make of him and the quality of his fiber, had a definite number, and when he had fought them he was done. Yes, he had had more fights in him than most of them, and he had had far more than his share of the hard, grueling fights—the kind that worked the heart and lungs to bursting, that took the elastic out of the arteries and made hard knots of muscle out of youth's sleek suppleness, that wore out nerve and stamina and made brain and bones weary from excess of effort and endurance overwrought. Yes, he had done better than all of them. There was none of his old fighting partners left. He was the last of the old guard. He had seen them all finished, and he had had a hand in finishing some of them.

They had tried him out against the old uns, and one after another he had put them away—laughing when, like old Stowsher Bill, they cried in the dressing room. And now he was an old un, and they tried out the youngsters on him. There was that bloke Sandel. He had come over from New Zealand with a record behind him. But nobody in Australia knew anything about him, so they put him up against old Tom King. If Sandel made a showing, he would be given better men to fight, with bigger purses to win; so it was to be depended upon that he would put up a fierce battle. He had everything to win by it—money and glory and career; and Tom King was the grizzled old chopping block that guarded the highway to fame and fortune. And he had nothing to win except thirty quid, to pay to the landlord and the tradesmen. And as Tom King thus ruminated, there came to his stolid vision the form of youth, glorious youth, rising exultant and invincible, supple of muscle and silken of skin, with heart and lungs that had never been tired and torn and that laughed at limitation of effort. Yes, youth was the nemesis. It destroyed the old uns and recked not that, in so doing, it destroyed itself. It enlarged its arteries and smashed its knuckles, and was in turn destroyed by youth. For youth was ever youthful. It was only age that grew old.

At Castlereagh Street he turned to the left, and three blocks along came to the Gayety. A crowd of young larrikins hanging outside the door made respectful way for him, and he heard one say to another: "That's 'im! That's Tom King!"

Inside, on the way to his dressing room, he encountered the secretary, a keen-eyed, shrewd-faced young man, who shook his hand.

"How are you feelin', Tom?" he asked.

"Fit as a fiddle," King answered, though he knew that he lied, and that if he had a quid he would give it right there for a good piece of steak.

When he emerged from the dressing room, his seconds behind him, and came down the aisle to the squared ring in the center of the hall, a burst of greeting and applause went up from the waiting crowd. He acknowledged salutations right and left, though few of the faces did he know. Most of them were the faces of kiddies unborn when he was winning his first laurels in the squared ring. He leaped lightly to the raised platform and ducked through the ropes to his corner, where he sat down on a folding stool. Jack Ball, the referee, came over and shook his hand. Ball was a broken-down pugilist who for over ten years had not entered the ring as a principal. King was glad that he had him for referee. They were both old uns. If he should rough it with Sandel a bit beyond the rules, he knew Ball could be depended upon to pass it by.

Aspiring young heavyweights, one after another, were climbing into the ring and being presented to the audience by the referee. Also he issued their challenges for them.

"Young Pronto," Bill announced, "from North Sydney, challenges the winner for fifty pounds side bet."

The audience applauded, and applauded again as Sandel himself sprang through the ropes and sat down in his corner. Tom King looked across the ring at him curiously, for in a few minutes they would be locked together in merciless combat, each trying with all the force of him to knock the other into unconsciousness. But little could he see, for Sandel, like himself, had trousers and sweater on over his ring costume. His face was strongly handsome, crowned with a curly mop of yellow hair, while his thick, muscular neck hinted at bodily magnificence.

Young Pronto went to one corner and then the other, shaking hands with the principals and dropping down out of the ring. The challenges went on. Ever youth climbed through the ropes—youth unknown but insatiable, crying out to mankind that with strength and skill it would match issues with the winner. A few years before, in his own heyday of invincibleness, Tom King would have been amused and bored by these preliminaries. But now he sat fascinated, unable to shake the vision of youth from his eyes. Always were these youngsters rising up in the boxing game, springing through the ropes and shouting their defiance; and always were the old uns going down before them. They climbed to success over the bodies of the old uns. And ever they came, more and more youngsters—youth unquenchable and irresistible—and ever they put the old uns away, themselves becoming old uns and traveling the same downward path, while behind them, ever pressing on them, was youth eternal—the new babies, grown lusty and dragging their elders down, with behind them more babies to the end of time—youth that must have its will and that will never die.

King glanced over to the press box and nodded to Morgan, of the *Sportsman*, and Corbett, of the *Referee*. Then he held out his hands, while Sid Sullivan and Charley Bates, his seconds, slipped on his gloves and laced them tight, closely watched by one of Sandel's seconds, who first examined critically the tapes on King's knuckles. A second of his own was in Sandel's corner, performing a like office. Sandel's trousers were pulled off, and as he stood up his sweater was skinned off over his head. And Tom King, looking, saw youth incarnate, deep-chested, heavy-thewed, with muscles that slipped and slid like live things under the white satin skin. The whole body was acrawl with life, and Tom King knew that it was a life that had never oozed its freshness out through the aching pores during the long fights wherein youth paid its toll and departed not quite so young as when it entered.

The two men advanced to meet each other, and as the gong sounded and the seconds clattered out of the ring with the folding stools, they shook hands and instantly took their fighting attitudes. And instantly, like a mechanism of steel and springs balanced on a hair trigger, Sandel was in and out and in again, landing a left to the eyes, a right to the ribs, ducking a counter, dancing lightly away and dancing menacingly back again. He was swift and clever. It was a dazzling exhibition. The house yelled its approbation. But King was not dazzled. He had fought too many fights and too many youngsters. He knew the blows for what they were—too quick and too deft to be dangerous. Evidently Sandel was going to rush things from the start. It was to be expected. It was the way of youth, expending its splendor and excellence in wild insurgence and furious onslaught, overwhelming opposition with its own unlimited glory of strength and desire.

Sandel was in and out, here, there, and everywhere, light-footed and eager-hearted, a living wonder of white flesh and stinging muscle that wove itself into a dazzling fabric of attack, slipping and leaping like a flying shuttle from action to action through a thousand actions, all of them centered upon the destruction of Tom King, who stood between him and fortune. And Tom King patiently endured. He knew his business, and he knew youth now that youth was no longer his. There was nothing to do till the other lost some of his steam, was his thought, and he grinned to himself as he deliberately ducked so as to receive a heavy blow on the top of his head. It was a wicked thing to do, yet eminently fair according to the rules of the boxing game. A man was supposed to take care of his own knuckles, and if he insisted on hitting an opponent on the top of the head he did so at his own peril. King could have ducked lower and let the blow whiz harmlessly past, but he remembered his own early fights and how he smashed his first knuckle on the head of the Welsh Terror. He was but playing the game. That duck had accounted for one of Sandel's knuckles. Not that Sandel would mind it now. He would go on, superbly regardless, hitting as hard as ever throughout the fight. But later on, when the long ring battles had begun to tell, he would regret that knuckle and look back and remember how he smashed it on Tom King's head.

The first round was all Sandel's, and he had the house yelling with the rapidity of his whirlwind rushes. He overwhelmed King with avalanches of punches, and King did nothing. He never struck once, contenting himself with

covering up, blocking and ducking and clinching to avoid
punishment. He occasionally feinted, shook his head when
the weight of a punch landed, and moved stolidly about,
never leaping or springing or wasting an ounce of strength.
Sandel must foam the froth of youth away before discreet
age could dare to retaliate. All King's movements were slow
and methodical, and his heavy-lidded, slow-moving eyes
gave him the appearance of being half asleep or dazed. Yet
they were eyes that saw everything, that had been trained
to see everything through all his twenty years and odd in
the ring. They were eyes that did not blink or waver before
an impending blow, but that coolly saw and measured
distance.

Seated in his corner for the minute's rest at the end of
the round, he lay back with outstretched legs, his arms resting on the right angle of the ropes, his chest and abdomen
heaving frankly and deeply as he gulped down the air
driven by the towels of his seconds. He listened with closed
eyes to the voices of the house, "Why don't yeh fight,
Tom?" many were crying. "Yeh ain't afraid of 'im, are
yeh?"

"Muscle-bound," he heard a man on a front seat com-
ment. "He can't move quicker. Two to one on Sandel, in
quids."

The gong struck and the two men advanced from their
corners. Sandel came forward fully three quarters of the distance, eager to begin again; but King was content to advance the shorter distance. It was in line with his policy
of economy. He had not been well trained, and he had not
had enough to eat, and every step counted. Besides, he had
already walked two miles to the ringside. It was a repeti-
tion of the first round, with Sandel attacking like a whirlwind and with the audience indignantly demanding why
King did not fight. Beyond feinting and several slowly delivered and ineffectual blows he did nothing save block and
stall and clinch. Sandel wanted to make the pace fast, while
King, out of his wisdom, refused to accommodate him. He
grinned with a certain wistful pathos in his ring-battered
countenance, and went on cherishing his strength with the
jealousy of which only age is capable. Sandel was youth,
and he threw his strength away with the munificent abandon
of youth. To King belonged the ring generalship, the wisdom bred of long, aching fights. He watched with cool

eyes and head, moving slowly and waiting for Sandel's froth
to foam away. To the majority of the onlookers it seemed
as though King was hopelessly outclassed, and they voiced
their opinion in offers of three to one on Sandel. But there
were wise ones, a few, who knew King of old time, and
who covered what they considered easy money.

The third round began as usual, one-sided, with Sandel
doing all the leading and delivering all the punishment. A
half minute had passed when Sandel, overconfident, left an
opening. King's eyes and right arm flashed in the same instant. It was his first real blow—a hook, with the twisted
arch of the arm to make it rigid, and with all the weight
of the half-pivoted body behind it. It was like a sleepy-
seeming lion suddenly thrusting out a lightning paw. Sandel,
caught on the side of the jaw, was felled like a bullock.
The audience gasped and murmured awestricken applause.
The man was not muscle-bound, after all, and he could
drive a blow like a trip hammer.

Sandel was shaken. He rolled over and attempted to rise,
but the sharp yells from his seconds to take the count
restrained him. He knelt on one knee, ready to rise, and
waited, while the referee stood over him, counting the seconds loudly in his ear. At the ninth he rose in fighting
attitude, and Tom King, facing him, knew regret that the
blow had not been an inch nearer the point of the jaw.
That would have been a knockout, and he could have carried the thirty quid home to the missus and the kiddies.

The round continued to the end of its three minutes,
Sandel for the first time respectful of his opponent and
King slow of movement and sleepy-eyed as ever. As the
round neared its close, King, warned of the fact by sight
of the seconds crouching outside ready for the spring in
through the ropes, worked the fight around to his own
corner. And when the gong struck, he sat down immediately on the waiting stool, while Sandel had to walk all
the way across the diagonal of the square to his own corner. It was a little thing, but it was the sum of little things
that counted. Sandel was compelled to walk that many
more steps, to give up that much energy, and to lose a part
of the precious minute of rest. At the beginning of every
round King loafed slowly out from his corner, forcing his
opponent to advance the greater distance. The end of every

round found the fight maneuvered by King into his own
corner so that he could immediately sit down.

Two more rounds went by, in which King was parsimon-
ious of effort and Sandel prodigal. The latter's attempt to
force a fast pace made King uncomfortable, for a fair per-
centage of the multitudinous blows showered upon him
went home. Yet King persisted in his dogged slowness, despite the crying of the young hotheads for him to go in
and fight. Again, in the sixth round, Sandel was careless,
again Tom King's fearful right flashed out to the jaw, and
again Sandel took the nine seconds' count.

By the seventh round Sandel's pink of condition was
gone, and he settled down to what he knew was to be the
hardest fight in his experience. Tom King was an old un,
but a better old un than he had ever encountered—an old
un who never lost his head, who was remarkably able at
defense, whose blows had the impact of a knotted club,
and who had a knockout in either hand. Nevertheless, Tom
King dared not hit often. He never forgot his battered
knuckles, and knew that every hit must count if the
knuckles were to last out the fight. As he sat in his corner,
glancing across at his opponent, the thought came to him
that the sum of his wisdom and Sandel's youth would con-
stitute a world's champion heavyweight. But that was the
trouble. Sandel would never become a world champion. He
lacked the wisdom, and the only way for him to get it was
to buy it with youth; and when wisdom was his, youth
would have been spent in buying it.

King took every advantage he knew. He never missed
an opportunity to clinch, and in effecting most of the
clinches his shoulder drove stiffly into the other's ribs. In
the philosophy of the ring a shoulder was as good as a
punch so far as damage was concerned, and a great deal
better so far as concerned expenditure of effort. Also in
the clinches King rested his weight on his opponent, and
was loath to let go. This compelled the interference of the
referee, who tore them apart, always assisted by Sandel, who
had not yet learned to rest. He could not refrain from using
those glorious flying arms and writhing muscles of his, and
when the other rushed into a clinch, striking shoulder
against ribs, and with head resting under Sandel's left arm,
Sandel almost invariably swung his right behind his own
back and into the projecting face. It was a clever stroke,

much admired by the audience, but it was not dangerous, and was, therefore, just that much wasted strength. But Sandel was tireless and unaware of limitations, and King grinned and doggedly endured.

Sandel developed a fierce right to the body, which made it appear that King was taking an enormous amount of punishment, and it was only the old ringsters who appreciated the deft touch of King's left glove to the other's biceps just before the impact of the blow. It was true, the blow landed each time; but each time it was robbed of its power by that touch on the biceps. In the ninth round, three times inside a minute, King's right hooked its twisted arch to the jaw; and three times Sandel's body, heavy as it was, was leveled to the mat. Each time he took the nine seconds allowed him and rose to his feet, shaken and jarred, but still strong. He had lost much of his speed, and he wasted less effort. He was fighting grimly; but he continued to draw upon his chief asset, which was youth. King's chief asset was experience. As his vitality had dimmed and his vigor abated, he had replaced them with cunning, with wisdom born of the long fights and with a careful shepherding of strength. Not alone had he learned never to make a superfluous movement, but he had learned how to seduce an opponent into throwing his strength away. Again and again, by feint of foot and hand and body, he continued to inveigle Sandel into leaping back, ducking, or countering. King rested, but he never permitted Sandel to rest. It was the strategy of age.

Early in the tenth round King began stopping the other's rushes with straight lefts to the face, and Sandel, grown wary, responded by drawing the left, then by ducking it and delivering his right in a swinging hook to the side of the head. It was too high up to be vitally effective; but when first it landed King knew the old, familiar descent of the black veil of unconsciousness across his mind. For the insant, or for the slightest fraction of an instant, rather, he ceased. In the one moment he saw his opponent ducking out of his field of vision and the background of white, watching faces; in the next moment he again saw his opponent and the background of faces. It was as if he had slept for a time and just opened his eyes again, and yet the interval of unconsciousness was so microscopically short that there had been no time for him to fall. The

audience saw him totter and his knees give, and then saw
him recover and tuck his chin deeper into the shelter of
his left shoulder.

Several times Sandel repeated the blow, keeping King par-
tially dazed, and then the latter worked out his defense,
which was also a counter. Feinting with his left, he took a
half step backward, at the same time uppercutting with the
whole strength of his right. So accurately was it timed that
it landed squarely on Sandel's face in the full, downward
sweep of the duck, and Sandel lifted in the air and curled
backward, striking the mat on his head and shoulders.
Twice King achieved this, then turned loose and hammered
his opponent to the ropes. He gave Sandel no chance to
rest or to set himself, but smashed blow in upon blow
till the house rose to its feet and the air was filled with
an unbroken roar of applause. But Sandel's strength and endurance were superb, and he continued to stay on his feet.
A knockout seemed certain, and a captain of police, appalled at the dreadful punishment, arose by the ringside
to stop the fight. The gong struck for the end of the round
and Sandel staggered to his corner, protesting to the captain
that he was sound and strong. To prove it, he threw two
back air-springs, and the police captain gave in.

Tom King, leaning back in his corner and breathing
hard, was disappointed. If the fight had been stopped, the
referee, perforce, would have rendered him the decision and
the purse would have been his. Unlike Sandel, he was not
fighting for glory or career, but for thirty quid. And now
Sandel would recuperate in the minute of rest.

Youth will be served—this saying flashed into King's
mind, and he remembered the first time he had heard it,
the night when he had put away Stowsher Bill. The toff
who had bought him a drink after the fight and patted
him on the shoulder had used those words. Youth will be
served! The toff was right. And on that night in the long
ago he had been youth. Tonight youth sat in the opposite
corner. As for himself, he had been fighting for half an hour
now, and he was an old man. Had he fought like Sandel,
he would not have lasted fifteen minutes. But the point
was that he did not recuperate. Those upstanding arteries
and that sorely tried heart would not enable him to gather
strength in the intervals between the rounds. And he had
not had sufficient strength in him to begin with. His legs

were heavy under him and beginning to cramp. He should not have walked those two miles to the fight. And there was the steak which he had got up longing for that morning. A great and terrible hatred rose up in him for the butchers who had refused him credit. It was hard for an old man to go into a fight without enough to eat. And a piece of steak was such a little thing, a few pennies at best; yet it meant thirty quid to him.

With the gong that opened the eleventh round Sandel rushed, making a show of freshness which he did not really possess. King knew it for what it was—a bluff as old as the game itself. He clinched to save himself, then, going free, allowed Sandel to get set. This was what King desired. He feinted with his left, drew the answering duck and swinging upward hook, then made the half step backward, delivered the uppercut full to the face and crumpled Sandel over to the mat. After that he never let him rest, receiving punishment himself, but inflicting far more, smashing Sandel to the ropes, hooking and driving all manner of blows into him, tearing away from his clinches or punching him out of attempted clinches, and ever when Sandel would have fallen, catching him with one uplifting hand and with the other immediately smashing him into the ropes where he could not fall.

The house by this time had gone mad, and it was his house, nearly every voice yelling: "Go it, Tom!" "Get 'im! Get 'im!" "You've got 'im, Tom! You've got 'im!" It was to be a whirlwind finish, and that was what a ringside audience paid to see.

And Tom King, who for half an hour had conserved his strength, now expended it prodigally in the one great effort he knew he had in him. It was his one chance— now or not at all. His strength was waning fast, and his hope was that before the last of it ebbed out of him he would have beaten his opponent down for the count. And as he continued to strike and force, coolly estimating the weight of his blows and the quality of the damage wrought, he realized how hard a man Sandel was to knock out. Stamina and endurance were his to an extreme degree, and they were the virgin stamina and endurance of youth. Sandel was certainly a coming man. He had it in him. Only out of such rugged fiber were successful fighters fashioned.

Sandel was reeling and staggering, but Tom King's legs

were cramping and his knuckles going back on him. Yet he steeled himself to strike the fierce blows, every one of which brought anguish to his tortured hands. Though now he was receiving practically no punishment, he was weakening as rapidly as the other. His blows went home, but there was no longer the weight behind them, and each blow was the result of a severe effort of will. His legs were like lead, and they dragged visibly under him; while Sandel's backers, cheered by this symptom, began calling encouragement to their man.

King was spurred to a burst of effort. He delivered two blows in succession—a left, a trifle too high, to the solar plexus, and a right cross to the jaw. They were not heavy blows, yet so weak and dazed was Sandel that he went down and lay quivering. The referee stood over him, shouting the count of the fatal seconds in his ear. If before the tenth second was called he did not rise, the fight was lost. The house stood in hushed silence. King rested on trembling legs. A mortal dizziness was upon him, and before his eyes the sea of faces sagged and swayed, while to his ears, as from a remote distance, came the count of the referee. Yet he looked upon the fight as his. It was impossible that a man so punished could rise.

Only youth could rise, and Sandel rose. At the fourth second he rolled over on his face and groped blindly for the ropes. By the seventh second he had dragged himself to his knee, where he rested, his head rolling groggily on his shoulders. As the referee cried "Nine!" Sandel stood upright, in proper stalling position, his left arm wrapped about his face, his right wrapped about his stomach. Thus were his vital points guarded, while he lurched forward toward King in the hope of effecting a clinch and gaining more time.

At the instant Sandel arose, King was at him, but the two blows he delivered were muffled on the stalled arms. The next moment Sandel was in the clinch and holding on desperately while the referee strove to drag the two men apart. King helped to force himself free. He knew the rapidity with which youth recovered, and he knew that Sandel was his if he could prevent that recovery. One stiff punch would do it. Sandel was his, indubitably his. He had outgeneraled him, outfought him, outpointed him. Sandel reeled out of the clinch, balanced on the hair line between defeat or survival. One good blow would topple him over and down and out. And Tom King, in a flash of bitterness, remembered the piece of steak and wished that he had it then behind that necessary punch he must deliver. He nerved himself for the blow, but it was not heavy enough nor swift enough. Sandel swayed but did not fall, staggering back to the ropes and holding on. King staggered after him, and, with a pang like that of dissolution, delivered another blow. But his body had deserted him. All that was left of him was a fighting intelligence that was dimmed and clouded from exhaustion. The blow that was aimed for the jaw struck no higher than the shoulder. He had willed the blow higher, but the tired muscles had not been able to obey. And, from the impact of the blow, Tom King himself reeled back and nearly fell. Once again he strove. This time his punch missed altogether, and from absolute weakness he fell against Sandel and clinched, holding on to him to save himself from sinking to the floor.

King did not attempt to free himself. He had shot his bolt. He was gone. And youth had been served. Even in the clinch he could feel Sandel growing stronger against him. When the referee thrust them apart, there, before his eyes, he saw youth recuperate. From instant to instant Sandel grew stronger. His punches, weak and futile at first, became stiff and accurate. Tom King's bleared eyes saw the gloved fist driving at his jaw, and he willed to guard it by interposing his arm. He saw the danger, willed the act; but the arm was too heavy. It seemed burdened with a hundredweight of lead. It would not lift itself, and he strove to lift it with his soul. Then the gloved fist landed home. He experienced a sharp snap that was like an electric spark, and simultaneously the veil of blackness enveloped him.

When he opened his eyes again he was in his corner, and he heard the yelling of the audience like the roar of the surf at Bondi Beach. A wet sponge was being pressed against the base of his brain, and Sid Sullivan was blowing cold water in a refreshing spray over his face and chest. His gloves had already been removed, and Sandel, bending over him, was shaking his hand. He bore no ill will toward the man who had put him out, and he returned the grip with a heartiness that made his battered knuckles protest. Then Sandel stepped to the center of the ring and the

audience hushed its pandemonium to hear him accept
young Pronto's challenge and offer to increase the side bet
to one hundred pounds. King looked on apathetically while
his seconds mopped the streaming water from him, dried
his face, and prepared him to leave the ring. He felt hungry. It was not the ordinary, gnawing kind, but a great
faintness, a palpitation at the pit of the stomach that communicated itself to all his body. He remembered back into
the fight to the moment when he had Sandel swaying and
tottering on the hairline balance of defeat. Ah, that piece of
steak would have done it! He had lacked just that for the
decisive blow, and he had lost. It was all because of the
piece of steak.

His seconds were half supporting him as they helped him
through the ropes. He tore free from them, ducked through
the ropes unaided, and leaped heavily to the floor, following on their heels as they forced a passage for him down
the crowded center aisle. Leaving the dressing room for the
street, in the entrance to the hall, some young fellow spoke
to him.

"W'y didn't yuh go in an' get 'im when yuh 'ad 'im?"
the young fellow asked.

"Aw, go to hell!" said Tom King, and passed down the
steps to the sidewalk.

The doors of the public house at the corner were swinging wide, and he saw the lights and the smiling barmaids,
heard the many voices discussing the fight and the prosperous chink of money on the bar. Somebody called to him
to have a drink. He hesitated perceptibly, then refused and
went on his way.

He had not a copper in his pocket, and the two-mile
walk home seemed very long. He was certainly getting old.
Crossing the Domain he sat down suddenly on a bench,
unnerved by the thought of the missus sitting up for him,
waiting to learn the outcome of the fight. That was harder
than any knockout, and it seemed almost impossible to face.

He felt weak and sore, and the pain of his smashed
knuckles warned him that, even if he could find a job
at navvy work, it would be a week before he could grip
a pick handle or a shovel. The hunger palpitation at the
pit of the stomach was sickening. His wretchedness overwhelmed him, and into his eyes came an unwonted moisture. He covered his face with his hands, and, as he cried,

he remembered Stowsher Bill and how he had served him that night in the long ago. Poor old Stowsher Bill! He could understand now why Bill had cried in the dressing room.

The Heathen

I MET HIM first in a hurricane; and though we had gone through the hurricane on the same schooner, it was not until the schooner had gone to pieces under us that I first laid eyes on him. Without doubt I had seen him with the rest of the Kanaka crew on board, but I had not consciously been aware of his existence, for the *Petite Jeanne* was rather overcrowded. In addition to her eight or ten Kanaka seamen, her white captain, mate, and supercargo, and her six cabin passengers, she sailed from Rangiroa with something like eighty-five deck passengers—Paumotans and Tahitians, men, women, and children each with a trade box, to say nothing of sleeping mats, blankets, and clothes bundles.

The pearling season in the Paumotus was over, and all hands were returning to Tahiti. The six of us cabin passengers were pearl buyers. Two were American, one was Ah Choon (the whitest Chinese I have ever known,, one was a German, one was a Polish Jew, and I completed the half dozen.

It had been a prosperous season. Not one of us had cause for complaint, nor one of the eighty-five deck passengers either. All had done well, and all were looking forward to a rest-off and a good time in Papeete.

Of course the *Petite Jeanne* was overloaded She was only seventy tons, and she had no right to carry a tithe of the mob she had on board. Beneath her hatches she was crammed and jammed with pearl shell and copra. Even the trade room was packed full with shell. It was a miracle that the sailors could work her. There was no moving about the decks. They simply climbed back and forth along the rails.

In the nighttime they walked upon the sleepers, who carpeted the deck, I'll swear, two deep. Oh, and there were pigs and chickens on deck, and sacks of yams, while every conceivable place was festooned with strings of drinking coconuts and bunches of bananas. On both sides, between the fore and main shrouds, guys had been stretched, just low enough for the foreboom to swing clear; and from each of these guys at least fifty bunches of bananas were suspended.

It promised to be a messy passage, even if we did make it in the two or three days that would have been required if the southeast trades had been blowing fresh. But they weren't blowing fresh. After the first five hours the trade died away in a dozen or so gasping fans. The calm continued all that night and the next day—one of those glaring, glassy calms, when the very thought of opening one's eyes to look at it is sufficient to cause a headache.

The second day a man died—an Easter Islander, one of the best divers that season in the lagoon. Smallpox—that is what it was; though how smallpox could come on board, when there had been no known cases ashore when we left Rangiroa, is beyond me. There it was, though—smallpox, a man dead, and three others down on their backs.

There was nothing to be done. We could not segregate the sick, nor could we care for them. We were packed like sardines. There was nothing to do but rot and die— that is, there was nothing to do after the night that followed the first death. On that night the mate, the supercargo, the Polish Jew, and four native divers sneaked away in the large whaleboat. They were never heard of again. In the morning the captain promptly scuttled the remaining boats, and there we were.

That day there were two deaths; the following day three; then it jumped to eight. It was curious to see how we took it. The natives, for instance, fell into a condition of dumb, stolid fear. The captain—Oudouse, his name was, a Frenchman—became very nervous and voluble. He actually got the twitches. He was a large, fleshy man, weighing at least two hundred pounds, and he quickly became a faithful representation of a quivering jelly mountain of fat.

The German, the two Americans, and myself bought up all the scotch whisky and proceeded to stay drunk. The theory was beautiful—namely, if we kept ourselves soaked in alcohol, every smallpox germ that came into contact with us would immediately be scorched to a cinder. And the theory worked, though I must confess that neither Captain

Oudouse nor Ah Choon were attacked by the disease either. The Frenchman did not drink at all, while Ah Choon restricted himself to one drink daily.

It was a pretty time. The sun, going into northern declination, was straight overhead. There was no wind, except for frequent squalls, which blew fiercely for from five minutes to half an hour, and wound up by deluging us with rain. After each squall the awful sun would come out, drawing clouds of steam from the soaked decks

The steam was not nice. It was the vapor of death, freighted with millions and millions of germs. We always took another drink when we saw it going up from the dead and dying, and usually we took two or three more drinks, mixing them exceptionally stiff. Also we made it a rule to take an additional several each time they hove the dead over to the sharks that swarmed about us.

We had a week of it, and then the whisky gave out. It is just as well, or I shouldn't be alive now. It took a sober man to pull through what followed, as you will agree when I mention the little fact that only two men did pull through. The other man was the heathen—at least, that was what I heard Captain Oudouse call him at the moment I first became aware of the heathen's existence. But to come back.

It was at the end of the week, with the whisky gone and the pearl buyers sober, that I happened to glance at the barometer that hung in the cabin companionway. Its normal register in the Paumotus was 29.90, and it was quite customary to see it vacillate between 29.85 and 30.00, or even 30.05; but to see it as I saw it, down to 29.62, was sufficient to sober the most drunken pearl buyer that ever incinerated smallpox microbes in scotch whisky.

I called Captin Oudouse's attention to it, only to be informed that he had watched it going down for several hours. There was little to do, but that little he did very well, considering the circumstances. He took off the light sails, shortened right down to storm canvas, spread life lines, and waited for the wind. His mistake lay in what he did after the wind came. He hove to on the port tack, which was the right thing to do south of the Equator if—and there was the rub—if one were not in the direct path of the hurricane.

We were in the direct path. I could see that by the

steady increase of the wind and the equally steady fall of the barometer. I wanted him to turn and run with the wind on the port quarter until the barometer ceased falling, and then to heave to. We argued till he was reduced to hysteria, but budge he would not. The worst of it was that I could not get the rest of the pearl buyers to back me up. Who was I, anyway, to know more about the sea and its ways than a properly qualified captain? was what was in their minds, I knew.

Of course the sea rose with the wind frightfully; and I shall never forget the first three seas the *Petite Jeanne* shipped. She had fallen off, as vessels do at times when hove to, and the first sea made a clean breach. The life lines were only for the strong and well, and little good were they even for them when the women and children, the bananas and coconuts, the pigs and trade boxes, the sick and the dying, were swept along in a solid, screeching, groaning mass.

The second sea filled the *Petite Jeanne's* decks flush with the rails; and as her stern sank down and her bow tossed skyward, all the miserable dunnage of life and luggage poured aft. It was a human torrent. They came head first, feet first, sidewise, rolling over and over, twisting, squirming, writhing, and crumpling up. Now and again one caught a grip on a stanchion or a rope; but the weight of the bodies behind tore such grips loose.

One man I noticed fetch up, head on and square on, with the starboard bitt. His head cracked like an egg. I saw what was coming, sprang on top of the cabin, and from there into the mainsail itself. Ah Choon and one of the Americans tried to follow me, but I was one jump ahead of them. The American was swept away and over the stern like a piece of chaff. Ah Choon caught a spoke of the wheel and swung in behind it. But a strappling Rarotonga *wahine* (woman)—she must have weighed two hundred and fifty—brought up against him and got an arm around his neck. He clutched the Kanaka steersman with his other hand; and just at that moment the schooner flung down to starboard.

The rush of bodies and sea that was coming along the port runway between the cabin and the rail turned abruptly and poured to starboard. Away they went—*wahine*, Ah Choon, and steersman; and I swear I saw Ah Choon grin at me with philosophic resignation as he cleared the rail and went under.

The third sea—the biggest of the three—did not do so much damage. By the time it arrived nearly everybody was in the rigging. On deck perhaps a dozen gasping, half-drowned, and half-stunned wretches were rolling about or attempting to crawl into safety. They went by the board, as did the wreckage of the two remaining boats. The other pearl buyers and myself, between seas, managed to get about fifteen women and children into the cabin and battened down. Little good it did the poor creatures in the end.

Wind? Out of all my experience I could not have believed it possible for the wind to blow as it did. There is no describing it. How can one describe a nightmare? It was the same way with that wind. It tore the clothes off our bodies. I say *tore them off*, and I mean it. I am not asking you to believe it. I am merely telling something that I saw and felt. There are times when I do not believe it myself. I went through it, and that is enough. One could not face that wind and live. It was a monstrous thing, and the most monstrous thing about it was that it increased and continued to increase.

Imagine countless millions and billions of tons of sand. Imagine this sand tearing along at ninety, a hundred, a hundred and twenty, or any other number of miles per hour. Imagine, further, this sand to be invisible, impalpable, yet to retain all the weight and density of sand. Do all this, and you may get a vague inkling of what that wind was like.

Perhaps sand is not the right comparison. Consider it mud, invisible, impalpable, but heavy as mud. Nay, it goes beyond that. Consider every molecule of air to be a mud-bank in itself. Then try to imagine the multitudinous impact of mudbanks. No; it is beyond me. Language may be adequate to express the ordinary conditions of life, but it cannot possibly express any of the conditions of so enormous a blast of wind. It would have been better had I stuck by my original intention of not attempting a description.

I will say this much: the sea, which had risen at first, was beaten down by that wind. More, it seemed as if the whole ocean had been sucked up in the maw of the hurricane, and hurled on through that portion of space which previously had been occupied by the air.

Of course our canvas had gone long before. But Captain Oudouse had on the *Petite Jeanne* something I had never before seen on a South Sea schooner—a sea anchor. It was a conical canvas bag, the mouth of which was kept open by a huge hoop of iron. The sea anchor was bridled something like a kite, so that it bit into the water as a kite bites into the air, but with a difference. The sea anchor remained just under the surface of the ocean in a perpendicular position. A long line, in turn, connected it with the schooner. As a result the *Petite Jeanne* rode bow on to the wind and to what sea there was.

The situation really would have been favorable had we not been in the path of the storm. True, the wind itself tore our canvas out of the gaskets, jerked out our topmasts, and made a raffle of our running gear, but still we would have come through nicely had we not been square in front of the advancing storm center. That was what fixed us. I was in a state of stunned, numbed, paralyzed collapse from enduring the impact of the wind, and I think I was just about ready to give up and die when the center smote us. The blow we received was an absolute lull. There was not a breath of air. The effect on one was sickening.

Remember that for hours we had been at terrific muscular tension, withstanding the awful pressure of that wind. And then, suddenly, the pressure was removed. I know that I felt as though I was about to expand, to fly apart in all directions. It seemed as if every atom composing my body was repelling every other atom and was on the verge of rushing off irresistibly into space. But that lasted only for a moment. Destruction was upon us.

In the absence of wind and pressure the sea rose. It jumped, it leaped, it soared straight toward the clouds. Remember, from every point of the compass that inconceivable wind was blowing in toward the center of calm. The result was that the seas sprang up from every point of the compass. There was no wind to check them. They popped up like corks released from the bottom of a pail of water. There was no system to them, no stability. They were hollow, maniacal seas. They were eighty feet high at the least. They were not seas at all. They resembled no sea a man had ever seen.

They were splashes, monstrous splashes—that is all. Splashes that were eighty feet high. Eighty! They were more than eighty. They went over our mastheads. They were spouts, explosions. They were drunken. They fell anywhere, anyhow. They jostled one another; they collided. They rushed together and collapsed upon one another, or fell apart like a thousand waterfalls all at once. It was no ocean any man had ever dreamed of, that hurricane center. It was confusion thrice confounded. It was anarchy. It was a hell pit of sea water gone mad.

The *Petite Jeanne?* I don't know. The heathen told me afterwards that he did not know. She was literally torn apart, ripped wide open, beaten into a pulp, smashed into kindling wood, annihilated. When I came to I was in the water, swimming automatically, though I was about two thirds drowned. How I got there I had no recollection. I remembered seeing the *Petite Jeanne* fly to pieces at what must have been the instant that my own consciousness was buffeted out of me. But there I was, with nothing to do but make the best of it, and in that best there was little promise. The wind was blowing again, the sea was much smaller and more regular, and I knew that I had passed through the center. Fortunately there were no sharks about. The hurricane had dissipated the ravenous horde that had surrounded the death ship and fed off the dead.

It was about midday when the *Petite Jeanne* went to pieces, and it must have been two hours afterward when I picked up with one of her hatch covers. Thick rain was driving at the time; and it was the merest chance that flung me and the hatch cover together. A short length of line was trailing from the rope handle; and I knew that I was good for a day, at least, if the sharks did not return. Three hours later, possibly a little longer, sticking close to the cover, and with closed eyes concentrating my whole soul upon the task of breathing in enough air to keep me going and at the same time of avoiding breathing in enough water to drown me, it seemed to me that I heard voices. The rain had ceased, and wind and sea were easing marvelously. Not twenty feet away from me, on another hatch cover, were Captain Oudouse and the heathen. They were fighting over the possession of the cover—at least, the Frenchman was.

"*Paĩen noir!*" I heard him scream, and at the same time I saw him kick the Kanaka.

Now Captain Oudouse had lost all his clothes except his shoes, and they were heavy brogans. It was a cruel blow, for it caught the heathen on the mouth and the point of the chin, half stunning him. I looked for him to retaliate, but he contented himself with swimming about forlornly a safe ten feet away. Whenever a fling of the sea threw him closer, the Frenchman, hanging on with his hands, kicked out at him with both feet. Also, at the moment of delivering each kick, he called the Kanaka a black heathen.

"For two centimes I'd come over there and drown you, you white beast!" I yelled.

The only reason I did not go was that I felt too tired. The very thought of the effort to swim over was nauseating. So I called to the Kanaka to come to me, and proceeded to share the hatch cover with him. Otoo, he told me his name was (pronounced ō-tō-ō); also he told me that he was a native of Borabora, the most westerly of the Society group. As I learned afterward, he had got the hatch cover first, and, after some time, encountering Captain Oudouse, had offered to share it with him, and had been kicked off for his pains.

And that was how Otoo and I first came together. He was no fighter. He was all sweetness and gentleness, a love creature, though he stood nearly six feet tall and was muscled like a gladiator. He was no fighter, but he was also no coward. He had the heart of a lion; and in the years that followed I have seen him run risks that I would never dream of taking. What I mean is that while he was no fighter, and while he always avoided precipitating a row, he never ran away from trouble when it started. And it was "'Ware shoal!" when once Otoo went into action. I shall never forget what he did to Bill King. It occurred in German Samoa. Bill King was hailed the champion heavyweight of the American Navy. He was a big brute of a man, a veritable gorilla, one of those hard-hitting, roughhousing chaps, and clever with his fists as well. He picked the quarrel, and he kicked Otoo twice and struck him once before Otoo felt it to be necessary to fight. I don't think it lasted four minutes, at the end of which time Bill King was the unhappy possessor of four broken ribs, a broken forearm, and a dislocated shoulder blade. Otoo knew nothing of scientific boxing. He was merely a manhandler; and Bill King was something like three months in recovering from the bit of manhandling he received that afternoon on Apia beach.

But I am running ahead of my yarn. We shared the hatch cover between us. We took turn and turn about, one lying flat on the cover and resting, while the other, submerged to the neck, merely held on with his hands. For two days and nights, spell and spell, on the cover and in the water, we drifted over the ocean. Toward the last I was delirious most of the time; and there were times, too, when I heard Otoo babbling and raving in his native tongue. Our continuous immersion prevented us from dying of thirst, though the sea water and the sunshine gave us the prettiest imaginable combination of salt pickle and sunburn.

In the end Otoo saved my life; for I came to lying on the beach twenty feet from the water, sheltered from the sun by a couple of coconut leaves. No one but Otoo could have dragged me there and stuck up the leaves for shade. He was lying beside me. I went off again; and the next time I came round it was cool and starry night, and Otoo was pressing a drinking coconut to my lips.

We were the sole survivors of the *Petite Jeanne*. Captain Oudouse must have succumbed to exhaustion, for several days later his hatch cover drifted ashore without him. Otoo and I lived with the natives of the atoll for a week, when we were rescued by the French cruiser and taken to Tahiti. In the meantime, however, we had performed the ceremony of exchanging names. In the South Seas such a ceremony binds two men closer together than blood brothership. The initiative had been mine; and Otoo was rapturously delighted when I suggested it.

"It is well," he said in Tahitian. "For we have been mates together for two days on the lips of Death."

"But Death stuttered." I smiled.

"It was a brave deed you did, master," he replied, "and Death was not vile enough to speak."

"Why do you 'master' me?" I demanded with a show of hurt feelings. "We have exchanged names. To you I am Otoo. To me you are Charley. And between you and me, forever and forever, you shall be Charley, and I shall be Otoo. It is the way of the custom. And when we die, if it does happen that we live again somewhere beyond the stars and the sky, still shall you be Charley to me, and I Otoo to you."

"Yes, master," he answered, his eyes luminous and soft with joy.

"There you go!" I cried indignantly.

"What does it matter what my lips utter?" he argued. "They are only my lips. But I shall think Otoo always. Whenever I think of myself, I shall think of you. Whenever men call me by name, I shall think of you. And beyond the sky and beyond the stars, always and forever, you shall be Otoo to me. Is it well, master?"

I hid my smile and answered that it was well.

We parted at Papeete. I remained ashore to recuperate; and he went on in a cutter to his own island, Borabora. Six weeks later he was back. I was surprised, for he had told me of his wife, and said that he was returning to her, and would give over sailing on far voyages.

"Where do you go, master?" he asked after our first greetings.

I shrugged my shoulders. It was a hard question.

"All the world," was my answer, "all the world, all the sea, and all the islands that are in the sea."

"I will go with you," he said simply. "My wife is dead."

I never had a brother; but from what I have seen of other men's brothers, I doubt if any man ever had a brother that was to him what Otoo was to me. He was brother and father and mother as well. And this I know: I lived a straighter and better man because of Otoo. I cared little for other men, but I had to live straight in Otoo's eyes. Because of him I dared not tarnish myself. He made me his ideal, compounding me, I fear, chiefly out of his own love and worship; and there were times when I stood close to the steep pitch of hell, and would have taken the plunge had not the thought of Otoo restrained me. His pride in me entered into me, until he became one of the major rules in my personal code to do nothing that would diminish that pride of his.

Naturally I did not learn right away what his feelings were toward me. He never criticized, never censured; and slowly the exalted place I held in his eyes dawned upon me, and slowly I grew to comprehend the hurt I could inflict upon him by being anything less than my best.

For seventeen years we were together; for seventeen years he was at my shoulder, watching while I slept, nursing me through fever and wounds—aye, and receiving wounds in fighting for me. He signed on the same ships with me; and together we ranged the Pacific from Hawaii to Sydney Head, and from Torres Straits to the Galápagos. We blackbirded from the New Hebrides and the Line Islands over to the westward clear through the Louisiades, New Britain, New Ireland, and New Hanover. We were wrecked three times— in the Gilberts, in the Santa Cruz group, and in the Fijis. And he traded and salved wherever a dollar promised in the way of pearl and pearl shell, copra, bêche-de-mer, hawkbill turtle shell, and stranded wrecks.

It began in Papeete, immediately after his announcement that he was going with me over all the sea, and the islands in the midst thereof. There was a club in those days in Papeete, where the pearlers, traders, captains, and riffraff of South Sea adventurers forgathered. The play ran high, and the drink ran high; and I am very much afraid that I kept later hours than were becoming or proper. No matter what the hour was when I left the club, there was Otoo waiting to see me safely home.

At first I smiled; next I chided him. Then I told him flatly that I stood in need of no wet-nursing. After that I did not see him when I came out of the club. Quite by accident, a week or so later, I discovered that he still saw me home, lurking across the street among the shadows of the mango trees. What could I do? I know what I did do.

Insensibly I began to keep better hours. On wet and stormy nights, in the thick of the folly and the fun, the thought would persist in coming to me of Otoo keeping his dreary vigil under the dripping mangoes. Truly, he made a better man of me. Yet he was not strait-laced. And he knew nothing of common Christian morality. All the people on Borabora were Christians; but he was a heathen, the only unbeliever on the island, a gross materialist, who believed that when he died he was dead. He believed merely in fair play and square dealing. Petty meanness, in his code, was almost as serious as wanton homicide; and I do believe that he respected a murderer more than a man given to small practices.

Concerning me, personally, he objected to my doing anything that was hurtful to me. Gambling was all right. He was an ardent gambler himself. But late hours, he explained, were bad for one's health. He had seen men who did not take care of themselves die of fever. He was no teetotaler, and welcomed a stiff nip any time when it was wet work in the boats. On the other hand, he believed in liquor in moderation. He had seen many men killed or disgraced by square-face or scotch.

Otoo had my welfare always at heart. He thought ahead for me, weighed my plans, and took a greater interest in them than I did myself. At first, when I was unaware of this interest of his in my affairs, he had to divine my intentions, as, for instance, at Papeete, when I contemplated going partners with a knavish fellow countryman on a guana venture. I did not know he was a knave. Nor did any white man in Papeete. Neither did Otoo know, but he saw how thick we were getting, and found out for me, and without my asking him. Native sailors from the ends of the seas knock about on the beach in Tahiti; and Otoo, suspicious merely, went among them till he had gathered sufficient data to justify his suspicions. Oh, it was a nice history, that of Randolph Waters. I couldn't believe it when Otoo first narrated it; but when I sheeted it home to Waters he gave in without a murmur and got away on the first steamer to Auckland.

At first, I am free to confess, I couldn't help resenting Otoo's poking his nose into my business. But I knew that he was wholly unselfish; and soon I had to acknowledge his wisdom and discretion. He had his eyes open always to my main chance, and he was both keen-sighted and farsighted. In time he became my counselor, until he knew more of my business than I did myself. He really had my interest at heart more than I did. Mine was the magnificent carelessness of youth, for I preferred romance to dollars, and adventure to a comfortable billet with all night in. So it was well that I had someone to look out for me. I know that if it had not been for Otoo I should not be here today.

Of numerous instances, let me give one. I had had some experience in blackbirding before I went pearling in the Paumotus. Otoo and I were on the beach in Samoa—we really were on the beach and hard aground—when my chance came to go as recruiter on a blackbird brig. Otoo signed on before the mast; and for the next half-dozen years, in as many ships, we knocked about the wildest portions of Melanesia. Otoo saw to it that he always pulled stroke oar in my boat. Our custom in recruiting labor was to land the recruiter on the beach. The covering boat always lay on its oars several hundred feet offshore, while the recruiter's boat, also lying on its oars, kept afloat on the edge of the beach. When I landed with my trade goods, leaving my steering sweep apeak, Otoo left his stroke position and came into the stern sheets, where a Winchester lay ready to hand under a flap of canvas. The boat's crew was also armed, the Sniders concealed under canvas flaps that ran the length of the gunwales. While I was busy arguing and persuading the woolly-headed cannibals to come and labor on the Queensland plantations, Otoo kept watch. And often and often his low voice warned me of suspicious actions and impending treachery. Sometimes it was the quick shot from his rifle that was the first warning I received. And in my rush to the boat his hand was always there to jerk me flying aboard. Once, I remember, on *Santa Anna*, the boat grounded just as the trouble began. The covering boat was dashing to our assistance, but the several score of savages would have wiped us out before it arrived. Otoo took a flying leap ashore, dug both hands into the trade goods, and scattered tobacco, beads, tomahawks, knives, and calicoes in all directions.

This was too much for the woolly-heads. While they scrambled for the treasures, the boat was shoved clear, and we were aboard and forty feet away. And I got thirty recruits off that very beach in the next four hours.

The particular instance I have in mind was on Malaita, the most savage island in the easterly Solomons. The natives had been remarkably friendly; and how were we to know that the whole village had been taking up a collection for over two years with which to buy a white's man's head? The beggars are all head-hunters, and they especially esteem a white man's head. The fellow who captured the head would receive the whole collection. As I say, they appeared very friendly; and on this day I was fully a hundred yards down the beach from the boat. Otoo had cautioned me; and, as usual when I did not heed him, I came to grief.

The first I knew, a cloud of spears sailed out of the mangrove swamp at me. At least a dozen were sticking into me. I started to run, but tripped over one that was fast in my calf, and went down. The woolly-heads made a run for me, each with a long-handled, fantail tomahawk with which to hack off my head. They were so eager for the prize that they

got in one another's way. In the confusion I avoided several
hacks by throwing myself right and left on the sand.

Then Otoo arrived—Otoo the manhandler. In some way
he had got hold of a heavy war club, and at close quarters it
was a far more efficient weapon than a rifle. He was right
in the thick of them, so that they could not spear him, while
their tomahawks seemed worse than useless. He was fighting
for me, and he was in a true berserker rage. The way he
handled that club was amazing. Their skulls squashed like
overripe oranges. It was not until he had driven them back,
picked me up in his arms, and started to run that he received
his first wounds. He arrived in the boat with four spear
thrusts, got his Winchester, and with it got a man for every
shot. Then we pulled aboard the schooner and doctored up.

Seventeen years we were together. He made me. I should
today be a supercargo, a recruiter, or a memory, if it had not
been for him.

"You spend your money, and you go out and get more,"
he said one day. "It is easy to get money now. But when you
get old, your money will be spent, and you will not be able
to go out and get more. I know, master. I have studied the
way of white men. On the beaches are many old men who
were young once, and who could get money just like you.
Now they are old, and they have nothing, and they wait
about for the young men like you to come ashore and buy
drinks for them.

"The black boy is a slave on the plantations. He gets twenty
dollars a year. He works hard. The overseer does not work
hard. He rides a horse and watches the black boy work. He
gets twelve hundred dollars a year. I am a sailor on the
schooner. I get fifteen dollars a month. That is because I am
a good sailor. I work hard. The captain has a double awning
and drinks beer out of long bottles. I have never seen him
haul a rope or pull an oar. He gets one hundred and fifty
dollars a month. I am a sailor. He is a navigator. Master, I
think it would be very good for you to know navigation."

Otoo spurred me on to it. He sailed with me as second
mate on my first schooner, and he was far prouder of my
command than I was myself. Later on it was:

"The captain is well paid, master; but the ship is in his
keeping, and he is never free from the burden. It is the owner
who is better paid—and the owner who sits ashore with
many servants and turns his money over."

"True, but a schooner costs five thousand dollars—an old schooner at that," I objected. "I should be an old man before I saved five thousand dollars."

"There be short ways for white men to make money," he went on, pointing ashore at the coconut-fringed beach.

We were in the Solomons at the time, picking up a cargo of ivory nuts along the east coast of Guadalcanal.

"Between this river mouth and the next it is two miles," he said. "The flat land runs far back. It is worth nothing now. Next year—who knows?—or the year after, men will pay much money for that land. The anchorage is good. Big steamers can lie close up. You can buy the land four miles deep from the old chief for ten thousand sticks of tobacco, ten bottles of squareface, and a Snider, which will cost you, maybe, one hundred dollars. Then you place the deed with the commissioner; and the next year, or the year after, you sell and become the owner of a ship."

I followed his lead, and his words came true, though in three years instead of two. Next came the grasslands deal on Guadalcanal—twenty thousand acres, on a governmental nine hundred and ninety-nine years' lease at a nominal sum. I owned the lease for precisely ninety days, when I sold it to a company for half a fortune. Always it was Otoo who looked ahead and saw the opportunity. He was responsible for the salving of the Doncaster—bought in at auction for a hundred pounds, and clearing three thousand after every expense was paid. He led me into the Savaii plantation and the cocoa venture on Upolu.

We did not go seafaring so much as in the old days. I was too well off. I married, and my standard of living rose; but Otoo remained the same old-time Otoo, moving about the house or trailing through the office, his wooden pipe in his mouth, a shilling undershirt on his back, and a four-shilling lava-lava about his loins. I could not get him to spend money. There was no way of repaying him except with love, and God knows he got that in full measure from all of us. The children worshipped him and if he had been spoilable, my wife would surely have been his undoing.

The children! He really was the one who showed them the way of their feet in the world practical. He began by teaching them to walk. He sat up with them when they were sick. One by one, when they were scarcely toddlers, he took them down to the lagoon and made them into amphibians. He taught them more than I ever knew of the habits of fish and the ways of catching them. In the bush it was the same thing. At seven Tom knew more woodcraft than I ever dreamed existed. At six Mary went over the Sliding Rock without a quiver, and I had seen strong men balk at that feat. And when Frank had just turned six he could bring up shillings from the bottom in three fathoms.

"My people in Borabora do not like heathen—they are all Christians; and I do not like Borabora Christians," he said one day, when I, with the idea of getting him to spend some of the money that was rightfully his, had been trying to persuade him to make a visit to his own island in one of our schooners—a special voyage which I had hoped to make a record breaker in the matter of prodigal expense.

I say one of our schooners, though legally at the time they belonged to me. I struggled long with him to enter into partnership.

"We have been partners from the day the *Petite Jeanne* went down," he said at last. "But if your heart so wishes, then shall we become partners by the law. I have no work to do, yet are my expenses large. I drink and eat and smoke in plenty—it costs much, I know. I do not pay for the playing of billiards, for I play on your table; but still the money goes. Fishing on the reef is only a rich man's pleasure. It is shocking, the cost of hooks and cotton line. Yes; it is necessary that we be partners by law. I need the money. I shall get it from the head clerk in the office."

So the papers were made out and recorded. A year later I was compelled to complain.

"Charley," said I, "you are a wicked old fraud, a miserly skinflint, a miserable land crab. Behold, your share for the year in all our partnership has been thousands of dollars. The head clerk has given me this paper. It says that in the year you have drawn just eighty-seven dollars and twenty cents."

"Is there any owing me?" he asked anxiously.

"I tell you thousands and thousands," I answered.

His face brightened, as with an immense relief.

"It is well," he said. "See that the head clerk keeps good account of it. When I want it, I shall want it, and there must not be a cent missing."

"If there is," he added fiercely, after a pause, "it must come out of the clerk's wages."

And all the time, as I afterward learned, his will, drawn up by Carruthers, and making me sole beneficiary, lay in the American consul's safe.

But the end came, as the end must come to all human associations. It occurred in the Solomons, where our wildest work had been done in the wild young days, and where we were once more—principally on a holiday, incidentally to look after our holdings on Florida Island and to look over the pearling possibilities of the Mboli Pass. We were lying at Savu, having run in to trade for curios.

Now Savu is alive with sharks. The custom of the woolly-heads of burying their dead in the sea did not tend to discourage the sharks from making the adjacent waters a hangout. It was my luck to be coming aboard in a tiny, overloaded, native canoe when the thing capsized. There were four woolly-heads and myself in it, or, rather hanging to it. The schooner was a hundred yards away. I was just hailing for a boat when one of the woolly-heads began to scream. Holding on to the end of the canoe, both he and that portion of the canoe were dragged under several times. Then he loosed his clutch and disappeared. A shark had got him.

The three remaining woolly-heads tried to climb out of the water upon the bottom of the canoe. I yelled and cursed and struck at the nearest with my fist, but it was no use. They were in a blind funk. The canoe could barely have supported one of them. Under the three it upended and rolled sidewise, throwing them back into the water.

I abandoned the canoe and started to swim toward the schooner, expecting to be picked up by the boat before I got there. One of the woolly-heads elected to come with me, and we swam along silently, side by side, now and again putting our faces into the water and peering about for sharks. The screams of the man who stayed by the canoe informed us that he was taken. I was peering into the water when I saw a big shark pass directly beneath me. He was fully sixteen feet in length. I saw the whole thing. He got the woolly-head by the middle, and away he went, the poor devil, head, shoulders, and arms out of water all the time, screeching in a heart-rending way. He was carried along in this fashion for several hundred feet, when he was dragged beneath the surface.

I swam doggedly on, hoping that that was the last unattached shark. But there was another. Whether it was one that had attacked the natives earlier, or whether it was one that had made a good meal elsewhere, I do not know. At any rate, he was not in such haste as the others. I could not swim so rapidly now, for a large part of my effort was devoted to keeping track of him. I was watching him when he made his first attack. By good luck I got both hands on his nose, and though his momentum nearly shoved me under, I managed to keep him off. He veered clear and began circling about again. A second time I escaped him by the same maneuver. The third rush was a miss on both sides. He sheered at the moment my hands should have landed on his nose, but his sandpaper hide (I had on a sleeveless undershirt) scraped the skin off one arm from elbow to shoulder.

By this time I was played out, and gave up hope. The schooner was still two hundred feet away. My face was in the water, and I was watching him maneuver for another attempt, when I saw a brown body pass between us. It was Otoo.

"Swim for the schooner, master!" he said. And he spoke gaily, as though the affair was a mere lark. "I know sharks. The shark is my brother."

I obeyed, swimming slowly on, while Otoo swam about me, keeping always between me and the shark, foiling his rushes and encouraging me.

"The davit tackle carried away, and they are rigging the falls," he explained a minute or so later, and then went under to head off another attack.

By the time the schooner was thirty feet away I was about done for. I could scarcely move. They were heaving lines at us from on board, but they continually fell short. The shark, finding that it was receiving no hurt, had become bolder. Several times it nearly got me, but each time Otoo was there just the moment before it was too late. Of course Otoo could have saved himself any time. But he stuck by me.

"Good-by, Charley! I'm finished!" I just managed to gasp.

I knew that the end had come, and that the next moment I should throw up my hands and go down.

But Otoo laughed in my face, saying:

"I will show you a new trick. I will make that shark feel sick!"

He dropped in behind me, where the shark was preparing to come at me.

"A little more to the left!" he next called out. "There is a line there on the water. To the left, master—to the left!"

I changed my course and struck out blindly. I was by that time barely conscious. As my hand closed on the line I heard an exclamation from on board. I turned and looked. There was no sign of Otoo. The next instant he broke surface. Both hands were off at the wrist, the stumps spouting blood.

"Otoo!" he called softly. And I could see in his gaze the love that thrilled in his voice.

Then, and then only, at the very last of all our years, he called me by that name.

"Good-by, Otoo!" he called.

Then he was dragged under, and I was hauled aboard, where I fainted in the captain's arms.

And so passed Otoo, who saved me and made me a man, and who saved me in the end. We met in the maw of a hurricane and parted in the maw of a shark, with seventeen intervening years of comradeship, the like of which I dare to assert has never befallen two men, the one brown and the other white. If Jehovah be from His high place watching every sparrow fall, not least in His kingdom shall be Otoo, the one heathen of Borabora.

The Law of Life

OLD KOSKOOSH LISTENED greedily. Though his sight had long since faded, his hearing was still acute, and the slightest sound penetrated to the glimmering intelligence which yet abode behind the withered forehead, but which no longer gazed forth upon the things of the world. Ah! That was Sit-cum-to-ha, shrilly anathematizing the dogs as she cuffed and beat them into the harnesses. Sit-cum-to-ha was his daughter's daughter, but she was too busy to waste a thought upon her broken grandfather, sitting alone there in the snow, forlorn and helpless. Camp must be broken. The long trail waited while the short day refused to linger. Life called her, and the duties of life, not death. And he was very close to death now.

The thought made the old man panicky for the moment, and he stretched forth a palsied hand which wandered tremblingly over the small heap of dry wood beside him. Reassured that it was indeed there, his hand returned to the shelter of his mangy furs, and he again fell to listening. The sulky crackling of half-frozen hides told him that the chief's moose-skin lodge had been struck, and even then was being rammed and jammed into portable compass. The chief was his son, stalwart and strong, headman of the tribesmen, and a mighty hunter. As the women toiled with the camp luggage, his voice rose, chiding them for their slowness. Old Koskoosh strained his ears. It was the last time he would hear that voice. There went Geehow's lodge! And Tusken's! Seven, eight, nine; only the shaman's could be still standing. There! They were at work upon it now. He could hear the shaman grunt as he piled it on the sled. A child whimpered, and a woman soothed it with soft, crooning gutturals. Little Koo-tee, the old man thought, a fretful child, and not overstrong. It would die soon, perhaps, and they would burn a hole through the frozen tundra and pile rocks above to keep the wolverines away. Well, what did it matter? A few years at best, and as many an empty belly as a full one. And in the end, Death waited, ever-hungry and hungriest of them all.

What was that? Oh, the men lashing the sleds and drawing tight the thongs. He listened, who would listen no more. The whiplashes snarled and bit among the dogs. Hear them whine! How they hated the work and the trail! They were off! Sled after sled churned slowly away into the silence. They were gone. They had passed out of his life, and he faced the last bitter hour alone. No. The snow crunched beneath a moccasin; a man stood beside him; upon his head a hand rested gently. His son was good to do this thing. He remembered other old men whose sons had not waited after the tribe. But his son had. He wandered away into the past, till the young man's voice brought him back.

"It is well with you?" he asked.

And the old man answered, "It is well."

"There be wood beside you," the younger man continued, "and the fire burns bright. The morning is gray, and the cold has broken. It will snow presently. Even now it is snowing."

"Aye, even now is it snowing."

"The tribesmen hurry. Their bales are heavy and their bellies flat with lack of feasting. The trail is long and they travel fast. I go now. It is well?"

"It is well. I am as a last year's leaf, clinging lightly to the stem. The first breath that blows, and I fall. My voice is become like an old woman's. My eyes no longer show me the way of my feet, and my feet are heavy, and I am tired. It is well."

He bowed his head in content till the last noise of the complaining snow had died away, and he knew his son was beyond recall. Then his hand crept out in haste to the wood. It alone stood between him and the eternity that yawned in upon him. At last the measure of his life was a handful of faggots. One by one they would go to feed the fire, and just so, step by step, death would creep upon him. When the last stick had surrendered up its heat, the frost would begin to gather strength. First his feet would yield, then his hands; and the numbness would travel, slowly, from the extremities to the body. His head would fall forward upon his knees, and he would rest. It was easy. All men must die.

He did not complain. It was the way of life, and it was just. He had been born close to the earth, close to the earth had he lived, and the law thereof was not new to him. It was the law of all flesh. Nature was not kindly to the flesh. She had no concern for that concrete thing called the individual. Her interest lay in the species, the race. This was the deepest abstraction old Koskoosh's barbaric mind was capable of, but he grasped it firmly. He saw it exemplified in all life. The rise of the sap, the bursting greenness of the willow bud, the fall of the yellow leaf—in this alone was told the whole history. But one task did Nature set the individual. Did he not perform it, he died. Did he perform it, it was all the same, he died. Nature did not care; there were plenty who were obedient, and it was only the obedience in this matter, not the obedient, which lived and lived always. The tribe of Koskoosh was very old. The old men he had known when a boy had known old men before them. Therefore it was true that the tribe lived, that it stood for the obedience of all its members, way down into the forgotten past, whose very resting places were unremembered. They did not count; they were episodes. They had passed away like clouds from a summer sky. He also was an episode and would pass away. Nature did not care. To life she set one task, gave one law. To perpetuate was the task of life, its law was death. A maiden was a good creature to look upon, full-breasted and strong, with spring to her step and light in her eyes. But her task was yet before her. The light in her eyes brightened, her step quickened, she was now bold with the young men, now timid, and she gave them of her own unrest. And ever she grew fairer and yet fairer to look upon, till some hunter, able no longer to withhold himself, took her to his lodge to cook and toil for him and to become the mother of his children. And with the coming of her offspring her looks left her. Her limbs dragged and shuffled, her eyes dimmed and bleared, and only the little children found joy against the withered cheek of the old squaw by the fire. Her task was done. But a little while, on the first pinch of famine or the first long trail, and she would be left, even as he had been left, in the snow, with a little pile of wood. Such was the law.

He placed a stick carefully upon the fire and resumed his meditations. It was the same everywhere, with all things. The mosquitoes vanished with the first frost. The little tree squirrel crawled away to die. When age settled upon the rabbit it became slow and heavy and could no longer outfoot its enemies. Even the big bald-face grew clumsy and blind and quarrelsome, in the end to be dragged down by a handful of yelp-ing huskies. He remembered how he had abandoned his own father on an upper reach of the Klondike one winter, the win-ter before the missionary came with his talk books and his box of medicines. Many a time had Koskoosh smacked his lips over the recollection of that box, though now his mouth refused to moisten. The "painkiller" had been especially good. But the missionary was a bother after all, for he brought no meat into the camp, and he ate heartily, and the hunters grumbled. But he chilled his lungs on the divide by the Mayo, and the dogs afterward nosed the stones away and fought over his bones.

Koskoosh placed another stick on the fire and harked back deeper into the past. There was the time of the great famine, when the old men crouched empty-bellied to the fire, and let fall from their lips dim traditions of the ancient day when the Yukon ran wide open for three winters, and then lay frozen for three summers. He had lost his mother in that famine. In the summer the salmon run had failed, and the tribe looked forward to the winter and the coming of the caribou. Then the winter came, but with it there were no caribou. Never had the like been known, not even in the lives of the old men. But the caribou did not come, and it was the seventh year, and the rabbits had not replenished, and the dogs were naught but bundles of bones. And through the long darkness the children wailed and died, and the women, and the old men; and not one in ten of the tribe lived to meet the sun when it came back in the spring. That was a famine!

But he had seen times of plenty, too, when the meat spoiled on their hands, and the dogs were fat and worthless with overeating—times when they let the game go unkilled, and the women were fertile, and the lodges were cluttered with sprawling men-children and women-children. Then it was the men became high-stomached, and revived ancient quarrels, and crossed the divides to the south to kill the Pellys, and to the west that they might sit by the dead fires of the Tananas. He remembered, when a boy, during a time of plenty, when he saw a moose pulled down by the wolves. Zing-ha lay with him in the snow and watched—Zing-ha, who later became the craftiest of hunters, and who, in the end, fell through an air hole on the Yukon. They found him, a month afterward, just as he had crawled halfway out and frozen stiff to the ice.

But the moose. Zing-ha and he had gone out that day to play at hunting after the manner of their fathers. On the bed of the creek they struck the fresh track of a moose, and with it the tracks of many wolves. "An old one," Zing-ha, who was quicker at reading the sign, said, "an old one who cannot keep up with the herd. The wolves have cut him out from his brothers, and they will never leave him." And it was so. It was their way. By day and by night, never resting, snarling on his heels, snapping at his nose, they would stay by him to the end. How Zing-ha and he felt the blood lust quicken! The finish would be a sight to see!

Eager-footed, they took the trail, and even he, Koskoosh, slow of sight and an unversed tracker, could have followed it blind, it was so wide. Hot were they on the heels of the chase, reading the grim tragedy, fresh-written, at every step. Now they came to where the moose had made a stand. Thrice the length of a grown man's body, in every direction, had the snow been stamped about and uptossed. In the midst were the deep impressions of the splay-hoofed game, and all about, everywhere, were the lighter footmarks of the wolves. Some, while their brothers harried the kill, had lain to one side and rested. The full-stretched impress of their bodies in the snow was as perfect as though made the moment before. One wolf had been caught in a wild lunge of the maddened victim and trampled to death. A few bones, well picked, bore witness.

Again, they ceased the uplift of their snowshoes at a second stand. Here the great animal had fought desperately. Twice had he been dragged down, as the snow attested, and twice had he shaken his assailants clear and gained footing once more. He had done his task long since, but none the less was life dear to him. Zing-ha said it was a strange thing, a moose once down to get free again; but this one certainly had. The shaman would see signs and wonders in this when they told him.

And yet again, they come to where the moose had made to mount the bank and gain the timber. But his foes had laid on from behind, till he reared and fell back upon them, crushing two deep into the snow. It was plain the kill was at hand, for their brothers had left them untouched. Two more stands were hurried past, brief in time length and very close together. The trail was red now, and the clean stride of the

great beast had grown short and slovenly. Then they heard
the first sounds of the battle—not the full-throated chorus of
the chase, but the short, snappy bark which spoke of close
quarters and teeth to flesh. Crawling up the wind, Zing-ha
bellied it through the snow, and with him crept he, Koskoosh,
who was to be chief of the tribesmen in the years to come.
Together they shoved aside the underbranches of a young
spruce and peered forth. It was the end they saw.

The picture, like all of youth's impressions, was still strong
with him, and his dim eyes watched the end played out as
vividly as in that far-off time. Koskoosh marveled at this, for
in the days which followed, when he was a leader of men
and a head of councilors, he had done great deeds and made
his name a curse in the mouths of the Pellys, to say naught
of the strange white man he had killed, knife to knife, in
open fight.

For long he pondered on the days of his youth, till the
fire died down and the frost bit deeper. He replenished it with
two sticks this time, and gauged his grip on life by what remained. If Sit-cum-to-ha had only remembered her grandfather, and gathered a larger armful, his hours would have
been longer. It would have been easy. But she was ever a
careless child, and honored not her ancestors from the time
the Beaver, son of the son of Zing-ha, first cast eyes upon her.
Well, what mattered it? Had he not done likewise in his own
quick youth? For a while he listened to the silence. Perhaps
the heart of his son might soften, and he would come back
with the dogs to take his old father on with the tribe to
where the caribou ran thick and the fat hung heavy upon
them.

He strained his ears, his restless brain for the moment
stilled. Not a stir, nothing. He alone took breath in the midst
of the great silence. It was very lonely. Hark! What was that?
A chill passed over his body. The familiar, long-drawn howl
broke the void, and it was close at hand. Then on his dark-
ened eyes was projected the vision of the moose—the old
bull moose—the torn flanks and bloody sides, the riddled
mane, and the great branching horns, down low and tossing
to the last. He saw the flashing forms of gray, the gleaming
eyes, the lolling tongues, the slavered fangs. And he saw the
inexorable circle close in till it became a dark point in the
midst of the stamped snow.

A cold muzzle thrust against his cheek, and at its touch his soul leaped back to the present. His hand shot into the fire and dragged out a burning faggot. Overcome for the nonce by his hereditary fear of man, the brute retreated, raising a prolonged call to his brothers; and greedily they answered, till a ring of crouching, jaw-slobbered gray was stretched round about. The old man listened to the drawing in of this circle. He waved his brand wildly, and sniffs turned to snarls; but the panting brutes refused to scatter. Now one wormed his chest forward, dragging his haunches after, now a second, now a third; but never a one drew back. Why should he cling to life? he asked, and dropped the blazing stick into the snow. It sizzled and went out. The circle grunted uneasily but held its own. Again he saw the last stand of the old bull moose, and Koskoosh dropped his head wearily upon his knees. What did it matter after all? Was it not the law of life?

To the Man On Trail

"DUMP IT IN."

"But I say, Kid, isn't that going it a little too strong? Whisky and alcohol's bad enough; but when it comes to brandy and pepper sauce and——"

"Dump it in. Who's making this punch, anyway?" And Malemute Kid smiled benignantly through the clouds of steam. "By the time you've been in this country as long as I have, my son, and lived on rabbit tracks and salmon belly, you'll learn that Christmas comes only once per annum. And a Christmas without punch is sinking a hole to bedrock with nary a pay streak."

"Stack up on that fer a high cyard," approved Big Jim Belden, who had come down from his claim on Mazy May to spend Christmas, and who, as everyone knew, had been living the two months past on straight moose meat. "Hain't fergot the hooch we-uns made on the Tanana, hev yeh?"

"Well, I guess yes. Boys, it would have done your hearts good to see that whole tribe fighting drunk—and all because of a glorious ferment of sugar and sour dough. That was before your time," Malemute Kid said as he turned to Stanley Prince, a young mining expert who had been in two years. "No white women in the country then, and Mason wanted to get married. Ruth's father was chief of the Tananas, and objected, like the rest of the tribe. Stiff? Why, I used my last pound of sugar; finest work in that line I ever did in my life. You should have seen the chase, down the river and across the portage."

"But the squaw?" asked Louis Savoy, the tall French Canadian, becoming interested; for he had heard of this wild deed when at Forty Mile the preceding winter.

The Malemute Kid, who was a born raconteur, told the

116

unvarnished tale of the Northland Lochinvar. More than one rough adventurer of the North felt his heartstrings draw closer and experienced vague yearnings for the sunnier pastures of the Southland, where life promised something more than a barren struggle with cold and death.

"We struck the Yukon just behind the first ice run," he concluded, "and the tribe only a quarter of an hour behind. But that saved us; for the second run broke the jam above and shut them out. When they finally got into Nuklukyeto, the whole post was ready for them. And as to the forgathering, ask Father Roubeau here: he performed the ceremony."

The Jesuit took the pipe from his lips but could only express his gratification with patriarchal smiles, while Protestant and Catholic vigorously applauded.

"By gar!" ejaculated Louis Savoy, who seemed overcome by the romance of it. "*La petite* squaw; mon Mason *brav*. By gar!"

Then, as the first tin cups of punch went round, Bettles the Unquenchable sprang to his feet and struck up his favorite drinking song:

> "There's Henry Ward Beecher
> And Sunday-school teachers,
>   All drink of the sassafras root;
> But you bet all the same,
> If it had its right name,
>   It's the juice of the forbidden fruit."

"Oh, the juice of the forbidden fruit,"

roared out the bacchanalian chorus,

> "Oh, the juice of the forbidden fruit;
>   But you bet all the same,
>   If it had its right name,
> It's the juice of the forbidden fruit."

Malemute Kid's frightful concoction did its work; the men of the camps and trails unbent in its genial glow, and jest and song and tales of past adventure went round the board. Aliens from a dozen lands, they toasted each and all. It was the Englishman, Prince, who pledged "Uncle Sam, the precocious infant of the New World"; the Yankee, Bettles, who drank to "The Queen, God bless her"; and together, Savoy and Meyers, the German trader, clanged their cups to Alsace and Lorraine.

Then Malemute Kid arose, cup in hand, and glanced at the greased-paper window, where the frost stood full three inches thick. "A health to the man on trail this night; may his grub hold out; may his dogs keep their legs; may his matches never miss fire."

Crack! Crack! They heard the familiar music of the dog whip, the whining howl of the Malemutes, and the crunch of a sled as it drew up to the cabin. Conversation languished while they waited the issue.

"An old-timer; cares for his dogs and then himself," whispered Malemute Kid to Prince as they listened to the snapping jaws and the wolfish snarls and yelps of pain which proclaimed to their practiced ears that the stranger was beating back their dogs while he fed his own.

Then came the expected knock, sharp and confident, and the stranger entered. Dazzled by the light, he hesitated a moment at the door, giving to all a chance for scrutiny. He was a striking personage, and a most picturesque one, in his Arctic dress of wool and fur. Standing six foot two or three, with proportionate breadth of shoulders and depth of chest, his smooth-shaven face nipped by the cold to a gleaming pink, his long lashes and eyebrows white with ice, and the ear and neck flaps of his great wolfskin cap loosely raised, he seemed, of a verity, the Frost King, just stepped in out of the night. Clasped outside his Mackinaw jacket, a beaded belt held two large Colt's revolvers and a hunting knife, while he carried, in addition to the inevitable dog whip, a smokeless rifle of the largest bore and latest pattern. As he came forward, for all his step was firm and elastic, they could see that fatigue bore heavily upon him.

An awkward silence had fallen, but his hearty "What cheer, my lads?" put them quickly at ease, and the next instant Malemute Kid and he had gripped hands. Though they had never met, each had heard of the other, and the recognition was mutual. A sweeping introduction and a mug of punch were forced upon him before he could explain his errand.

"How long since that basket sled, with three men and eight dogs, passed?" he asked.

"An even two days ahead. Are you after them?"

"Yes; my team. Run them off under my very nose, the cusses. I've gained two days on them already—pick them up on the next run."

"Reckon they'll show spunk?" asked Belden, in order to keep up the conversation, for Malemute Kid already had the coffee-pot on and was busily frying bacon and moose meat.

The stranger significantly tapped his revolvers.

"When'd yeh leave Dawson?"

"Twelve o'clock."

"Last night?"—as a matter of course.

"Today."

A murmur of surprise passed round the circle. And well it might; for it was just midnight, and seventy-five miles of rough river trail was not to be sneered at for a twelve hours' run.

The talk soon became impersonal, however, harking back to the trails of childhood. As the young stranger ate of the rude fare Malemute Kid attentively studied his face. Nor was he long in deciding that it was fair, honest, and open, and that he liked it. Still youthful, the lines had been firmly traced by toil and hardship. Though genial in conversation, and mild when at rest, the blue eyes gave promise of the hard steel-glitter which comes when called into action, especially against odds. The heavy jaw and square-cut chin demonstrated rugged pertinacity and indomitability. Nor, though the attributes of the lion were there, was there wanting the certain softness, the hint of womanliness, which bespoke the emotional nature.

"So thet's how me an' the ol' woman got spliced," said Belden, concluding the exciting tale of his courtship. " 'Here we be, Dad,' sez she. 'An' may yeh be damned,' sez he to her, an' then to me, 'Jim, yeh—yeh git outen them good duds o' yourn; I want a right peart slice o' thet forty acre plowed 'fore dinner.' An' then he turns on her an' sez, 'An' yeh, Sal; yeh sail inter them dishes.' An' then he sort o' sniffled an' kissed her. An' I was thet happy—but he seen me an' roars out, 'Yeh, Jim!' An' yeh bet I dusted fer the barn."

"Any kids waiting for you back in the States?" asked the stranger.

"Nope; Sal died 'fore any come. Thet's why I'm here." Belden abstractedly began to light his pipe, which had failed to go out, and then brightened up with, "How 'bout yerself, stranger—married man?"

For reply, he opened his watch, slipped it from the thong which served for a chain, and passed it over. Belden pricked up the slush lamp, surveyed the inside of the case critically, and, swearing admiringly to himself, handed it over to Louis Savoy. With numerous "By gars!" he finally surrendered it to Prince, and they noticed that his hands trembled and his eyes took on a peculiar softness. And so it passed from horny hand to horny hand—the pasted photograph of a woman, the clinging kind that such men fancy, with a babe at the breast. Those who had not yet seen the wonder were keen with curiosity; those who had became silent and retrospective. They could face the pinch of famine, the grip of scurvy, or the quick death by field or flood; but the pictured semblance of a stranger woman and child made women and children of them all.

"Never have seen the youngster yet—he's a boy, she says, and two years old," said the stranger as he received the treasure back. A lingering moment he gazed upon it, then snapped the case and turned away, but not quick enough to hide the restrained rush of tears.

Malemute Kid led him to a bunk and bade him turn in.

"Call me at four sharp. Don't fail me," were his last words, and a moment later he was breathing in the heaviness of exhausted sleep.

"By Jove! He's a plucky chap," commented Prince. "Three hours' sleep after seventy-five miles with the dogs, and then the trail again. Who is he, Kid?"

"Jack Westondale. Been in going on three years, with nothing but the name of working like a horse, and any amount of bad luck to his credit. I never knew him, but Sitka Charley told me about him."

"It seems hard that a man with a sweet young wife like his should be putting in his years in this Godforsaken hole, where every year counts two on the outside."

"The trouble with him is clean grit and stubbornness. He's cleaned up twice with a stake, but lost it both times."

Here the conversation was broken off by an uproar from Bettles, for the effect had begun to wear away. And soon the bleak years of monotonous grub and deadening toil were being forgotten in rough merriment. Malemute Kid alone seemed unable to lose himself, and cast many an anxious look at his watch. Once he put on his mittens and beaver-skin cap, and, leaving the cabin, fell to rummaging about in the cache.

Nor could he wait the hour designated; for he was fifteen minutes ahead of time in rousing his guest. The young giant had stiffened badly, and brisk rubbing was necessary to bring him to his feet. He tottered painfully out of the cabin, to find his dogs harnessed and everything ready for the start. The company wished him good luck and a short chase, while Father Roubeau, hurriedly blessing him, led the stampede for the cabin; and small wonder, for it is not good to face seventy-four degrees below zero with naked ears and hands.

Malemute Kid saw him to the main trail, and there, gripping his hand heartily, gave him advice.

"You'll find a hundred pounds of salmon eggs on the sled," he said. "The dogs will go as far on that as with one hundred and fifty of fish, and you can't get dog food at Pelly, as you probably expected." The stranger started, and his eyes flashed, but he did not interrupt. "You can't get an ounce of food for dog or man till you reach Five Fingers, and that's a stiff two hundred miles. Watch out for open water on the Thirty Mile River, and be sure you take the big cutoff above Le Barge."

"How did you know it? Surely the news can't be ahead of me already?"

"I don't know it; and what's more, I don't want to know it. But you never owned that team you're chasing. Sitka Charley sold it to them last spring. But he sized you up to me as square once, and I believe him. I've seen your face; I like it. And I've seen—why, damn you, hit the high places for salt water and that wife of yours, and——" Here the Kid unmittened and jerked out his sack.

"No; I don't need it," and the tears froze on his cheeks as he convulsively gripped Malemute Kid's hand.

"Then don't spare the dogs; cut them out of the traces as fast as they drop; buy them, and think they're cheap at ten dollars a pound. You can get them at Five Fingers, Little Salmon, and Hootalinqua. And watch out for wet feet," was his parting advice. "Keep a-traveling up to twenty-five, but if it gets below that, build a fire and change your socks."

Fifteen minutes had barely elapsed when the jingle of bells announced new arrivals. The door opened, and a mounted policeman of the Northwest Territory entered, followed by two half-breed dog drivers. Like Westondale, they were heavily armed and showed signs of fatigue. The half-breeds had been born to the trail and bore it easily; but the young policeman was badly exhausted. Still, the dogged obstinacy of his race held him to the pace he had set, and would hold him till he dropped in his tracks.

"When did Westondale pull out?" he asked. "He stopped here, didn't he?" This was supererogatory, for the tracks told their own tale too well.

Malemute Kid had caught Belden's eye, and he, scenting the wind, replied evasively, "A right peart while back."

"Come, my man; speak up," the policeman admonished.

"Yeh seem to want him right smart. Hez he ben gittin' cantankerous down Dawson way?"

"Held up Harry McFarland's for forty thousand; exchanged it at the P. C. store for a check on Seattle; and who's to stop the cashing of it if we don't overtake him? When did he pull out?"

Every eye suppressed its excitement, for Malemute Kid had given the cue, and the young officer encountered wooden faces on every hand.

Striding over to Prince, he put the question to him. Though it hurt him, gazing into the frank, earnest face of his fellow countryman, he replied inconsequentially on the state of the trail.

Then he espied Father Roubeau, who could not lie. "A quarter of an hour ago," the priest answered; "but he had four hours' rest for himself and dogs."

"Fifteen minutes' start, and he's fresh! My God!" The poor fellow staggered back, half fainting from exhaustion and disappointment, murmuring something about the run from Dawson in ten hours and the dogs being played out.

Malemute Kid forced a mug of punch upon him; then he turned for the door, ordering the dog drivers to follow. But the warmth and promise of rest were too tempting, and they objected strenuously. The Kid was conversant with their French patois, and followed it anxiously.

They swore that the dogs were gone up; that Siwash and Babette would have to be shot before the first mile was covered; that the rest were almost as bad; and that it would be better for all hands to rest up.

"Lend me five dogs?" he asked, turning to Malemute Kid. But the Kid shook his head.

"I'll sign a check on Captain Constantine for five thousand—here's my papers—I'm authorized to draw at my own discretion."

Again the silent refusal.

"Then I'll requisition them in the name of the Queen."

Smiling incredulously, the Kid glanced at his well-stocked arsenal, and the Englishman, realizing his impotency, turned for the door. But the dog drivers still objecting, he whirled upon them fiercely, calling them women and curs. The swart face of the older half-breed flushed angrily as he drew himself up and promised in good, round terms that he would travel his leader off his legs, and would then be delighted to plant him in the snow.

The young officer—and it required his whole will—walked steadily to the door, exhibiting a freshness he did not possess. But they all knew and appreciated his proud effort; nor could he veil the twinges of agony that shot across his face. Covered with frost, the dogs were curled up in the snow, and it was almost impossible to get them to their feet. The poor brutes whined under the stinging lash, for the dog drivers were angry and cruel; nor till Babette, the leader, was cut from the traces, could they break out the sled and get under way.

"A dirty scoundrel and a liar!" "By gar! Him no good!" "A thief!" "Worse than an Indian!" It was evident that they were angry—first at the way they had been deceived; and second at the outraged ethics of the Northland, where honesty, above all, was man's prime jewel. "An' we gave the cuss a hand, after knowin' what he'd did." All eyes turned accusingly upon Malemute Kid, who rose from the corner where he had been making Babette comfortable, and silently emptied the bowl for a final round of punch.

"It's a cold night, boys—a bitter cold night," was the irrelevant commencement of his defense. "You've all traveled trail, and know what that stands for. Don't jump a dog when he's down. You've only heard one side. A whiter man than Jack Westondale never ate from the same pot nor stretched blanket with you or me. Last fall he gave his whole clean-up, forty thousand, to Joe Castrell, to buy in on Dominion. Today he'd be a millionaire. But while he stayed behind at Circle City, taking care of his partner with the scurvy, what does Castrell do? Goes into McFarland's, jumps the limit, and drops the whole sack. Found him dead in the snow the next day. And poor Jack laying his plans to go out this winter to his wife and the boy he's never seen. You'll notice he took exactly what his partner lost—forty thousand. Well, he's gone out; and what are you going to do about it?"

The Kid glanced round the circle of his judges, noted the softening of their faces, then raised his mug aloft. "So a health to the man on trail this night; may his grub hold out; may his dogs keep their legs; may his matches never miss fire. God prosper him; good luck go with him; and——"

"Confusion to the Mounted Police!" cried Bettles, to the crash of the empty cups.

The Wit of Porportuk

EL-SOO HAD BEEN a mission girl. Her mother had died when she was very small, and Sister Alberta had plucked El-Soo as a brand from the burning, one summer day, and carried her away to Holy Cross Mission and dedicated her to God. El-Soo was a full-blooded Indian, yet she exceeded all the half-breed and quarter-breed girls. Never had the good sisters dealt with a girl so adaptable and at the same time so spirited.

El-Soo was quick, and deft, and intelligent; but above all she was fire, the living flame of life, a blaze of personality that was compounded of will, sweetness, and daring. Her father was a chief, and his blood ran in her veins. Obedience, on the part of El-Soo, was a matter of terms and arrangement. She had a passion for equity, and perhaps it was because of this that she excelled in mathematics.

But she excelled in other things. She learned to read and write English as no girl had ever learned in the mission. She led the girls in singing, and into song she carried her sense of equity. She was an artist, and the fire of her flowed toward creation. Had she from birth enjoyed a more favorable environment, she would have made literature or music.

Instead she was El-Soo, daughter of Klakee-Nah, a chief, and she lived in the Holy Cross Mission where were no artists, but only pure-souled sisters who were interested in cleanliness and righteousness and the welfare of the spirit in the land of immortality that lay beyond the skies.

The years passed. She was eight years old when she entered the mission; she was sixteen, and the sisters were corresponding with their superiors in the order concerning the sending of El-Soo to the United States to complete her education, when a man of her own tribe arrived at Holy Cross and had talk with her. El-Soo was somewhat appalled by him. He was dirty. He was a Caliban-like creature, primitive-

125

ly ugly, with a mop of hair that had never been combed. He looked at her disappprovingly and refused to sit down.

"Thy brother is dead," he said shortly.

El-Soo was not particularly shocked. She remembered little of her brother. "Thy father is an old man, and alone," the messenger went on. "His house is large and empty, and he would hear thy voice and look upon thee."

Him she remembered—Klakee-Nah, the headman of the village, the friend of the missionaries and the traders, a large man thewed like a giant, with kindly eyes and masterful ways, and striding with a consciousness of crude royalty in his carriage.

"Tell him that I will come," was El-Soo's answer.

Much to the despair of the sisters, the brand plucked from the burning went back to the burning. All pleading with El-Soo was vain. There was much argument, expostulation, and weeping. Sister Alberta even revealed to her the project of sending her to the United States. El-Soo stared wide-eyed into the golden vista thus opened up to her, and shook her head. In her eyes persisted another vista. It was the mighty curve of the Yukon at Tanana Station, with the St. George Mission on one side, and the trading post on the other, and midway between the Indian village and a certain large log house where lived an old man tended upon by slaves.

All dwellers on the Yukon bank for twice a thousand miles knew the large log house, the old man, and the tending slaves; and well did the sisters know the house, its unending revelry, its feasting, and its fun. So there was weeping at Holy Cross when El-Soo departed.

There was a great cleaning up in the large house when El-Soo arrived. Klakee-Nah, himself masterful, protested at this masterful conduct of his young daughter; but in the end, dreaming barbarically of magnificence, he went forth and borrowed a thousand dollars from old Porportuk, than whom there was no richer Indian on the Yukon. Also Klakee-Nah ran up a heavy bill at the trading post. El-Soo re-created the large house. She invested it with new splendor, while Klakee-Nah maintained its ancient traditions of hospitality and revelry.

All this was unusual for a Yukon Indian, but Klakee-Nah was an unusual Indian. Not alone did he like to render inordinate hospitality, but, what of being a chief and of ac-

quiring much money, he was able to do it. In the primitive
trading days he had been a power over his people, and he had
dealt profitably with the white trading companies. Later on,
with Porportuk, he had made a gold strike on the Koyukuk
River. Klakee-Nah was by training and nature an aristocrat.
Porportuk was bourgeois, and Porportuk bought him out of
the gold mine. Porportuk was content to plod and accumu-
late. Klakee-Nah went back to his large house and proceeded
to spend. Porportuk was known as the richest Indian in Alaska. Klakee-Nah was known as the whitest. Porportuk was
a moneylender and a usurer. Klakee-Nah was an anachro-
nism—a medieval ruin, a fighter and a feaster, happy with
wine and song.

El-Soo adapted herself to the large house and its ways as
readily as she had adapted herself to Holy Cross Mission and
its ways. She did not try to reform her father and direct his
footsteps toward God. It is true, she reproved him when he
drank overmuch and profoundly, but that was for the sake of
his health and the direction of his footsteps on solid earth.

The latchstring to the large house was always out. What
with the coming and the going, it was never still. The rafters
of the great living room shook with the roar of wassail and of
song. At table sat men from all the world and chiefs from
distant tribes—Englishmen and colonials, lean Yankee
traders and rotund officials of the great companies, cowboys
from the Western ranges, sailors from the sea, hunters and
dog mushers of a score of nationalities.

El-Soo drew breath in a cosmopolitan atmosphere. She
could speak English as well as she could her native tongue,
and she sang English songs and ballads. The passing Indian
ceremonials she knew, and the perishing traditions. The
tribal dress of the daughter of a chief she knew how to wear
upon occasion. But for the most part she dressed as white
women dress. Not for nothing was her needlework at the
mission and her innate artistry. She carried her clothes like a
white woman, and she made clothes that could be so carried.

In her way she was as unusual as her father, and the position she occupied was as unique as his. She was the one Indian woman who was the social equal with the several white
women at Tanana Station. She was the one Indian woman to
whom white men honorably made proposals of marriage.
And she was the one Indian woman whom no white man
ever insulted.

For El-Soo was beautiful—not as white women are beautiful, not as Indian women are beautiful. It was the flame of her, that did not depend upon feature, that was her beauty. So far as mere line and feature went, she was the classic Indian type. The black hair and the fine bronze were hers, and the black eyes, brilliant and bold, keen as sword light, proud; and hers the delicate eagle nose with the thin, quivering nostrils, the high cheekbones that were not broad apart, and the thin lips that were not too thin. But over all and through all poured the flame of her—the unanalyzable something that was fire and that was the soul of her, that lay mellow-warm or blazed in her eyes, that sprayed the cheeks of her, that distended the nostrils, that curled the lip, or, when the lip was in repose, that was still there in the lip, the lip palpitant with its presence.

And El-Soo had wit—rarely sharp to hurt, yet quick to search out forgivable weakness. The laughter of her mind played like lambent flame over all about her, and from all about her arose answering laughter. Yet she was never the center of things. This she would not permit. The large house, and all of which it was significant, was her father's; and through it, to the last, moved his heroic figure—host, master of the revels, and giver of the law. It is true, as the strength oozed from him, that she caught up responsibilities from his failing hands. But in appearance he still ruled, dozing oft-times at the board, a bacchanalian ruin, yet in all seeming the ruler of the feast.

And through the large house moved the figure of Porportuk, ominous, with shaking head, coldly disapproving, paying for it all. Not that he really paid, for he compounded interest in weird ways, and year by year absorbed the properties of Klakee-Nah. Porportuk once took it upon himself to chide El-Soo upon the wasteful way of life in the large house —it was when he had about absorbed the last of Klakee-Nah's wealth—but he never ventured so to chide again. El-Soo, like her father, was an aristocrat, as disdainful of money as he, and with an equal sense of honor as finely strung.

Porportuk continued grudgingly to advance money, and ever the money flowed in golden foam away. Upon one thing El-Soo was resolved—her father should die as he had lived. There should be for him no passing from high to low, no diminution of the revels, no lessening of the lavish hospital-

ity. When there was famine, as of old, the Indians came
groaning to the large house and went away content. When
there was famine and no money, money was borrowed from
Porportuk, and the Indians still went away content. El-Soo
might well have repeated, after the aristocrats of another
time and place, that after her came the deluge. In her case
the deluge was old Porportuk. With every advance of money
he looked upon her with a more possessive eye, and felt
burgeoning within him ancient fires.

But El-Soo had no eyes for him. Nor had she eyes for the
white men who wanted to marry her at the mission with
ring and priest and book. For at Tanana Station was a young
man, Akoon, of her own blood and tribe and village. He
was strong and beautiful to her eyes, a great hunter, and, in
that he had wandered far and much, very poor; he had been
to all the unknown wastes and places; he had journeyed to
Sitka and to the United States; he had crossed the continent
to Hudson Bay and back again, and as seal hunter on a ship
he had sailed to Siberia and for Japan.

When he returned from the gold strike in Klondike he
came, as was he wont, to the large house to make report to
old Klakee-Nah of all the world that he had seen; and there
he first saw El-Soo, three years back from the mission. Thereat Akoon wandered no more. He refused a wage of twenty
dollars a day as pilot on the big steamboats. He hunted some
and fished some, but never far from Tanana Station, and he
was at the large house often and long. And El-Soo measured
him against many men and found him good. He sang songs to
her, and was ardent and glowed until all Tanana Station knew
he loved her. And Porportuk but grinned and advanced more
money for the upkeep of the large house.

Then came the death table of Klakee-Nah. He sat at feast,
with death in his throat, that he could not drown with wine.
And laughter and joke and song went around, and Akoon
told a story that made the rafters echo. There were no tears
or sighs at that table. It was no more than fit that Klakee-
Nah should die as he had lived, and none knew this better than
El-Soo, with her artist sympathy. The old roistering crowd
was there, and, as of old, three frostbitten sailors were there,
fresh from the long traverse from the Arctic, survivors of a
ship's company of seventy-four. At Klakee-Nah's back were
four old men, all that were left him of the slaves of his youth.
With rheumy eyes they saw to his needs, with palsied hands

filling his glass or striking him on the back between the
shoulders when death stirred and he coughed and gasped.

It was a wild night, and as the hours passed and the fun
laughed and roared along, death stirred more restlessly in
Klakee-Nah's throat.

Then it was that he sent for Porportuk. And Porportuk
came in from the outside frost to look with disapproving
eyes upon the meat and wine on the table for which he had
paid. But as he looked down the length of flushed faces to
the far end and saw the face of El-Soo, the light in his eyes
flared up, and for a moment the disapproval vanished.

Place was made for him at Klakee-Nah's side, and a glass
placed before him. Klakee-Nah, with his own hands, filled
the glass with fervent spirits. "Drink!" he cried. "Is it not
good?"

And Porportuk's eyes watered as he nodded his head and
smacked his lips.

"When, in your own house, have you had such drink?"
Klakee-Nah demanded.

"I will not deny that the drink is good to this old throat
of mine," Porportuk made answer, and hesitated for the
speech to complete the thought.

"But it costs overmuch," Klakee-Nah roared, completing
it for him.

Porportuk winced at the laughter that went down the table. His eyes burned malevolently. "We were boys together, of
the same age," he said. "In your throat is death. I am still
alive and strong."

An ominous murmur arose from the company. Klakee-Nah
coughed and strangled, and the old slaves smote him between
the shoulders. He emerged gasping, and waved his hand to
still the threatening rumble.

"You have grudged the very fire in your house because the
wood cost overmuch!" he cried. "You have grudged life. To
live cost overmuch, and you have refused to pay the price.
Your life has been like a cabin where the fire is out and there
are no blankets on the floor." He signaled to a slave to fill
his glass, which he held aloft. "But I have lived. And I have
been warm with life as you have never been warm. It is
true, you shall live long. But the longest nights are the cold
nights when a man shivers and lies awake. My nights have
been short, but I have slept warm."

He drained the glass. The shaking hand of a slave failed

to catch it as it crashed to the floor. Klakee-Nah sank back, panting, watching the upturned glasses at the lips of the drinkers, his own lips slightly smiling to the applause. At a sign, two slaves attempted to help him sit upright again. But they were weak, his frame was mighty, and the four old men tottered and shook as they helped him forward.

"But manner of life is neither here nor there," he went on. "We have other business, Porportuk, you and I, tonight. Debts are mischances, and I am in mischance with you. What of my debt, and how great is it?"

Porportuk searched in his pouch and brought forth a memorandum. He sipped at his glass and began. "There is the note of August 1889 for three hundred dollars. The interest has never been paid. And the note of the next year for five hundred dollars. This note was included in the note of two months later for a thousand dollars. Then there is the note——"

"Never mind the many notes!" Klakee-Nah cried out impatiently. "They make my head go around and all the things inside my head. The whole! The round whole! How much is it?"

Porportuk referred to his memorandum. "Fifteen thousand nine hundred and sixty-seven dollars and seventy-five cents," he read with careful precision.

"Make it sixteen thousand, make it sixteen thousand," Klakee-Nah said grandly. "Odd numbers were ever a worry. And now—and it is for this that I have sent for you—make me out a new note for sixteen thousand, which I shall sign. I have no thought of the interest. Make it as large as you will, and make it payable in the next world, when I shall meet you by the fire of the Great Father of all Indians. Then the note will be paid. This I promise you. It is the word of Klakee-Nah."

Porportuk looked perplexed, and loudly the laughter arose and shook the room. Klakee-Nah raised his hands. "Nay," he cried. "It is not a joke. I but speak in fairness. It was for this I sent for you, Porportuk. Make out the note."

"I have no dealings with the next world," Porportuk made answer slowly.

"Have you no thought to meet me before the Great Father!" Klakee-Nah demanded. Then he added, "I shall surely be there."

"I have no dealings with the next world," Porportuk repeated sourly.

The dying man regarded him with frank amazement.

"I know naught of the next world," Porportuk explained. "I do business in this world."

Klakee-Nah's face cleared. "This comes of sleeping cold of nights," he laughed. He pondered for a space, then said, "It is in this world that you must be paid. There remains to me this house. Take it, and burn the debt in the candle there."

"It is an old house and not worth the money," Porportuk made answer.

"There are my mines on the Twisted Salmon."

"They have never paid to work," was the reply.

"There is my share in the steamer Koyukuk. I am half owner."

"She is at the bottom of the Yukon."

Klakee-Nah started. "True, I forgot. It was last spring when the ice went out." He mused for a time, while the glasses remained untasted, and all the company waited upon his utterance.

"Then it would seem I owe you a sum of money which I cannot pay . . . in this world?" Porportuk nodded and glanced down the table.

"Then it would seem that you, Porportuk, are a poor businessman," Klakee-Nah said slyly.

And boldly Porportuk made answer, "No; there is security yet untouched."

"What!" cried Klakee-Nah. "Have I still property? Name it, and it is yours, and the debt is no more."

"There it is." Porportuk pointed at El-Soo.

Klakee-Nah could not understand. He peered down the table, brushed his eyes, and peered again.

"Your daughter El-Soo—her will I take and the debt be no more. I will burn the debt there in the candle."

Klakee-Nah's great chest began to heave. "Ho! Ho!—a joke—Ho! Ho! Ho!" he laughed homerically. "And with your cold bed and daughters old enough to be the mother of El-Soo! Ho! Ho! Ho!" He began to cough and strangle, and the old slaves smote him on the back. "Ho! Ho!" he began again, and went off into another paroxysm.

Porportuk waited patiently, sipping from his glass and studying the double row of faces down the board. "It is no joke," he said finally. "My speech is well meant."

Klakee-Nah sobered and looked at him, then reached for his glass, but could not touch it. A slave passed it to him, and glass and liquor he flung into the face of Porportuk.

"Turn him out!" Klakee-Nah thundered to the waiting table that strained like a pack of hounds in leash. "And roll him in the snow!"

As the mad riot swept past him and out of doors he signaled to the slaves, and the four tottering old men supported him on his feet as he met the returning revelers, upright, glass in hand, pledging them a toast to the short night when a man sleeps warm.

It did not take long to settle the estate of Klakee-Nah. Tommy, the little Englishman, clerk at the trading post, was called in by El-Soo to help. There was nothing but debts, notes overdue, mortgaged properties, and properties mortgaged but worthless. Notes and mortgages were held by Porportuk. Tommy called him a robber many times as he pondered the compounding of the interest.

"Is it a debt, Tommy?" El-Soo asked.

"It is a robbery," Tommy answered.

"Nevertheless, it is a debt," she persisted.

The winter wore away, and the early spring, and still the claims of Porportuk remained unpaid. He saw El-Soo often and explained to her at length, as he had explained to her father, the way the debt could be canceled. Also he brought with him old medicine men, who elaborated to her the everlasting damnation of her father if the debt were not paid. One day, after such an elaboration, El-Soo made final announcement to Porportuk.

"I shall tell you two things," she said. "First, I shall not be your wife. Will you remember that? Second, you shall be paid the last cent of the sixteen thousand dollars——"

"Fifteen thousand nine hundred and sixty-seven dollars and seventy-five cents," Porportuk corrected.

"My father said sixteen thousand," was her reply. "You shall be paid."

"How?"

"I know not how, but I shall find out how. Now go, and bother me no more. If you do"—she hesitated to find fitting penalty—"if you do, I shall have you rolled in the snow again as soon as the first snow flies."

This was still in the early spring, and a little later El-Soo surprised the country. Word went up and down the Yukon from Chilkoot to the Delta, and was carried from camp to camp to the farthermost camps that in June, when the first salmon ran, El-Soo, daughter of Klakee-Nah, would sell herself at public auction to satisfy the claims of Porportuk. Vain were the attempts to dissuade her. The missionary at St. George wrestled with her, but she replied:

"Only the debts to God are settled in the next world. The debts of men are of this world, and in this world are they settled."

Akoon wrestled with her, but she replied: "I do love thee, Akoon; but honor is greater than love, and who am I that I should blacken my father?" Sister Alberta journeyed all the way up from Holy Cross on the first steamer, and to no better end.

"My father wanders in the thick and endless forests," said El-Soo. "And there will he wander, with the lost souls crying, till the debt be paid. Then, and not until then, may he go on to the house of the Great Father."

"And you believe this?" Sister Alberta asked.

"I do not know," El-Soo made answer. "It was my father's belief."

Sister Alberta shrugged her shoulders incredulously.

"Who knows but that the things we believe come true?" El-Soo went on. "Why not? The next world to you may be heaven and harps . . . because you have believed heaven and harps; to my father the next world may be a large house where he will sit always at table feasting with God."

"And you?" Sister Alberta asked. "What is your next world?"

El-Soo hesitated but for a moment. "I should like a little of both," she said. "I should like to see your face as well as the face of my father."

The day of the auction came. Tanana Station was populous. As was their custom, the tribes had gathered to await the salmon run, and in the meantime spent the time in dancing and frolicking, trading and gossiping. Then there was the ordinary sprinkling of white adventurers, traders, and prospectors, and in addition a large number of white men who had come because of curiosity or interest in the affair.

It had been a backward spring, and the salmon were late in running. This delay but keyed up the interest. Then, on the day of the auction, the situation was made tense by

Akoon. He arose and made public and solemn announcement that whosoever bought El-Soo would forthwith and immediately die. He flourished the Winchester in his hand to indicate the manner of the taking off. El-Soo was angered thereat; but he refused to speak with her, and went to the trading post to lay in extra ammunition.

The first salmon was caught at ten o'clock in the evening, and at midnight the auction began. It took place on top of the high bank alongside the Yukon. The sun was due north just below the horizon, and the sky was lurid red. A great crowd gathered about the table and the two chairs that stood near the edge of the bank. To the fore were many white men and several chiefs. And most prominently to the fore, rifle in hand, stood Akoon. Tommy, at El-Soo's request, served as auctioneer, but she made the opening speech and described the goods about to be sold. She was in native costume, in the dress of a chief's daughter, splendid and barbaric, and she stood on a chair, that she might be seen to advantage.

"Who will buy a wife?" she asked. "Look at me. I am twenty years old and a maid. I will be a good wife to the man who buys me. If he is a white man, I shall dress in the fashion of white women; if he is an Indian, I shall dress as"—she hesitated a moment—"a squaw. I can make my own clothes, and sew, and wash, and mend. I was taught for eight years to do these things at Holy Cross Mission. I can read and write English, and I know how to play the organ. Also I can do arithmetic and some algebra—a little. I shall be sold to the highest bidder, and to him I will make out a bill of sale of myself. I forgot to say that I can sing very well, and that I have never been sick in my life. I weigh one hundred and thirty-two pounds; my father is dead and I have no relatives. Who wants me?"

She looked over the crowd with flaming audacity and stepped down. At Tommy's request she stood upon the chair again, while he mounted the second chair and started the bidding.

Surrounding El-Soo stood the four old slaves of her father. They were age-twisted and palsied, faithful to their meat, a generation out of the past that watched unmoved the antics of younger life. In the front of the crowd were several Eldorado and Bonanza kings from the upper Yukon, and beside them, on crutches, swollen with scurvy, were two broken prospectors. From the midst of the crowd, thrust out by its own vividness, appeared the face of a wild-eyed squaw from the remote regions of the upper Tanana; a strayed Sitkan from the coast stood side by side with a Stick from Lake Le Barge, and, beyond, a half-dozen French-Canadian voyageurs, grouped by themselves. From afar came the faint cries of myriads of wild fowl on the nesting grounds. Swallows were skimming up overhead from the placid surface of the Yukon, and robins were singing. The oblique rays of the hidden sun shot through the smoke, high-dissipated from forest fires a thousand miles away, and turned the heavens to somber red, while the earth shone red in the reflected glow. This red glow shone in the faces of all, and made everything seem unearthly and unreal.

The bidding began slowly. The Sitkan, who was a stranger in the land and who had arrived only half an hour before, offered one hundred dollars in a confident voice, and was surprised when Akoon turned threateningly upon him with the rifle. The bidding dragged. An Indian from the Tozikakat, a pilot, bid one hundred and fifty, and after some time a gambler, who had been ordered out of the upper country, raised the bid to two hundred. El-Soo was saddened; her pride was hurt; but the only effect was that she flamed more audaciously upon the crowd.

There was a disturbance among the onlookers as Porportuk forced his way to the front. "Five hundred dollars!" he bid in a loud voice, then looked about him proudly to note the effect.

He was minded to see his great wealth as a bludgeon with which to stun all competition at the start. But one of the voyageurs, looking on El-Soo with sparkling eyes, raised the bid a hundred.

"Seven hundred!" Porportuk returned promptly.

And with equal promptness came the "Eight hundred" of the voyageur.

Then Porportuk swung his club again. "Twelve hundred!" he shouted.

With a look of poignant disappointment the voyageur succumbed. There was no further bidding. Tommy worked hard but could not elicit a bid.

El-Soo spoke to Porportuk. "It were good, Porportuk, for you to weigh well your bid. Have you forgotten the thing I told you—that I would never marry you!"

"It is a public auction," he retorted. "I shall buy you with a bill of sale. I have offered twelve hundred dollars. You come cheap."

"Too damned cheap!" Tommy cried. "What if I am auctioneer? That does not prevent me from bidding. I'll make it thirteen hundred."

"Fourteen hundred," from Porportuk.

"I'll buy you in to be my—my sister," Tommy whispered to El-Soo, then called aloud, "Fifteen hundred!"

At two thousand one of the Eldorado kings took a hand, and Tommy dropped out.

A third time Porportuk swung the club of his wealth, making a clean raise of five hundred dollars. But the Eldorado king's pride was touched. No man could club him. And he swung back another five hundred.

El-Soo stood at three thousand. Porportuk made it thirty-five hundred, and gasped when the Eldorado king raised it a thousand dollars. Porportuk again raised it five hundred, and again gasped when the king raised a thousand more.

Porportuk became angry. His pride was touched; his strength was challenged, and with him strength took the form of wealth. He would not be ashamed for weakness before the world. El-Soo became incidental. The savings and scrimpings from the cold nights of all his years were ripe to be squandered. El-Soo stood at six thousand. He made it seven thousand. And then, in thousand-dollar bids, as fast as they could be uttered, her price went up. At fourteen thousand the two men stopped for breath.

Then the unexpected happened. A still heavier club was swung. In the pause that ensued the gambler, who had scented a speculation and formed a syndicate with several of his fellows, bid sixteen thousand dollars.

"Seventeen thousand," Porportuk said weakly.

"Eighteen thousand," said the king.

Porportuk gathered his strength. "Twenty thousand."

The syndicate dropped out. The Eldorado king raised a thousand, and Porportuk raised back; and as they bid, Akoon turned from one to the other, half menacingly, half curiously, as though to see what manner of man it was that he would have to kill. When the king prepared to make his next bid, Akoon having pressed closer, the king first loosed the revolver at his hip, then said:

"Twenty-three thousand."

"Twenty-four thousand," said Porportuk. He grinned vi-

ciously, for the certitude of his bidding had at last shaken
the king. The latter moved over close to El-Soo. He studied
her carefully for a long while.

"And five hundred," he said at last.

"Twenty-five thousand," came Porportuk's raise.

The king looked for a long space and shook his head. He
looked again and said reluctantly, "And five hundred."

"Twenty-six thousand," Porportuk snapped.

The king shook his head and refused to meet Tommy's
pleading eye. In the meatime Akoon had edged close to
Porportuk. El-Soo's quick eye noted this, and while Tommy
wrestled with the Eldorado king for another bid she bent and
spoke in a low voice in the ear of a slave. And while Tommy's
"Going . . . going . . . going . . ." dominated the air, the
slave went up to Akoon and spoke in a low voice in his ear.
Akoon made no sign that he had heard, though El-Soo
watched him anxiously.

"Gone!" Tommy's voice rang out. "To Porportuk, for
twenty-six thousand dollars."

Porportuk glanced uneasily at Akoon. All eyes were centered upon Akoon, but he did nothing.

"Let the scales be brought," said El-Soo.

"I shall make payment at my house," said Porportuk.

"Let the scales be brought," El-Soo repeated. "Payment
shall be made here where all can see."

So the gold scales were brought from the trading post,
while Porportuk went away and came back with a man at his
heels, on whose shoulders was a weight of gold dust in moose-
hide sacks. Also, at Porportuk's back walked another man
with a rifle, who had eyes only for Akoon.

"Here are the notes and mortgages," said Porportuk, "for
fifteen thousand nine hundred and sixty-seven dollars and
seventy-five cents."

El-Soo received them into her hands and said to Tommy,
"Let them be reckoned as sixteen thousand."

"There remains ten thousand dollars to be paid in gold,"
Tommy said.

Porportuk nodded and untied the mouths of the sacks.
El-Soo, standing at the edge of the bank, tore the papers to
shreds and sent them fluttering out over the Yukon. The
weighing began, but halted.

"Of course, at seventeen dollars," Porportuk had said to
Tommy as he adjusted the scales.

"At sixteen dollars," El-Soo said sharply.

"It is the custom of all the land to reckon gold at seventeen dollars for each ounce," Porportuk replied. "And this is a business transaction."

El-Soo laughed. "It is a new custom," she said. "It began this spring. Last year, and the years before, it was sixteen dollars an ounce. When my father's debt was made it was sixteen dollars. When he spent at the store the money he got from you, for one ounce he was given sixteen dollars' worth of flour, not seventeen. Wherefore shall you pay for me at sixteen and not at seventeen." Porportuk grunted and allowed the weighing to proceed.

"Weigh it in three piles, Tommy," she said. "A thousand dollars here, three thousand here, and here six thousand."

It was slow work, and while the weighing went on Akoon was closely watched by all.

"He but waits till the money is paid," one said; and the word went around and was accepted, and they waited for what Akoon should do when the money was paid. And Porportuk's man with the rifle waited and watched Akoon.

The weighing was finished, and the gold dust lay on the table in three dark yellow heaps. "There is a debt of my father to the company for three thousand dollars," said El-Soo. "Take it, Tommy, for the company. And here are four old men, Tommy. You know them. And here is one thousand dollars. Take it, and see that the old men are never hungry and never without tobacco."

Tommy scooped the gold into separate sacks. Six thousand dollars remained on the table. El-Soo thrust the scoop into the heap and with a sudden turn whirled the contents out and down to the Yukon in a golden shower. Porportuk seized her wrist as she thrust the scoop a second time into the heap.

"It is mine," she said calmly. Porportuk released his grip, but he gritted his teeth and scowled darkly as she continued to scoop the gold into the river till none was left.

The crowd had eyes for naught but Akoon, and the rifle of Porportuk's man lay across the hollow of his arm, the muzzle directed at Akoon a yard away, the man's thumb on the hammer. But Akoon did nothing.

"Make out the bill of sale," Porportuk said grimly.

And Tommy made out the bill of sale, wherein all right and title in the woman El-Soo was vested in the man Porportuk. El-Soo signed the document, and Porportuk folded it and put it away in his pouch. Suddenly his eyes flashed, and in sudden speech he addressed El-Soo.

"But it was not your father's debt," he said. "What I paid was the price for you. Your sale is business of today and not of last year and the years before. The ounces paid for you will buy at the post today seventeen dollars of flour, and not sixteen. I have lost a dollar on each ounce. I have lost six hundred and twenty-five dollars."

El-Soo thought for a moment, and saw the error she had made. She smiled, and then she laughed.

"You are right," she laughed. "I made a mistake. But it is too late. You have paid, and the gold is gone. You did not think quick. It is your loss. Your wit is slow these days, Porportuk. You are getting old."

He did not answer. He glanced uneasily at Akoon and was reassured. His lips tightened, and a hint of cruelty came into his face. "Come," he said, "we will go to my house."

"Do you remember the two things I told you in the spring?" El-Soo asked, making no movement to accompany him.

"My head would be full with the things women say, did I heed them," he answered.

"I told you that you would be paid," El-Soo went on carefully. "And I told you that I would never be your wife."

"But that was before the bill of sale." Porportuk crackled the paper between his fingers inside the pouch. "I have bought you before all the world. You belong to me. You will not deny that you belong to me."

"I belong to you," El-Soo said steadily.

"I own you."

"You own me."

Porportuk's voice rose slightly and triumphantly. "As a dog, I own you."

"As a dog, you own me," El-Soo continued calmly. "But, Porportuk, you forget the thing I told you. Had any other man bought me, I should have been that man's wife. I should have been a good wife to that man. Such was my will. But my will with you was that I should never be your wife. Wherefore, I am your dog."

Porportuk knew that he played with fire, and he resolved to play firmly. "Then I speak to you not as El-Soo but as a dog," he said; "and I tell you to come with me." He half reached to grip her arm, but with a gesture she held him back.

"Not so fast, Porportuk. You buy a dog. The dog runs away. It is your loss. I am your dog. What if I run away?"

"As the owner of the dog, I shall beat you——"

"When you catch me?"

"When I catch you."

"Then catch me."

He reached swiftly for her, but she eluded him. She laughed as she circled around the table. "Catch her!" Porportuk commanded the Indian with the rifle, who stood near to her. But as the Indian stretched forth his arm to her the Eldorado king felled him with a fist blow under the ear. The rifle clattered to the ground. Then was Akoon's chance. His eyes glittered, but he did nothing.

Porportuk was an old man, but his cold nights retained for him his activity. He did not circle the table. He came across suddenly, over the top of the table. El-Soo was taken off her guard. She sprang back with a sharp cry of alarm, and Porportuk would have caught her had it not been for Tommy. Tommy's leg went out. Porportuk tripped and pitched forward on the ground. El-Soo got her start.

"Then catch me," she laughed over her shoulder as she fled away.

She ran lightly and easily, but Porportuk ran swiftly and savagely. He outran her. In his youth he had been swiftest of all the young men. But El-Soo dodged in a willowy, elusive way. Being in native dress, her feet were not cluttered with skirts, and her pliant body curved a flight that defied the gripping fingers of Porportuk.

With laughter and tumult the great crowd scattered out to see the chase. It led through the Indian encampment; and ever dodging, circling, and reversing, El-Soo and Porportuk appeared and disappeared among the tents. El-Soo seemed to balance herself against the air with her arms, now one side, now on the other, and sometimes her body, too, leaned out upon the air far from the perpendicular as she achieved her sharpest curves. And Porportuk, always a leap behind, or a leap this side or that, like a lean hound strained after her.

They crossed the open ground beyond the encampment and disappeared in the forest. Tanana Station waited their reappearance, and long and vainly it waited.

In the meantime Akoon ate and slept, and lingered much at the steamboat landing, deaf to the rising resentment of Tanana Station in that he did nothing. Twenty-four hours

later Porportuk returned. He was tired and savage. He spoke
to no one but Akoon, and with him tried to pick a quarrel.
But Akoon shrugged his shoulders and walked away. Porportuk did not waste time. He outfitted half a dozen of the
young men, selecting the best trackers and travelers, and at
their head plunged into the forest.

Next day the steamer *Seattle*, bound upriver, pulled in to
the shore and wooded up. When the lines were cast off and
she churned out from the bank Akoon was on board in the
pilothouse. Not many hours afterward, when it was his turn
at the wheel, he saw a small birchbark canoe put off from the
shore. There was only one person in it. He studied it carefully, put the wheel over, and slowed down.

The captain entered the pilothouse.

"What's the matter?" he demanded. "The water's good."

Akoon grunted. He saw a larger canoe leaving the bank,
and in it were a number of persons. As the *Seattle* lost headway he put the wheel over some more.

The captain fumed. "It's only a squaw," he protested.

Akoon did not grunt. He was all eyes for the squaw and
the pursuing canoe. In the latter six paddles were flashing,
while the squaw paddled slowly.

"You'll be aground," the captain protested, seizing the
wheel.

But Akoon coutered his strength on the wheel and looked
him in the eyes. The captain slowly released the spokes.

"Queer beggar," he sniffed to himself.

Akoon held the *Seattle* on the edge of the shoal water
and waited till he saw the squaw's fingers clutch the forward
rail. Then he signaled for full speed ahead and ground the
wheel over. The large canoe was very near, but the gap between it and the steamer was widening.

The squaw laughed and leaned over the rail. "Then catch
me, Porportuk!" she cried.

Akoon left the steamer at Fort Yukon. He outfitted a
small poling boat and went up the Porcupine River. And with
him went El-Soo. It was a weary journey, and the way led
across the backbone of the world; but Akoon had traveled it
before. When they came to the head waters of the Porcupine
they left the boat and went on foot across the Rocky Mountains.

Akoon greatly liked to walk behind El-Soo and watch the
movement of her. There was a music in it that he loved.

And especially he loved the well-rounded calves in their sheaths of soft-tanned leather, the slim ankles, and the small moccasined feet that were tireless through the longest days.

"You are light as air," he said, looking up at her. "It is no labor for you to walk. You almost float, so lightly do your feet rise and fall. You are like a deer, El-Soo; you are like a deer, and your eyes are like deer's eyes, sometimes when you look at me, or when you hear a quick sound and wonder if it be danger that stirs. Your eyes are like a deer's eyes now as you look at me."

And El-Soo, luminous and melting, bent and kissed Akoon.

"When we reach the Mackenzie we will not delay," Akoon said later. "We will go south before the winter catches us. We will go to the sun lands where there is no snow. But we will return. I have seen much of the world, and there is no land like Alaska, no sun like our sun, and the snow is good after the long summer."

"And you will learn to read," said El-Soo.

And Akoon said, "I will surely learn to read."

But there was delay when they reached the Mackenzie. They fell in with a band of Mackenzie Indians and, hunting, Akoon was shot by accident. The rifle was in the hands of a youth. The bullet broke Akoon's right arm and, ranging farther, broke two of his ribs. Akoon knew rough surgery, while El-Soo had learned some refinements at Holy Cross. The bones were finally set, and Akoon lay by the fire for them to knit. Also he lay by the fire so that the smoke would keep the mosquitoes away.

Then it was that Porportuk, with his six young men, arrived. Akoon groaned in his helplessness and made appeal to the Mackenzies. But Porportuk made demand, and the Mackenzies were perplexed. Porportuk was for seizing upon El-Soo, but this they would not permit. Judgment must be given, and, as it was an affair of man and woman, the council of the old men was called—this that warm judgment might not be given by the young men, who were warm of heart.

The old men sat in a circle about the smudge fire. Their faces were lean and wrinkled, and they gasped and panted for air. The smoke was not good for them. Occasionally they struck with withered hands at the mosquitoes that braved the smoke. After such exertion they coughed hollowly and painfully. Some spat blood, and one of them sat a bit apart with head bowed forward, and bled slowly and continuously at the mouth; the coughing sickness had gripped them. They were as dead men; their time was short. It was a judgment of the dead.

"And I paid for her a heavy price," Porportuk concluded his complaint. "Such a price you have never seen. Sell all that is yours—sell your spears and arrows and rifles, sell your skins and furs, sell your tents and boats and dogs, sell everything, and you will not have maybe a thousand dollars. Yet did I pay for the woman, El-Soo, twenty-six times the price of all your spears and arrows and rifles, your skins and furs, your tents and boats and dogs. It was a heavy price."

The old men nodded gravely, though their wizened eye slits widened with wonder that any woman should be worth such a price. The one that bled at the mouth wiped his lips. "Is it true talk?" he asked each of Porportuk's six young men. And each answered that it was true.

"Is it true talk?" he asked El-Soo, and she answered, "It is true."

"But Porportuk has not told that he is an old man," Akoon said, "and that he has daughters older than El-Soo."

"It is true, Porportuk is an old man," said El-Soo.

"It is for Porportuk to measure the strength of his age," said he who bled at the mouth. "We be old men. Behold! Age is never so old as youth would measure it."

And the circle of old men champed their gums, and nodded approvingly, and coughed.

"I told him that I would never be his wife," said El-Soo.

"Yet you took from him twenty-six times all that we possess?" asked a one-eyed old man.

El-Soo was silent.

"Is it true?" And his one eye burned and bored into her like a fiery gimlet.

"It is true," she said.

"But I will run away again," she broke out passionately a moment later. "Always will I run away."

"That is for Porportuk to consider," said another of the old men. "It is for us to consider the judgment."

"What price did you pay for her?" was demanded of Akoon.

"No price did I pay for her," he answered. "She was above price. I did not measure her in gold dust, nor in dogs and tents and furs."

The old men debated among themselves and mumbled in undertones. "These old men are ice," Akoon said in English.

"I will not listen to their judgment, Porportuk. If you take El-Soo, I will surely kill you."

The old men ceased and regarded him suspiciously. "We do not know the speech you make," one said.

"He but said that he would kill me," Porportuk volunteered. "So it were well to take from him his rifle, and to have some of your young men sit by him, that he may not do me hurt. He is a young man, and what are broken bones to youth!"

Akoon, lying helpless, had rifle and knife taken from him, and to either side of his shoulders sat young men of the Mackenzies. The one-eyed old man arose and stood upright. "We marvel at the price paid for one mere woman," he began; "but the wisdom of the price is no concern of ours. We are here to give judgment, and judgment we give. We have no doubt. It is known to all that Porportuk paid a heavy price for the woman El-Soo. Wherefore does the woman El-Soo belong to Porportuk and none other." He sat down heavily and coughed. The old men nodded and coughed.

"I will kill you," Akoon cried in English.

Porportuk smiled and stood up. "You have given true judgment," he said to the council, "and my young men will give to you much tobacco. Now let the woman be brought to me."

Akoon gritted his teeth. The young men took El-Soo by the arms. She did not resist, and was led, her face a sullen flame, to Porportuk.

"Sit there at my feet till I have made my talk," he commanded. He paused a moment. "It is true," he said, "I am an old man. Yet can I understand the ways of youth. The fire has not all gone out of me. Yet am I no longer young, nor am I minded to run these old legs of mine through all the years that remain to me. El-Soo can run fast and well. She is a deer. This I know, for I have seen and run after her. It is not good that a wife should run so fast. I paid for her a heavy price, yet does she run away from me. Akoon paid no price at all, yet does she run to him.

"When I came among you people of the Mackenzie, I was of one mind. As I listened in the council and thought of the swift legs of El-Soo, I was of many minds. Now am I of one mind again, but it is a different mind from the one I brought to the council. Let me tell you my mind. When a dog runs once away from a master, it will run away again. No matter how many times it is brought back, each time it will run away again. When we have such dogs we sell them. El-Soo is like a dog that runs away. I will sell her. Is there any man of the council that will buy?"

The old men coughed and remained silent.

"Akoon would buy," Porportuk went on, "but he has no money. Wherefore I will give El-Soo to him, as he said, without price. Even now will I give her to him."

Reaching down, he took El-Soo by the hand and led her across the space to where Akoon lay on his back.

"She has a bad habit, Akoon," he said, seating her at Akoon's feet. "As she has run away from me in the past, in the days to come she may run away from you. But there is no need to fear that she will ever run away, Akoon. I shall see to that. Never will she run away from you—this the word of Porportuk. She has great wit. I know, for often has it bitten into me. Yet am I minded myself to give my wit play for once. And by my wit will I secure her to you, Akoon."

Stooping, Porportuk crossed El-Soo's feet, so that the instep of one lay over that of the other; and then, before his purpose could be divined, he discharged his rifle through the two ankles. As Akoon struggled to rise against the weight of the young men there was heard the crunch of the broken bone rebroken.

"It is just," said the old men, one to another.

El-Soo made no sound. She sat and looked at her shattered ankles, on which she would never walk again.

"My legs are strong, El-Soo," Akoon said. "But never will they bear me away from you."

El-Soo looked at him, and for the first time in all the time he had known her Akoon saw tears in her eyes.

"Your eyes are like deer's eyes, El-Soo," he said.

"Is it just?" Porportuk asked, and grinned from the edge of the smoke as he prepared to depart.

"It is just," the old men said. And they sat on in the silence.

Love of Life

This out of all will remain—
They have lived and have tossed:
So much of the game will be gain,
Though the gold of the dice has been lost.

THEY LIMPED PAINFULLY down the bank, and once the foremost of the two men staggered among the rough-strewn rocks. They were tired and weak, and their faces had the drawn expression of patience which comes of hardship long endured. They were heavily burdened with blanket packs which were strapped to their shoulders. Head straps, passing across the forehead, helped support these packs. Each man carried a rifle. They walked in a stooped posture, the shoulders well forward, the head still farther forward, the eyes bent upon the ground.

"I wish we had just about two of them cartridges that's layin' in that cache of ourn," said the second man.

His voice was utterly and drearily expressionless. He spoke without enthusiasm; and the first man, limping into the milky stream that foamed over the rocks, vouchsafed no reply.

The other man followed at his heels. They did not remove their footgear, though the water was icy cold—so cold that their ankles ached and their feet went numb. In places the water dashed against their knees, and both men staggered for footing.

The man who followed slipped on a smooth boulder, nearly fell, but recovered himself with a violent effort, at the same time uttering a sharp exclamation of pain. He seemed faint and dizzy and put out his free hand while he reeled, as though seeking support against the air. When he had steadied himself he stepped forward, but reeled again and nearly fell. Then he stood still and looked at the other man, who had never turned his head.

The man stood still for fully a minute, as though debating with himself. Then he called out:

"I say, Bill, I've sprained my ankle."

Bill staggered on through the milky water. He did not look around. The man watched him go, and though his face was expressionless as ever, his eyes were like the eyes of a wounded deer.

The other man limped up the farther bank and continued straight on without looking back. The man in the stream watched him. His lips trembled a little, so that the rough thatch of brown hair which covered them was visibly agitated. His tongue even strayed out to moisten them.

"Bill!" he cried out.

It was the pleading cry of a strong man in distress, but Bill's head did not turn. The man watched him go, limping grotesquely and lurching forward with stammering gait up the slow slope toward the soft sky line of the low-lying hill. He watched him go till he passed over the crest and disappeared. Then he turned his gaze and slowly took in the circle of the world that remained to him now that Bill was gone.

Near the horizon the sun was smoldering dimly, almost obscured by formless mists and vapors, which gave an impression of mass and density without outline or tangibility. The man pulled out his watch, the while resting his weight on one leg. It was four o'clock, and as the season was near the last of July or first of August—he did not know the precise date within a week or two—he knew that the sun roughly marked the northwest. He looked to the south and knew that somewhere beyond those bleak hills lay the Great Bear Lake; also he knew that in that direction the Arctic Circle cut its forbidding way across the Canadian Barrens. This stream in which he stood was a feeder to the Coppermine River, which in turn flowed north and emptied into Coronation Gulf and the Arctic Ocean. He had never been there, but he had seen it, once, on a Hudson's Bay Company chart.

Again his gaze completed the circle of the world about him. It was not a heartening spectacle. Everywhere was soft sky line. The hills were all low-lying. There were no trees, no shrubs, no grasses—naught but a tremendous and terrible desolation that sent fear swiftly dawning into his eyes.

"Bill!" he whispered, once and twice; "Bill!"

He cowered in the midst of the milky water, as though the vastness were pressing in upon him with overwhelming force, brutally crushing him with its complacent awfulness. He began to shake as with an ague fit, till the gun fell from his hand with a splash. This served to rouse him. He fought with his fear and pulled himself together, groping in the water and recovering the weapon. He hitched his pack farther over on his left shoulder, so as to take a portion of its weight from off the injured ankle. Then he proceeded, slowly and carefully, wincing with pain, to the bank.

He did not stop. With a desperation that was madness, unmindful of the pain, he hurried up the slope to the crest of the hill over which his comrade had disappeared—more grotesque and comical by far than that limping, jerking comrade. But at the crest he saw a shallow valley, empty of life. He fought with his fear again, overcame it, hitched the pack still farther over on his left shoulder, and lurched on down the slope.

The bottom of the valley was soggy with water, which the thick moss held, spongelike, close to the surface. This water squirted out from under his feet at every step, and each time he lifted a foot the action culminated in a sucking sound as the wet moss reluctantly released its grip. He picked his way from muskeg to muskeg, and followed the other man's footsteps along and across the rocky ledges which thrust like islets through the sea of moss.

Though alone, he was not lost. Farther on, he knew, he would come to where dead spruce and fir, very small and wizened, bordered the shore of a little lake, the *titchinnichilie*, in the tongue of the country, the "land of little sticks." And into that lake flowed a small stream, the water of which was not milky. There was rush grass on that stream —this he remembered well—but no timber, and he would follow it till its first trickle ceased at a divide. He would cross this divide to the first trickle of another stream, flowing to the west, which he would follow until it emptied into the river Dease, and here he would find a cache under an upturned canoe and piled over with many rocks. And in this cache would be ammunition for his empty gun, fishhooks and lines, a small net—all the utilities for the killing and snaring of food. Also he would find flour—not much—a piece of bacon, and some beans.

Bill would be waiting for him there, and they would paddle away south down the Dease to the Great Bear Lake. And south across the lake they would go, ever south, till they gained the Mackenzie. And south, still south, they would go, while the winter raced vainly after them, and the ice formed in the eddies, and the days grew chill and crisp, south to some warm Hudson's Bay Company post, where timber grew tall and generous and there was grub without end.

These were the thoughts of the man as he strove onward. But hard as he strove with his body, he strove equally hard with his mind, trying to think that Bill had not deserted him, that Bill would surely wait for him at the cache. He was compelled to think this thought, or else there would not be any use to strive, and he would have lain down and died. And as the dim ball of the sun sank slowly into the northwest he covered every inch—and many times—of his and Bill's flight south before the downcoming winter. And he conned the grub of the cache and the grub of the Hudson's Bay Company post over and over again. He had not eaten for two days; for a far longer time he had not had all he wanted to eat. Often he stooped and picked pale muskeg berries, put them into his mouth, and chewed and swallowed them. A muskeg berry is a bit of seed enclosed in a bit of water. In the mouth the water melts away and the seed chews sharp and bitter. The man knew there was no nourishment in the berries, but he chewed them patiently with a hope greater than knowledge and defying experience.

At nine o'clock he stubbed his toe on a rocky ledge, and from sheer weariness and weakness staggered and fell. He lay for some time, without movement, on his side. Then he slipped out of the pack straps and clumsily dragged himself into a sitting posture. It was not yet dark, and in the lingering twilight he groped about among the rocks for shreds of dry moss. When he had gathered a heap he built a fire—a smoldering, smudgy fire—and put a tin pot of water on to boil.

He unwrapped his pack and the first thing he did was to count his matches. There were sixty-seven. He counted them three times to make sure. He divided them into several portions, wrapping them in oil paper, disposing of one bunch in his empty tobacco pouch, of another bunch in the inside band of his battered hat, of a third bunch under his shirt on the chest. This accomplished, a panic came upon him, and he unwrapped them all and counted them again. There were still sixty-seven.

He dried his wet footgear by the fire. The moccasins were in soggy shreds. The blanket socks were worn through in places, and his feet were raw and bleeding. His ankle was throbbing, and he gave it an examination. It had swollen to the size of his knee. He tore a long strip from one of his two blankets and bound the ankle tightly. He tore other strips and bound them about his feet to serve for both moccasins and socks. Then he drank the pot of water, steaming hot, wound his watch, and crawled between his blankets.

He slept like a dead man. The brief darkness around midnight came and went. The sun arose in the northeast—at least the day dawned in that quarter, for the sun was hidden by gray clouds.

At six o'clock he awoke, quietly lying on his back. He gazed straight up into the gray sky and knew that he was hungry. As he rolled over on his elbow he was startled by a loud snort, and saw a bull caribou regarding him with alert curiosity. The animal was not more than fifty feet away, and instantly into the man's mind leaped the vision and the savor of a caribou steak sizzling and frying over a fire. Mechanically he reached for the empty gun, drew a bead, and pulled the trigger. The bull snorted and leaped away, his hoofs rattling and clattering as he fled across the ledges.

The man cursed and flung the empty gun from him. He groaned aloud as he started to drag himself to his feet. It was a slow and arduous task. His joints were like rusty hinges. They worked harshly in their sockets, with much friction, and each bending or unbending was accomplished only through a sheer exertion of will. When he finally gained his feet, another minute or so was consumed in straightening up, so that he could stand erect as a man should stand.

He crawled up a small knoll and surveyed the prospect. There were no trees, no bushes, nothing but a gray sea of moss scarcely diversified by gray rocks, gray lakelets, and gray streamlets. The sky was gray. There was no sun nor hint of sun. He had no idea of north, and he had forgotten the way he had come to this spot the night before. But he

was not lost. He knew that. Soon he would come to the
land of the little sticks. He felt that it lay off to the left
somewhere, not far—possibly just over the next low hill.

He went back to put his pack into shape for traveling.
He assured himself of the existence of his three separate
parcels of matches, though he did not stop to count them.
But he did linger, debating, over a squat moose-hide sack.
It was not large. He could hide it under his two hands.
He knew that it weighed fifteen pounds—as much as all
the rest of the pack—and it worried him. He finally set
it to one side and proceeded to roll the pack. He paused
to gaze at the squat moose-hide sack. He picked it up
hastily with a defiant glance about him, as though the desolation were trying to rob him of it; and when he rose to
his feet to stagger on into the day, it was included in the
pack on his back.

He bore away to the left, stopping now and again to
eat muskeg berries. His ankle had stiffened, his limp was
more pronounced, but the pain of it was as nothing com-
pared with the pain of his stomach. The hunger pangs were
sharp. They gnawed and gnawed until he could not keep
his mind steady on the course he must pursue to gain the
land of little sticks. The muskeg berries did not allay this
gnawing, while they made his tongue and the roof of his
mouth sore with their irritating bite.

He came upon a valley where rock ptarmigan rose on
whirring wings from the ledges and muskegs. "Ker—ker—
ker" was the cry they made. He threw stones at them but
could not hit them. He placed his pack on the ground and
stalked them as a cat stalks a sparrow. The sharp rocks cut
through his pants legs till his knees left a trail of blood;
but the hurt was lost in the hurt of his hunger. He squirmed
over the wet moss, saturating his clothes and chilling his
body; but he was not aware of it, so great was his fever
for food. And always the ptarmigan rose, whirring, before
him, till their "Ker—ker—ker" became a mock to him, and
he cursed them and cried aloud at them with their own
cry.

Once he crawled upon one that must have been asleep.
He did not see it till it shot up in his face from its rocky
nook. He made a clutch as startled as was the rise of the
ptarmigan, and there remained in his hand three tail feathers.
As he watched its flight he hated it, as though it had done

him some terrible wrong. Then he returned and shouldered his pack.

As the day wore along he came into valleys or swales where game was more plentiful. A band of caribou passed by, twenty and odd animals, tantalizingly within rifle range. He felt a wild desire to run after them, a certitude that he could run them down. A black fox came toward him, carrying a ptarmigan in his mouth. The man shouted. It was a fearful cry, but the fox, leaping away in fright, did not drop the ptarmigan.

Late in the afternoon he followed a stream, milky with lime, which ran through sparse patches of rush grass. Grasping these rushes firmly near the root, he pulled up what resembled a young onion sprout no larger than a shingle nail. It was tender, and his teeth sank into it with a crunch that promised deliciously of food. But its fibers were tough. It was composed of stringy filaments saturated with water, like the berries, and devoid of nourishment. He threw off his pack and went into the rush grass on hands and knees, crunching and munching, like some bovine creature.

He was very weary and often wished to rest—to lie down and sleep; but he was continually driven on, not so much by his desire to gain the land of little sticks as by his hunger. He searched little ponds for frogs and dug up the earth with his nails for worms, though he knew in spite that neither frogs nor worms existed so far north.

He looked into every pool of water vainly, until, as the long twilight came on, he discovered a solitary fish, the size of a minnow, in such a pool. He plunged his arm in up to the shoulder, but it eluded him. He reached for it with both hands and stirred up the milky mud at the bottom. In his excitement he fell in, wetting himself to the waist. Then the water was too muddy to admit of his seeing the fish, and he was compelled to wait until the sediment had settled.

The pursuit was renewed, till the water was again muddied. But he could not wait. He unstrapped the tin bucket and began to bail the pool. He bailed wildly at first, splashing himself and flinging the water so short a distance that it ran back into the pool. He worked more carefully, striving to be cool, though his heart was pounding against his chest and his hands were trembling. At the end of half an hour the pool was nearly dry. Not a cupful of water remained. And there was no fish. He found a hidden crevice among the stones through which it had escaped to the adjoining and larger pool—a pool which he could not empty in a night and a day. Had he known of the crevice, he could have closed it with a rock at the beginning and the fish would have been his.

Thus he thought, and crumpled up and sank down upon the wet earth. At first he cried softly to himself, then he cried loudly to the pitiless desolation that ringed him around; and for a long time after he was shaken by great dry sobs.

He built a fire and warmed himself by drinking quarts of hot water, and made camp on a rocky ledge in the same fashion he had the night before. The last thing he did was to see that his matches were dry and to wind his watch. The blankets were wet and clammy. His ankle pulsed with pain. But he knew only that he was hungry, and through his restless sleep he dreamed of feasts and banquets and of food served and spread in all imaginable ways.

He awoke chilled and sick. There was no sun. The gray of earth and sky had become deeper, more profound. A raw wind was blowing, and the first flurries of snow were whitening the hilltops. The air about him thickened and grew white while he made a fire and boiled more water. It was wet snow, half rain, and the flakes were large and soggy. At first they melted as soon as they came in contact with the earth, but ever more fell, covering the ground, putting out the fire, spoiling his supply of moss fuel.

This was a signal for him to strap on his pack and stumble onward, he knew not where. He was not concerned with the land of little sticks, nor with Bill and the cache under the upturned canoe by the river Dease. He was mastered by the verb "to eat." He was hunger-mad. He took no heed of the course he pursued, so long as that course led him through the swale bottoms. He felt his way through the wet snow to the watery muskeg berries, and went by feel as he pulled up the rush grass by the roots. But it was tasteless stuff and did not satisfy. He found a weed that tasted sour and he ate all he could find of it, which was not much, for it was a creeping growth, easily hidden under the several inches of snow.

He had no fire that night, nor hot water, and crawled under his blanket to sleep the broken hunger sleep. The snow turned into a cold rain. He awakened many times to feel it falling on his upturned face. Day came—a gray day and no sun. It had ceased raining. The keenness of his hunger had departed. Sensibility, as far as concerned the yearning for food, had been exhausted. There was a dull, heavy ache in his stomach, but it did not bother him so much. He was more rational, and once more he was chiefly interested in the land of little sticks and the cache by the river Dease.

He ripped the remnant of one of his blankets into strips and bound his bleeding feet. Also he recinched the injured ankle and prepared himself for a day of travel. When he came to his pack he paused long over the squat moose-hide sack, but in the end it went with him.

The snow had melted under the rain, and only the hill-tops showed white. The sun came out, and he succeeded in locating the points of the compass, though he knew now that he was lost. Perhaps, in his previous days' wanderings, he had edged away too far to the left. He now bore off to the right to counteract the possible deviation from his true course.

Though the hunger pangs were no longer so exquisite, he realized that he was weak. He was compelled to pause for frequent rests, when he attacked the muskeg berries and rush-grass patches. His tongue felt dry and large, as though covered with a fine hairy growth, and it tasted bitter in his mouth. His heart gave him a great deal of trouble. When he had traveled a few minutes it would begin a remorseless thump, thump, thump, and then leap up and away in a painful flutter of beats that choked him and made him go faint and dizzy.

In the middle of the day he found two minnows in a large pool. It was impossible to bail it, but he was calmer now and managed to catch them in his tin bucket. They were no longer than his little finger, but he was not particularly hungry. The dull ache in his stomach had been growing duller and fainter. It seemed almost that his stomach was dozing. He ate the fish raw, masticating with painstaking care, for the eating was an act of pure reason. While he had no desire to eat, he knew that he must eat to live.

In the evening he caught three more minnows, eating two and saving the third for breakfast. The sun had dried

stray shreds of moss, and he was able to warm himself
with hot water. He had not covered more than ten miles
that day; and the next day, traveling whenever his heart
permitted him, he covered no more than five miles. But his
stomach did not give him the slightest uneasiness. It had
gone to sleep. He was in a strange country, too, and the
caribou were growing more plentiful, also the wolves. Often
their yelps drifted across the desolation, and once he saw
three of them slinking away before his path.

Another night; and in the morning, being more rational,
he untied the leather string that fastened the squat moose-
hide sack. From its open mouth poured a yellow stream
of coarse gold dust and nuggets. He roughly divided the
gold in halves, caching one half on a prominent ledge,
wrapped in a piece of blanket, and returning the other half
to the sack. He also began to use strips of the one remaining blanket for his feet. He still clung to his gun, for
there were cartridges in that cache by the river Dease.

This was a day of fog, and this day hunger awoke in him
again. He was very weak and was afflicted with a giddiness
which at times blinded him. It was no uncommon thing
now for him to stumble and fall; and stumbling once, he
fell squarely into a ptarmigan nest. There were four newly
hatched chicks, a day old—little specks of pulsating life
no more than a mouthful; and he ate them ravenously,
thrusting them alive into his mouth and crunching them
like eggshells between his teeth. The mother ptarmigan beat
about him with great outcry. He used his gun as a club
with which to knock her over, but she dodged out of reach.
He threw stones at her and with one chance shot broke
a wing. Then she fluttered away, running, trailing the
broken wing, with him in pursuit.

The little chicks had no more than whetted his appetite.
He hopped and bobbed clumsily along on his injured ankle,
throwing stones and screaming hoarsely at times; at other
times hopping and bobbing silently along, picking himself
up grimly and patiently when he fell, or rubbing his eyes
with his hand when the giddiness threatened to overpower
him.

The chase led him across swampy ground in the bottom
of the valley, and he came upon footprints in the soggy
moss. They were not his own—he could see that. They
must be Bill's. But he could not stop, for the mother

ptarmigan was running on. He would catch her first, then he would return and investigate.

He exhausted the mother ptarmigan; but he exhausted himself. She lay panting on her side. He lay panting on his side, a dozen feet away, unable to crawl to her. And as he recovered she recovered, fluttering out of reach as his hungry hand went out to her. The chase was resumed. Night settled down and she escaped. He stumbled from weakness and pitched head foremost on his face, cutting his cheek, his pack upon his back. He did not move for a long while; then he rolled over on his side, wound his watch, and lay there until morning.

Another day of fog. Half of his last blanket had gone into foot-wrappings. He failed to pick up Bill's trail. It did not matter. His hunger was driving him too compellingly —only—only he wondered if Bill, too, were lost. By midday the irk of his pack became too oppressive. Again he divided the gold, this time merely spilling half of it on the ground. In the afternoon he threw the rest of it away, there remaining to him only the half blanket, the tin bucket, and the rifle.

A hallucination began to trouble him. He felt confident that one cartridge remained to him. It was in the chamber of the rifle and he had overlooked it. On the other hand, he knew all the time that the chamber was empty. But the hallucination persisted. He fought it off for hours, then threw his rifle open and was confronted with emptiness. The disappointment was as bitter as though he had really expected to find the cartridge.

He plodded on for half an hour, when the hallucination arose again. Again he fought it, and still it persisted, till for very relief he opened his rifle to unconvince himself. At times his mind wandered farther afield, and he plodded on, a mere automaton, strange conceits and whimsicalities gnawing at his brain like worms. But these excursions out of the real were of brief duration, for ever the pangs of the hunger bite called him back. He was jerked back abruptly once from such an excursion by a sight that caused him nearly to faint. He reeled and swayed, doddering like a drunken man to keep from falling. Before him stood a horse. A horse! He could not believe his eyes. A thick mist was in them, intershot with sparkling points of light. He rubbed his eyes savagely to clear his vision, and beheld not a horse but a great brown bear. The animal was studying him with bellicose curiosity.

The man had brought his gun halfway to his shoulder before he realized. He lowered it and drew his hunting knife from its beaded sheath at his hip. Before him was meat and life. He ran his thumb along the edge of his knife. It was sharp. The point was sharp. He would fling himself upon the bear and kill it. But his heart began its warning thump, thump, thump. Then followed the wild upward leap and tattoo of flutters, the pressing as of an iron band about his forehead, the creeping of the dizziness into his brain.

His desperate courage was evicted by a great surge of fear. In his weakness, what if the animal attacked him? He drew himself up to his most imposing stature, gripping the knife and staring hard at the bear. The bear advanced clumsily a couple of steps, reared up, and gave vent to a tentative growl. If the man ran, he would run after him; but the man did not run. He was animated now with the courage of fear. He, too, growled, savagely, terribly, voicing the fear that is to life germane and that lies twisted about life's deepest roots.

The bear edged away to one side, growling menacingly, himself appalled by this mysterious creature that appeared upright and unafraid. But the man did not move. He stood like a statue till the danger was past, when he yielded to a fit of trembling and sank down into the wet moss.

He pulled himself together and went on, afraid now in a new way. It was not the fear that he should die passively from lack of food, but that he should be destroyed violently before starvation had exhausted the last particle of the endeavor in him that made toward surviving. There were the wolves. Back and forth across the desolation drifted their howls, weaving the very air into a fabric of menace that was so tangible that he found himself, arms in the air, pressing it back from him as it might be the walls of a windblown tent.

Now and again the wolves, in packs of two and three, crossed his path. But they sheered clear of him. They were not in sufficient numbers, and besides, they were hunting the caribou, which did not battle, while this strange creature that walked erect might scratch and bite.

In the late afternoon he came upon scattered bones where the wolves had made a kill. The debris had been a caribou

calf an hour before, squawking and running and very much
alive. He contemplated the bones, clean-picked and polished,
pink with the cell life in them which had not yet died.
Could it possibly be that he might be that ere the day
was done! Such was life, eh? A vain and fleeting thing. It
was only life that pained. There was no hurt in death. To
die was to sleep. It meant cessation, rest. Then why was
he not content to die?

But he did not moralize long. He was squatting in the
moss, a bone in his mouth, sucking at the shreds of life
that still dyed it faintly pink. The sweet meaty taste, thin
and elusive almost as a memory, maddened him. He closed
his jaws on the bones and crunched. Sometimes it was
the bone that broke, sometimes his teeth. Then he crushed
the bones between rocks, pounded them to a pulp, and
swallowed them. He pounded his fingers, too, in his haste,
and yet found a moment in which to feel surprise at the
fact that his fingers did not hurt much when caught under
the descending rock.

Came frightful days of snow and rain. He did not know
when he made camp, when he broke camp. He traveled in
the night as much as in the day. He rested wherever he
fell, crawled on whenever the dying life in him flickered up
and burned less dimly. He, as a man, no longer strove. It
was the life in him, unwilling to die, that drove him on.
He did not suffer. His nerves had become blunted, numb,
while his mind was filled with weird visions and delicious
dreams.

But ever he sucked and chewed on the crushed bones of
the caribou calf, the least remnants of which he had
gathered up and carried with him. He crossed no more hills
or divides, but automatically followed a large stream which
flowed through a wide and shallow valley. He did not see
this stream nor this valley. He saw nothing save visions.
Soul and body walked or crawled side by side, yet apart,
so slender was the thread that bound them.

He awoke in his right mind, lying on his back on a rocky
ledge. The sun was shining bright and warm. Afar off he
heard the squawking of caribou calves. He was aware of
vague memories of rain and wind and snow, but whether
he had been beaten by the storm for two days or two
weeks he did not know.

For some time he lay without movement, the genial sun-

shine pouring upon him and saturating his miserable body
with its warmth. A fine day, he thought. Perhaps he could
manage to locate himself. By a painful effort he rolled
over on his side. Below him flowed a wide and sluggish
river. Its unfamiliarity puzzled him. Slowly he followed it
with his eyes, winding in wide sweeps among the bleak,
bare hills, bleaker and barer and lower-lying than any hills
he had yet encountered. Slowly, deliberately, without excitement or more than the most casual interest, he followed
the course of the strange stream toward the sky line and
saw it emptying into a bright and shining sea. He was
still unexcited. Most unusual, he thought, a vision or a mi-
rage—more likely a vision, a trick of his disordered mind.
He was confirmed in this by sight of a ship lying at anchor
in the midst of the shining sea. He closed his eyes for a
while, then opened them. Strange how the vision persisted!
Yet not strange. He knew there were no seas or ships in
the heart of the barren lands, just as he had known there
was no cartridge in the empty rifle.

He heard a snuffle behind him—a half-choking gasp or
cough. Very slowly, because of his exceeding weakness and
stiffness, he rolled over on his other side. He could see
nothing near at hand, but he waited patiently. Again came
the snuffle and cough, and outlined between two jagged
rocks not a score of feet away he made out the gray head
of a wolf. The sharp ears were not pricked so sharply as he
had seen them on other wolves; the eyes were bleared and
bloodshot, the head seemed to droop limply and forlornly.
The animal blinked continually in the sunshine. It seemed
sick. As he looked it snuffled and coughed again.

This, at least, was real, he thought, and turned on the
other side so that he might see the reality of the world
which had been veiled from him before by the vision. But
the sea still shone in the distance and the ship was plainly
discernible. Was it reality after all? He closed his eyes for a
long while and thought, and then it came to him. He had
been making north by east, away from the Dease Divide
and into the Coppermine Valley. This wide and sluggish
river was the Coppermine. That shining sea was the Arctic
Ocean. That ship was a whaler, strayed east, far east, from
the mouth of the Mackenzie, and it was lying at anchor in
Coronation Gulf. He remembered the Hudson's Bay Com-

pany chart he had seen long ago, and it was all clear and reasonable to him.

He sat up and turned his attention to immediate affairs. He had worn through the blanket wrappings, and his feet were shapeless lumps of raw meat. His last blanket was gone. Rifle and knife were both missing. He had lost his hat somewhere, with the bunch of matches in the band, but the matches against his chest were safe and dry inside the tobacco pouch and oil paper. He looked at his watch. It marked eleven o'clock and was still running. Evidently he had kept it wound.

He was calm and collected. Though extremely weak, he had no sensation of pain. He was not hungry. The thought of food was not even pleasant to him, and whatever he did was done by his reason alone. He ripped off his pants legs to the knees and bound them about his feet. Somehow he had succeeded in retaining the tin bucket. He would have some hot water before he began what he foresaw was to be a terrible journey to the ship.

His movements were slow. He shook as with a palsy. When he started to collect dry moss he found he could not rise to his feet. He tried again and again, then contented himself with crawling about on hands and knees. Once he crawled near to the sick wolf. The animal dragged itself reluctantly out of his way, licking its chops with a tongue which seemed hardly to have the strength to curl. The man noticed that the tongue was not the customary healthy red. It was a yellowish brown and seemed coated with a rough and half-dry mucus.

After he had drunk a quart of hot water the man found he was able to stand, and even to walk as well as a dying man might be supposed to walk. Every minute or so he was compelled to rest. His steps were feeble and uncertain, just as the wolf's that trailed him were feeble and uncertain; and that night, when the shining sea was blotted out by blackness, he knew he was nearer to it by no more than four miles.

Throughout the night he heard the cough of the sick wolf, and now and then the squawking of the caribou calves. There was life all around him, but it was strong life, very much alive and well, and he knew the sick wolf clung to the sick man's trail in the hope that the man would die first. In the morning, on opening his eyes, he beheld

it regarding him with a wistful and hungry stare. It stood
crouched, with tail between its legs, like a miserable and
woebegone dog. It shivered in the chill morning wind and
grinned dispiritedly when the man spoke to it in a voice
that achieved no more than a hoarse whisper.

The sun rose brightly, and all morning the man tottered
and fell toward the ship on the shining sea. The weather
was perfect. It was the brief Indian summer of the high
latitudes. It might last a week. Tomorrow or next day it
might be gone.

In the afternoon the man came upon a trail. It was of
another man, who did not walk, but who dragged himself
on all fours. The man thought it might be Bill, but he
thought in a dull, uninterested way. He had no curiosity.
In fact sensation and emotion had left him. He was no
longer susceptible to pain. Stomach and nerves had gone to
sleep. Yet the life that was in him drove him on. He was
very weary, but it refused to die. It was because it refused
to die that he still ate muskeg berries and minnows, drank
his hot water, and kept a wary eye on the sick wolf.

He followed the trail of the other man who dragged himself along, and soon came to the end of it—a few fresh-
picked bones where the soggy moss was marked by the foot
pads of many wolves. He saw a squat moose-hide sack,
mate to his own, which had been torn by sharp teeth. He
picked it up, though its weight was almost too much for
his feeble fingers. Bill had carried it to the last. Ha-ha!
He would have the laugh on Bill. He would survive and
carry it to the ship in the shining sea. His mirth was hoarse
and ghastly, like a raven's croak, and the sick wolf joined
him, howling lugubriously. The man ceased suddenly. How
could he have the laugh on Bill if that were Bill; if those
bones, so pinky-white and clean, were Bill?

He turned away. Well, Bill had deserted him; but he
would not take the gold, nor would he suck Bill's bones.
Bill would have, though, had it been the other way around,
he mused as he staggered on.

He came to a pool of water. Stooping over in quest of
minnows, he jerked his head back as though he had been
stung. He had caught sight of his reflected face. So horrible
was it that sensibility awoke long enough to be shocked.
There were three minnows in the pool, which was too large
to drain; and after several ineffectual attempts to catch

them in the tin bucket he forbore. He was afraid, because
of his great weakness, that he might fall in and drown. It
was for this reason that he did not trust himself to the
river astride one of the many drift logs which lined its
sandspits.

That day he decreased the distance between him and the
ship by three miles; the next day by two—for he was
crawling now as Bill had crawled; and the end of the fifth
day found the ship still seven miles away and him unable
to make even a mile a day. Still the Indian summer held
on, and he continued to crawl and faint, turn and turn
about; and ever the sick wolf coughed and wheezed at his
heels. His knees had become raw meat like his feet, and
though he padded them with the shirt from his back it
was a red track he left behind him on the moss and
stones. Once, glancing back, he saw the wolf licking hun-
grily his bleeding trail, and he saw sharply what his own
end might be—unless—unless he could get the wolf. Then
began as grim a tragedy of existence as was ever played—a
sick man that crawled, a sick wolf that limped, two creatures dragging their dying carcasses across the desolation
and hunting each other's lives.

Had it been a well wolf, it would not have mattered so
much to the man; but the thought of going to feed the
maw of that loathsome and all but dead thing was repug-
nant to him. He was finicky. His mind had begun to wander again and to be perplexed by hallucinations, while his
lucid intervals grew rarer and shorter.

He was awakened once from a faint by a wheeze close
in his ear. The wolf leaped lamely back, losing its footing
and falling in its weakness. It was ludicrous, but he was
not amused. Nor was he even afraid. He was too far gone
for that. But his mind was for the moment clear, and he
lay and considered. The ship was no more than four miles
away. He could see it quite distinctly when he rubbed the
mists out of his eyes, and he could see the white sail of
a small boat cutting the water of the shining sea. But he
could never crawl those four miles. He knew that, and was
very calm in the knowledge. He knew that he could not
crawl half a mile. And yet he wanted to live. It was un-
reasonable that he should die after all he had undergone.
Fate asked too much of him. And, dying, he declined

to die. It was stark madness, perhaps, but in the very grip
of death he defied death and refused to die.

He closed his eyes and composed himself with infinite
precaution. He steeled himself to keep above the suffocating
languor that lapped like a rising tide through all the wells
of his being. It was very like a sea, this deadly languor
that rose and rose and drowned his consciousness bit by
bit. Sometimes he was all but submerged, swimming
through oblivion with a faltering stroke; and again, by some
strange alchemy of soul, he would find another shred of
will and strike out more strongly.

Without movement he lay on his back, and he could
hear, slowly drawing near and nearer, the wheezing intake
and output of the sick wolf's breath. It drew closer, ever
closer, through an infinitude of time, and he did not move.
It was at his ear. The harsh dry tongue grated like sandpaper against his cheek. His hands shot out—or at least he
willed them to shoot out. The fingers were curved like talons,
but they closed on empty air. Swiftness and certitude require
strength, and the man had not this strength.

The patience of the wolf was terrible. The man's patience
was no less terrible. For half a day he lay motionless, fighting off unconsciousness and waiting for the thing that was
to feed upon him and upon which he wished to feed.
Sometimes the languid sea rose over him and he dreamed
long dreams; but ever through it all, waking and dreaming,
he waited for the wheezing breath and the harsh caress of
the tongue.

He did not hear the breath, and he slipped slowly from
some dream to the feel of the tongue along his hand. He
waited. The fangs pressed softly; the pressure increased; the
wolf was exerting its last strength in an effort to sink teeth
in the food for which it had waited so long. But the man
had waited long, and the lacerated hand closed on the jaw.
Slowly, while the wolf struggled feebly and the hand
clutched feebly, the other hand crept across to a grip. Five
minutes later the whole weight of the man's body was on
top of the wolf. The hands had not sufficient strength to
choke the wolf, but the face of the man was pressed close
to the throat of the wolf and the mouth of the man was
full of hair. At the end of half an hour the man was aware
of a warm trickle in his throat. It was not pleasant. It was
like molten lead being forced into his stomach, and it was

forced by his will alone. Later the man rolled over on his back and slept.

There were some members of a scientific expedition on the whaleship *Bedford*. From the deck they remarked a strange object on the shore. It was moving down the beach toward the water. They were unable to classify it, and, being scientific men, they climbed into the whaleboat alongside and went ashore to see. And they saw something that was alive but which could hardly be called a man. It was blind, unconscious. It squirmed along the ground like some monstrous worm. Most of its efforts were ineffectual, but it was persistent, and it writhed and twisted and went ahead perhaps a score of feet an hour.

Three weeks afterward the man lay in a bunk on the whaleship *Bedford*, and with tears streaming down his wasted cheeks told who he was and what he had undergone. He also babbled incoherently of his mother, of sunny southern California, and a home among the orange groves and flowers.

The days were not many after that when he sat at table with the scientific men and ship's officers. He gloated over the spectacle of so much food, watching it anxiously as it went into the mouths of others. With the disappearance of each mouthful an expression of deep regret came into his eyes. He was quite sane, yet he hated those men at mealtime. He was haunted by a fear that the food would not last. He inquired of the cook, the cabin boy, the captain, concerning the food stores. They reassured him countless times; but he could not believe them, and pried cunningly about the lazaret to see with his own eyes.

It was noticed that the man was getting fat. He grew stouter with each day. The scientific men shook their heads and theorized. They limited the man at his meals, but still his girth increased and he swelled prodigiously under his shirt.

The sailors grinned. They knew. And when the scientific men set a watch on the man they knew. They saw him slouch for'ard after breakfast, and, like a mendicant, with outstretched palm, accost a sailor. The sailor grinned and passed him a fragment of sea biscuit. He clutched it avariciously, looked at it as a miser looks at gold, and thrust it into his shirt bosom. Similar were the donations from other grinning sailors.

The scientific men were discreet. They let him alone. But they privily examined his bunk. It was lined with hardtack; the mattress was stuffed with hardtack; every nook and cranny was filled with hardtack. Yet he was sane. He was taking precautions against another possible famine—that was all. He would recover from it, the scientific men said; and he did, ere the *Bedford's* anchor rumbled down in San Francisco Bay.

The Pearls of Parlay

THE KANAKA HELMSMAN put the wheel down and the *Malahini* slipped into the eye of the wind and righted to an even keel. Her headsails emptied; there was a rat-tat of reef points and quick shifting of boom tackles, and she heeled over and filled away on the other tack. Though it was early morning and the wind brisk the five white men who lounged on the poop deck were scantily clad. David Grief and his guest, Gregory Mulhall, an Englishman, were still in pajamas, their naked feet thrust into Chinese slippers. The captain and mate were in thin undershirts and unstarched duck trousers, while the supercargo still held in his hands the undershirt he was reluctant to put on. The sweat stood out on his forehead and he seemed to thrust his bare chest thirstily into the wind that did not cool.

"Pretty muggy for a breeze like this," he complained.

"And what's it doing around in the west? That's what I want to know," was Grief's contribution to the general plaint.

"It won't last and it ain't been there long," said Hermann, the Holland mate. "She is been chop round all night —five minutes here, ten minutes there, one hour somewhere other quarter."

"Something makin', something makin'," Captain Warfield croaked, spreading his bushy beard with the fingers of both hands and shoving the thatch of his chin into the breeze in a vain search for coolness. "Weather's been crazy for a fortnight. Haven't had the proper trades in three weeks. Everything's mixed up. Barometer was pumping at sunset last night and it's pumping now, though the weather sharps say it don't mean anything. All the same, I've got a prejudice against seeing it pump. Gets on my nerves, sort of, you know. She was pumping that way the time we lost the *Lancaster*. I was only an apprentice, but I can remember

167

that well enough. Brand-new four-masted steel ship; first voyage—broke the old man's heart. He'd been forty years in the company. Just faded away and died the next year."

Despite the wind and the early hour, the heat was suffocating. The wind whispered coolness but did not deliver coolness. It might have blown off the Sahara, save for the extreme humidity with which it was laden. There was no fog or mist, nor hint of fog or mist; yet the dimness of distance produced the impression.

There were no defined clouds; yet so thickly were the heavens covered by a messy cloud pall that the sun failed to shine through.

"Ready about!" Captain Warfield ordered with slow sharpness.

The brown, breechclouted Kanaka sailors moved languidly but quickly to head sheets and boom tackles.

"Hard alee!"

The helmsman ran the spokes over with no hint of gentling and the *Malahini* darted prettily into the wind and about.

"Jove! She's a witch!" was Mulhall's appreciation. "I didn't know you South Sea traders sailed yachts."

"She was a Gloucester fisherman originally," Grief explained, "and the Gloucester boats are all yachts when it comes to build, rig, and sailing."

"But you're heading right in—why don't you make it?" came the Englishman's criticism.

"Try it, Captain Warfield," Grief suggested. "Show him what a lagoon entrance is on a strong ebb."

"Close and by!" the captain ordered.

"Close and by!" the Kanaka repeated, easing half a spoke.

The *Malahini* laid squarely into the narrow passage, which was the lagoon entrance of a large, long, and narrow oval of an atoll. The atoll was shaped as if three atolls, in the course of building, had collided and coalesced and failed to rear the partition walls. Coconut palms grew in spots on the circle of sand and there were many gaps where the sand was too low to the sea for coconuts, through which could be seen the protected lagoon where the water lay flat like the ruffled surface of a mirror. Many square miles of water were in the irregular lagoon, all of which surged out on the ebb through the one narrow channel. So narrow was the channel, so large the outflow of water, that the passage was more like the rapids of a river than the mere tidal entrance to an atoll. The water boiled and whirled and swirled and drove outward in a white foam of stiff, serrated waves. Each heave and blow on her bows of the upstanding waves of the current swung the *Malahini* off the straight lead and wedged her as with wedges of steel toward the side of the passage. Part way in she was when her closeness to the coral edge compelled her to go about. On the opposite tack, broadside to the current, she swept seaward with the current's speed.

"Now's the time for that new and expensive engine of yours," Grief jeered good-naturedly.

That the engine was a sore point with Captain Warfield was patent. He had begged and badgered for it until, in the end, Grief had given his consent.

"It will pay for itself yet," the captain retorted. "You wait and see. It beats insurance; and you know the underwriters won't stand for insurance in the Paumotus."

Grief pointed to a small cutter beating up astern of them on the same course.

"I'll wager five francs the little *Nuhiva* beats us in."

"Sure!" Captain Warfield agreed. "She's overpowered. We're like a liner alongside of her and we've only got forty horsepower. She's got ten horse, and she's a little skimming dish. She could skate across the froth of hell; but just the same she can't buck this current. It's running ten knots right now."

And at the rate of ten knots, buffeted and jerkily rolled, the *Malahini* went out to sea with the tide.

"She'll slacken in half an hour—then we'll make headway," Captain Warfield said with an irritation explained by his next words. "He has no right to call it Parlay. It's down on the Admiralty charts, and the French charts too, as Hikihoho. Bougainville discovered it and named it from the natives."

"What's the name matter?" the supercargo demanded, taking advantage of speech to pause with arms shoved into the sleeves of the undershirt. "There it is, right under our nose; and old Parlay is there with the pearls."

"Who see them pearls?" Hermann queried, looking from one to another.

"It's well known," was the supercargo's reply. He turned to the steersman. "Tell them, Tai-Hotauri."

The Kanaka, pleased and self-conscious, took and gave a spoke. "My brother dive for Parlay three-four month and he make much talk about pearl. Hikihoho very good place for pearl."

"And the pearl buyers have never got him to part with a pearl," the captain broke in.

"And they say the old man had a hatful for Armande when he sailed for Tahiti," the supercargo carried on the tale.

"That's fifteen years ago and he's been adding to it ever since—stored the shell as well. Everybody's seen that—hundreds of tons of it. They say the lagoon's fished clean now. Maybe that's why he's announced the auction."

"If he really sells what he has, this will be the biggest year's output of pearls in the Paumotus," Grief said.

"I say, now, look here!" Mulhall burst forth, harried by the humid heat as much as the rest of them. "What's it all about? Who's the old beachcomber anyway? What are all these pearls? Why so secretive about it?"

"Hikihoho belongs to old Parlay," the supercargo answered. "He's got a fortune in pearls, saved up for years and years; and he sent the word out weeks ago that he'd auction them off to the buyers tomorrow. See those schooners' masts sticking up inside the lagoon?"

"Eight—so I see," said Hermann.

"What are they doing in a dinky atoll like this?" the supercargo went on. "There isn't a schoonerload of copra a year in the place. They've come for the auction. That's why we're here. That's why the little Nuhiva's bumping along astern there—though what she can buy is beyond me. Narii Herring—he's an English Jew half-caste—owns and runs her, and his only assets are his nerve, his debts, and his whisky bills. He's a genius in such things. He owes so much there isn't a merchant in Papeete who isn't interested in his welfare. They go out of their way to throw work in his way. They've got to—and a dandy stunt it is for Narii. Now I owe nobody. What's the result? If I fell down in a fit on the beach they'd let me lie there and die. They wouldn't lose anything. But Narii Herring! What wouldn't they do if he fell in a fit? Their best wouldn't be too good for him. They've got too much money tied up in him to let him lie. They'd take him into their homes and hand-nurse him like

a brother. Let me tell you, honesty in paying bills ain't
what it's cracked up to be."

"What's this Narii chap got to do with it?" was the
Englishman's short-tempered demand. And, turning to Grief,
he said: "What's all this pearl nonsense? Begin at the beginning."

"You'll have to help me out," Grief warned the others
as he began. "Old Parlay is a character. From what I've
seen of him, I believe he's partly and mildly insane. Anyway, here's the story. Parlay's a full-blooded Frenchman. He
told me once that he came from Paris. His accent is the
true Parisian. He arrived down here in the old days. Went
to trading and all the rest. That's how he got in on Hikihoho. Came in trading when trading was the real thing.
About a hundred miserable Paumotans lived on the island.
He married the Queen—native fashion. When she died
everything was his. Measles came through and there weren't
more than a dozen survivors. He fed them and worked
them, and was King. Now before the Queen died she gave
birth to a girl. That's Armande. When she was three he
sent her to the convent at Papeete. When she was seven
or eight he sent her to France. You begin to glimpse the
situation. The best and most aristocratic convent in France
was none too good for the only daughter of a Paumotan
island king and capitalist—and you know the old-country
French draw no color line. She was educated like a princess
and she accepted herself in much the same way. Also she
thought she was all white and never dreamed of a bar sinister.

"Now comes the tragedy. The old man had always been
cranky and erratic, and he'd played the despot on Hikihoho
so long that he'd got the idea in his head that there was
nothing wrong with the King—or the princess either. When
Armande was eighteen he sent for her. He had slews and
slathers of money, as Yankee Bill would say. He'd built the
big house on Hikihoho and a whacking fine bungalow in
Papeete. She was to arrive on the mail boat from New
Zealand and he sailed in his schooner to meet her at
Papeete. And he might have carried the situation off, despite the hens and bull beasts of Papeete, if it hadn't been
for the hurricane. That was the year, wasn't it, when Manu-
Huni was swept and eleven hundred drowned?"

The others nodded and Captain Warfield said: "I was in
the Magpie that blow and we went ashore, all hands and

the cook—*Magpie* and all—a quarter of a mile into the
coconuts at the head of Taiohae Bay—and it a supposedly
hurricane-proof harbor."

"Well," Grief continued, "old Parlay got caught in the
same blow and arrived in Papeete with his hatful of pearls
three weeks too late. He'd had to jack up his schooner and
build half a mile of ways before he could get her back into
the sea.

"Meantime there was Armande at Papeete. Nobody called
on her. She did, French fashion, make the initial calls on
the governor and the port doctor. They saw her, but neither
of their hen wives was at home to her or returned the
call. She was out of caste—without caste—though she had
never dreamed it; and that was the gentle way they broke
the information to her. There was a gay young lieutenant
on the French cruiser. He lost his heart to her, but not his
head. You can imagine the shock to this young woman,
refined, beautiful, raised like an aristocrat, pampered with
the best of old France that money could buy! And you
can guess the end." He shrugged his shoulders. "There was
a Japanese servant in the bungalow. He saw it—said she
did it with the proper spirit of the samurai. Took a stiletto
—no thrust, no drive, no wild rush for annihilation—took
the stiletto, placed the point carefully against her heart, and
with both hands slowly and steadily pressed home.

"Old Parlay arrived after that with his pearls. There was
one single one of them, they say, worth sixty thousand
francs. Peter Gee saw it and has told me he offered that
much for it. The old man went clean off for a while. They
had him strait-jacketed in the Colonial Club for two
days——"

"His wife's uncle, an old Paumotan, cut him out of the
jacket and turned him loose," the supercargo corroborated.

"And then old Parlay proceeded to eat things up," Grief
went on. "Pumped three bullets into the scalawag of a lieutenant——"

"Who lay in sick bay for three months," Captain Warfield contributed.

"Flung a glass of wine in the governor's face; fought a
duel with the port doctor; beat up his native servants,
wrecked the hospital; broke two ribs and the collarbone of
a man nurse—and escaped; went down to his schooner, a
gun in each hand, daring the chief of police and all the

gendarmes to arrest him, and sailed for Hikihoho. And they say he's never left the island since."

The supercargo nodded. "That was fifteen years ago, and he's never budged."

"And added to his pearls," said the captain. "He's a blithering old lunatic. Makes my flesh creep. He's a regular Finn."

"What's that?" Mulhall asked.

"Bosses the weather—that's what the natives believe, at any rate. Ask Tai-Hotauri there. Hey, Tai-Hotauri, what you think old Parlay do along weather?"

"Just the same one big weather devil!" came the Kanaka's answer. "I know. He want big blow, he make big blow. He want no wind, no wind come."

"A regular old warlock," said Mulhall.

"No good luck, them pearl," Tai-Hotauri blurted out, rolling his head ominously. "He say he sell. Plenty schooner come. Then he make big hurricane; everybody finish, you see. All native men say so."

"It's hurricane season now," Captain Warfield laughed morosely. "They're not far wrong. It's making for something right now; and I'd feel better if the Malahini was a thousand miles away from here."

"He is a bit mad," Grief concluded. "I've tried to get his point of view. It's—well, it's mixed. For eighteen years he'd centered everything on Armande. Half the time he believes she's still alive—not yet come back from France. That's one of the reasons he held on to the pearls. And all the time he hates white men. He never forgets they killed her, though a great deal of the time he forgets she's dead."

"Hello! Where's your wind?"

The sails bellied emptily overhead and Captain Warfield grunted his disgust. Intolerable as the heat had been, in the absence of wind it was almost overpowering. The sweat oozed out on all their faces; and now one and then another drew deep breaths, involuntarily questing for more air.

"Here she comes again—an eight-point haul! Boom tackles across! Jump!"

The Kanakas sprang to the captain's orders and for five minutes the schooner laid directly into the passage—and even gained on the current. Again the breeze fell flat, then puffed from the old quarter, compelling a shift back of sheets and tackles.

"Here comes the *Nuhiva*," Grief said. "She's got her engine on. Look at her skim!"

"All ready?" the captain asked the engineer, a Portuguese half-caste, whose head and shoulders protruded from the small hatch just for'ard of the cabin, and who wiped the dripping sweat from his face with a bunch of greasy waste.

"Sure!" he replied.

"Then let her go!"

The engineer disappeared into his den and a moment later the exhaust muffler coughed and sputtered overside; but the schooner could not hold her lead. The little cutter traveled three feet to her two and was quickly alongside and forging ahead.

Only natives were on her deck and the man who was steering waved his hand in derisive greeting and farewell.

"That's Narii Herring," Grief told Mulhall, "the big fellow at the wheel—the nerviest and most conscienceless scoundrel in the Paumotus."

Five minutes later a cry of joy from their own Kanakas centered all eyes on the *Nuhiva*. Her engine had broken down and they were overtaking her. The *Malahini's* sailors sprang into the rigging and jeered as they went by; the little cutter, heeled over by the wind, was going backward on the tide.

"Some engine, that of ours!" Grief approved as the lagoon opened before them and the course was changed across it to the anchorage.

Captain Warfield was visibly cheered, though he merely grunted: "It'll pay for itself; never fear."

The *Malahini* ran well into the center of the little fleet ere she found swinging room to anchor.

"There's Isaacs on the *Dolly*," Grief observed with a hand wave of greeting. "And Peter Gee's on the *Roberta*. Couldn't keep him away from a pearl sale like this. And there's Francini on the *Cactus*. They're all here—all the buyers. Old Parlay will surely get a price."

"They haven't repaired the engine yet," Captain Warfield grumbled gleefully. He was looking across the lagoon to where the *Nuhiva's* sails showed through the sparse coconuts.

II

The house of Parlay was a big two-story frame affair, built of California lumber, with a galvanized iron roof. So disproportionate was it to the slender ring of the atoll that it showed out upon the sand strip and above it like some monstrous excrescence. They of the *Malahini* paid the courtesy visit ashore immediately after anchoring. Other captains and buyers were in the big room examining the pearls that were to be auctioned next day. Paumotan servants, natives of Hikihoho and relatives of the owner, moved about, dispensing whisky and absinthe. And through the curious company moved Parlay himself, cackling and sneering, the withered wreck of what had once been a tall and powerful man. His eyes were deep-sunken and feverish, his cheeks fallen in and cavernous. The hair of his head seemed to have come out in patches and his mustache and imperial had been shed in the same lopsided way.

"Jove!" Mulhall muttered under his breath. "A long-legged Napoleon III—but burnt out, baked, and fire-crackled. And mangy! No wonder he crooks his head to one side. He's got to keep the balance."

"Goin' to have a blow," was the old man's greeting to Grief. "You must think a lot of pearls to come a day like this."

"They're worth going to inferno for," Grief laughed genially back, running his eyes over the surface of the table covered by the display.

"Other men have already made that journey for them," old Parlay cackled. "See this one!" He pointed to a large, perfect pearl, the size of a small walnut, that lay apart on a piece of chamois. "They offered me sixty thousand francs for it in Tahiti. They'll bid as much and more for it tomorrow if they aren't blown away. Well, that pearl was found by my cousin—my cousin by marriage. He was a native, you see. Also he was a thief. He hid it. It was mine. His cousin, who was also my cousin—we're all related here—killed him for it and fled away in a cutter to Noo-Nau. I pursued; but the chief of Noo-Nau had killed him for it before I got there. Oh yes, there are many dead men represented on the table there. Have a drink, Captain? Your face is not familiar. You are new in the islands?"

"It's Captain Robinson, of the *Roberta*," Grief said, introducing them.

Meantime Mulhall had shaken hands with Peter Gee.

"I never fancied there were so many pearls in the world," Mulhall said.

"Nor have I ever seen so many together at one time," Peter Gee admitted.

"What ought they to be worth?" asked Mulhall.

"Fifty or sixty thousand pounds—and that's to us buyers. In Paris . . ." He shrugged his shoulders.

Mulhall wiped the sweat from his eyes. All were sweating profusely and breathing hard. There was no ice, and the whisky and absinthe went down lukewarm.

"Yes, yes!" Parlay was cackling. "Many dead men lie on the table there. I know those pearls, all of them. You see those three—perfectly matched, aren't they? A diver from Easter Island got them for me inside a week. Next week a shark got him—took his arm off and blood poison did the business. And that big baroque there—nothing much; if I'm offered twenty francs for it tomorrow I'll be in luck—it came out of twenty-two fathoms of water. The man was from Rarotonga. He broke all diving records. He got it out of twenty-two fathoms. I saw him. And he burst his lungs at the same time, or got the bends; for he died in two hours. He died screaming. They could hear him for miles. He was the most powerful native I ever saw. Half a dozen of my divers have died of the bends. And more men will die—more men will die!"

"Oh, hush your croaking, Parlay!" chided one of the captains. "It ain't going to blow."

"If I was a strong young man I couldn't get up hook and get out fast enough," the old man retorted in the falsetto of age. "Not if I was a strong young man with the taste for wine yet in my mouth. But not you. You'll all stay. I wouldn't advise you if I thought you'd go. You can't drive buzzards away from the carrion. Have another drink, my brave sailormen. Well, well! What men will dare for a few little oyster drops! There they are, the beauties! Auction tomorrow at ten sharp. Old Parlay's selling out and the buzzards are gathering—old Parlay, who was a stronger man in his day than any of them and who will see most of them dead yet!"

"If he isn't a vile old beast!" the supercargo of the *Malahini* whispered to Peter Gee.

"What if she does blow?" said the captain of the *Dolly*. "Hikihoho's never been swept."

"The more reason she will be, then," Captain Warfield answered back. "I wouldn't trust her."

"Who's croaking now?" Grief reproved.

"I'd hate to lose that new engine before it paid for itself," Captain Warfield replied gloomily.

Parlay skipped with astonishing nimbleness across the crowded room to where a ship's barometer hung on the wall.

"Take a look, my brave sailormen!" he cried exultantly.

The man nearest read the glass. The sobering effect showed plainly on his face.

"It's dropped ten," was all he said, yet every face went anxious and there was a restlessness as if every man desired immediately to start for the door.

"Listen!" Parlay commanded.

In the silence the outer surf seemed to have become unusually loud. There was a great, rumbling roar.

"A big sea is beginning to set," someone said; and there was a movement to the windows, where all gathered.

Through the sparse coconuts they gazed seaward. An orderly succession of huge, smooth seas was rolling down upon the coral shore. For some minutes they gazed on the strange sight and talked in low voices, and in those few minutes it was manifest to all that the waves were increasing in size. It was uncanny, this rising sea in a dead calm, and their voices unconsciously sank lower. Old Parlay shocked them with his abrupt cackle.

"There is yet time to get away to sea, brave gentlemen. You can tow across the lagoon with your whaleboats."

"It's all right, old man," said Darling, the mate of the *Cactus*, a stalwart youngster of twenty-five. "The blow's to the south'ard and passing on. We'll not get a whiff of it."

An air of relief went through the room. Conversations were started, and the voices became louder. Several of the buyers even went back to the table to continue the examination of the pearls. Parley's cackle rose higher.

"That's right," he encouraged. "If the world was coming to an end you'd go on buying."

"We'll buy these tomorrow," Isaacs assured him.

"Then you'll be doing your buying in hell!"

The chorus of incredulous laughter incensed the old man. He turned fiercely on Darling.

"Since when have children like you come to the knowledge of storms? And who is the man who has plotted the hurricane courses of the Paumotus? What books will you find it in? I sailed the Paumotus before the oldest of you drew breath. I know! To the eastward the paths of the hurricanes are on so wide a circle they make a straight line. To the westward here they make a sharp curve. Remember your chart. How did it happen the hurricane of '91 swept Auri and Hiolau? The curve, my brave boy, the curve! In an hour, or two or three at most, will come the wind. Listen to that!"

A vast, rumbling crash shook the coral foundations of the atoll. The house quivered to it. The native servants, with bottles of whisky and absinthe in their hands, shrank together as if for protection and stared with fear through the windows at the mighty wash of the wave lapping far up the beach to the corner of a copra shed.

Parlay looked at the barometer, giggled, and leered around at his guests. Captain Warfield strode across to see.

"Twenty-nine seventy-five!" he read. "She's gone down five more. The old devil's right. She's a-coming—and it's me, for one, for aboard!"

"It's growing dark," Isaacs half whimpered.

"Jove! It's like a stage," Mulhall said to Grief, looking at his watch. "Ten o'clock in the morning and it's like twilight. Down go the lights for the tragedy. Where's the slow music?"

In answer another rumbling crash shook the atoll and the house. Almost in a panic the company started for the door. In the dim light their sweaty faces appeared ghastly. Isaacs panted asthmatically in the suffocating heat.

"What's your haste?" Parlay chuckled and girded at his departing guests. "A last drink, brave gentlemen!" No one noticed him. As they took the shell-bordered path to the beach he stuck his head out at the door and called: "Don't forget, gentlemen—at ten tomorrow old Parlay sells his pearls!"

III

On the beach a curious scene took place. Whaleboat after whaleboat was being hurriedly manned and shoved off. It had grown still darker. The stagnant calm continued and the sand shook under their feet with each buffet of the sea on the outer shore. Narii Herring walked leisurely along the sand. He grinned at the very evident haste of the captains and buyers. With him were three of his Kanakas and also Tai-Hotauri.

"Get into the boat and take an oar," Captain Warfield ordered the latter.

Tai-Hotauri came over jauntily, while Narii Herring and his Kanakas paused and looked on from forty feet away.

"I work no more for you, skipper," Tai-Hotauri said insolently and loudly; but his face belied his words, for he was guilty of a prodigious wink. "Fire me, skipper," he huskily whispered with a second significant wink.

Captain Warfield took the cue and proceeded to do some acting himself. He raised his fist and his voice.

"Get into that boat, you swine," he thundered, "or I'll knock seven bells out of you!"

The Kanaka drew back truculently and Grief stepped between to placate his captain.

"I go to work on the *Nuhiva*," Tai-Hotauri said, rejoining the other group.

"Come back here!" the captain threatened.

"He's a free man, skipper," Narii Herring spoke up. "He's sailed with me in the past and he's sailing with me again —that's all."

"Come on; we must get on board," Grief urged. "Look how dark it's getting!"

Captain Warfield gave in, but as the boat shoved off he stood up in the stern sheets and shook his fist ashore.

"I'll settle with you yet, Narii!" he cried. "You're the only skipper in the group who steals other men's sailors." He sat down and in a lowered voice queried: "Now what's Tai-Hotauri up to? He's on to something; but what is it?"

IV

As the boat came alongside the *Malahini*, Hermann's anxious face greeted them over the rail.

"Bottom fall out from barometer," he announced. "She's goin' to blow. I got starboard anchor overhaul."

"Overhaul the big one too," Captain Warfield ordered, taking charge. "And here, some of you, hoist in this boat. Lower her down to the deck and lash her, bottom up."

Men were busy at work on the decks of all the schooners. There was a great clanking of chains being overhauled; and now one craft and now another hove in, veered, and dropped a second anchor.

Like the *Malahini*, those that had third anchors were preparing to drop them when the wind showed what quarter it was to blow from.

The roar of the big surf continually grew, though the lagoon lay in mirrorlike calm. There was no sign of life where Parlay's big house perched on the sand. Boat and copra sheds and the sheds where the shell was stored were deserted.

"For two cents I'd up anchors and get out," Grief said. "I'd do it anyway if it were open sea; but those chains of atolls to the north and east have us pocketed. We've a better chance right there. What do you think, Captain Warfield?"

"I agree with you, though a lagoon is no millpond for riding it out. I wonder where she's going to start from? Hello! There goes one of Parlay's copra sheds!"

They could see the grass-thatched shed lift and collapse, while a froth of foam cleared the crest of the sand and ran down to the lagoon.

"Breached across!" Mulhall exclaimed. "That's something for a starter. There she comes again!"

The wreck of the shed was now flung up and left on the sand crest. A third wave buffeted it into fragments, which washed down the slope toward the lagoon.

"If she blow I would as be cooler yet," Hermann grunted. "No longer can I breathe. It is damn hot. I am dry like a stove."

He chopped open a drinking coconut with his heavy

sheath knife and drained the contents. The rest of them followed his example, pausing once to watch one of Parlay's shell sheds go down in ruin. The barometer now registered 29.50.

"Must be pretty close to the center of the area of low pressure," Grief remarked cheerfully. "I was never through the eye of a hurricane before. It will be an experience for you too, Mulhall. From the speed the barometer's dropped it's going to be a big one."

Captain Warfield groaned, and all eyes were drawn to him. He was looking through the glasses down the length of the lagoon to the southeast.

"There she comes," he said quietly.

They did not need glasses to see. A flying film, strangely marked, seemed drawing over the surface of the lagoon. Abreast of it, along the atoll, traveling with equal speed, was a stiff bending of the coconut palms and a blur of flying leaves. The front of the wind on the water was a solid, sharply defined strip of dark-colored, wind-vexed water. In advance of this strip, like skirmishers, were flashes of windflaws. Behind this strip, a quarter of a mile in width, was a strip of what seemed glassy calm. Next came another dark strip of wind—and behind that the lagoon was all crisping, boiling whiteness.

"What is that calm streak?" Mulhall asked.

"Calm," Warfield answered.

"But it travels as fast as the wind," was the other's objection.

"It has to, or it would be overtaken and there wouldn't be any calm. It's a double-header. I saw a big squall like that off Savaii once. A regular double-header. Smash! It hit us; then it lulled to nothing and smashed us a second time. Stand by and hold on. Here she is on top of us. Look at the *Roberta!*"

The *Roberta*, lying nearest to the wind at slack chains, was swept off broadside like a straw. Then her chains brought her up, bow on to the wind, with an astonishing jerk. Schooner after schooner—the *Malahini* with them— was now sweeping away with the first gust and fetching up on taut chains.

Mulhall and several of the Kanakas were taken off their feet when the *Malahini* jerked to her anchor.

And then there was no wind. The flying calm streak had

reached them. Grief lighted a match and the unshielded
flame burned without flickering in the still air. A very dim
twilight prevailed. The cloud-sky, lowering as it had been
for hours, seemed now to have descended quite down upon
the sea.

The *Roberta* tightened to her chains when the second
head of the hurricane hit, as did schooner after schooner
in swift succession. The sea, white with fury, boiled in tiny,
spitting wavelets. The deck of the *Malahini* vibrated under
their feet. The taut-stretched halyards beat a tattoo against
the masts, and all the rigging, as if smitten by some mighty
hand, set up a wild thrumming. It was impossible to face
the wind and breathe. Mulhall, crouching with the others
behind the shelter of the cabin, discovered this; and his
lungs were filled in an instant with so great a volume of
driven air which he could not expel that he nearly strangled
ere he could turn his head away.

"It's incredible!" he gasped; but no one heard him.

Hermann and several Kanakas were crawling for'ard on
hands and knees to let go the third anchor. Grief touched
Captain Warfield and pointed to the *Roberta*. She was dragging down upon them. Warfield put his mouth to Grief's
ear and shouted:

"We're dragging too!"

Grief sprang to the wheel and put it hard over, veering
the *Malahini* to port. The third anchor took hold and the
Roberta went by, stern first, a dozen yards away. They
waved their hands to Peter Gee and Captain Robinson,
who, with a number of sailors, were at work on the bow.

"He's knocking out the shackles!" Grief shouted. "Going
to chance the passage! Got to! Anchors skating!"

"We're holding now!" came the answering shout. "There
goes the *Cactus* down on the *Misi*. That settles them!"

The *Misi* had been holding, but the added windage of
the *Cactus* was too much and the entangled schooners slid
away across the boiling white. Their men could be seen
chopping and fighting to get them apart. The *Roberta*,
cleared of her anchors, with a patch of tarpaulin set for'ard,
was heading for the passage at the northwestern end of the
lagoon. They saw her make it and drive out to sea. The
Misi and the *Cactus*, however, unable to get clear of each
other, went ashore on the atoll half a mile from the passage.

The wind merely increased on itself and continued to

increase. To face the full blast of it required all one's strength, and several minutes of crawling on deck against it tired a man to exhaustion. Hermann, with his Kanakas, plodded steadily, lashing and making secure, putting ever more gaskets on the sails. The wind ripped and tore their thin undershirts from their backs. They moved slowly, as if their bodies weighed tons, never releasing a handhold until another had been secured. Loose ends of rope stood out stiffly horizontal, and after whipping the loose ends frazzled and blew away.

Mulhall touched one and then another and pointed to the shore. The grass sheds had disappeared and Parlay's house rocked drunkenly. Because the wind blew lengthwise along the atoll the house had been sheltered by the miles of coconut trees; but the big seas, breaking across from outside, were undermining it and hammering it to pieces. Already tilted down the slope of sand, its end was imminent. Here and there in the coconut trees people had lashed themselves. The trees did not sway or thresh about. Bent over rigidly by the wind, they remained in that position and vibrated monstrously. Underneath, across the sand, surged the white spume of the breakers.

A big sea was likewise making down the length of the lagoon. It had plenty of room to kick up in the ten-mile stretch from the windward rim of the atoll, and all the schooners were bucking and plunging into it. The *Malahini* had begun shoving her bow and fo'c'sle head under the bigger ones, and at times her waist was filled rail-high with water.

"Now's the time for your engine!" Grief bellowed; and Captain Warfield, crawling over to where the engineer lay, shouted emphatic commands.

Under the engine, going full speed ahead, the *Malahini* behaved better. Though she continued to ship seas over her bow, she was not jerked down so fiercely by her anchors. On the other hand, she was unable to get any slack in the chains. The best her forty horsepower could do was to ease the strain.

Still the wind increased. The little *Nuhiva*, lying abreast of the *Malahini* and closer in to the beach, her engine still unrepaired and her captain ashore, was having a bad time of it. She buried herself so frequently and so deeply that they wondered each time if she could clear herself of the water.

At three in the afternoon, buried by a second sea before she could free herself of the preceding one, she did not come up.

Mulhall looked at Grief.

"Burst in her hatches!" was the bellowed answer.

Captain Warfield pointed to the *Winifred*, a little schooner plunging and burying outside of them, and shouted in Grief's ear. His voice came in patches of dim words, with intervals of silence when whisked away by the roaring wind.

"Rotten little tub! . . . Anchors hold. . . . But how she holds together! . . . Old as the ark."

An hour later Hermann pointed to her. Her for'ard bitts, foremast, and most of her bow were gone, having been jerked out of her by her anchors. She swung broadside, rolling in the trough and settling by the head; and in this plight she was swept away to leeward.

Five vessels now remained, and of them the *Malahini* was the only one with an engine. Fearing either the *Nuhiva's* or the *Mildred's* fate, two of them followed the *Roberta's* example, knocking out the chain shackles and running for the passage. The *Dolly* was the first, but her tarpaulin was carried away and she went to destruction on the lee rim of the atoll, near the *Misi* and the *Cactus*. Undeterred by this, the *Moana* let go and followed with the same result.

"Pretty good engine that, eh?" Captain Warfield yelled to his owner.

Grief put out his hand and shook. "She's paying for herself!" he yelled back. "The wind's shifting round to the south'ard and we ought to lie easier!"

Slowly and steadily, but with ever-increasing velocity, the wind veered round to the south and the southwest, till the three schooners that were left pointed directly in toward the beach. The wreck of Parlay's house was picked up, hurled into the lagoon, and blown out upon them. Passing the *Malahini*, it crashed into the *Papara*, lying a quarter of a mile astern. There was wild work for'ard on her and in a quarter of an hour the house went clear, but it had taken the *Papara's* foremast and bowsprit with it.

Inshore, on their port bow, lay the *Tahaa*, slim and yacht-like, but excessively oversparred. Her anchors still held, but her captain, finding no abatement in the wind, proceeded to reduce windage by chopping down his masts.

"Pretty good engine that!" Grief congratulated his skipper. "It will save our sticks for us yet."

Captain Warfield shook his head dubiously.

The sea on the lagoon went swiftly down with the change of wind, but they were beginning to feel the heave and lift of the outer sea breaking across the atoll. There were not so many trees remaining. Some had been broke short off, others uprooted. One tree they saw snapped off halfway up, three persons clinging to it, and whirled away by the wind into the lagoon. Two detached themselves from it and swam to the *Tahaa*. Not long after, just before darkness, they saw a man jump overboard from that schooner's stern and strike out strongly for the *Malahini* through the white, spitting wavelets.

"It's Tai-Hotauri," was Grief's judgment. "Now we'll have the news."

The Kanaka caught the bobstay, climbed over the bow, and crawled aft. Time was given him to breathe and then, behind the part shelter of the cabin, in broken snatches and largely by signs he told his story:

"Narii . . . Damn robber! . . . He want steal . . . pearls. . . . Kill Parlay. . . . One man kill Parlay. . . . No man know what man. . . . Three Kanakas, Narii, me . . . five beans . . . hat. . . . Narii say one bean black. . . . Nobody know. . . . Kill Parlay. . . . Narii damn liar. . . . All beans black. . . . Five black. . . . Copra shed dark. . . . Every man get black bean. . . . Big wind come . . . no chance. . . . Everybody get up tree. . . . No good luck, them pearls, I tell you before . . . no good luck."

"Where's Parlay?" Grief shouted.

"Up tree. . . . Three of his Kanakas same tree; Narii and one Kanaka 'nother tree. . . . My tree blow to hell; then I come on board."

"Where are the pearls?"

"Up tree along Parlay. Mebbe Narii get them pearl yet."

In the ear of one after another Grief shouted Tai-Hotauri's story. Captain Warfield was particularly incensed and they could see him grinding his teeth.

Hermann went below and returned with a riding light, but the moment it was lifted above the level of the cabin wall the wind blew it out. He had better success with the binnacle lamp, which was lighted only after many collective attempts.

"A fine night of wind," Grief yelled in Mulhall's ear, "and blowing harder all the time!"

"How hard?"

"A hundred miles an hour—two hundred! I don't know. Harder than I've ever seen it."

The lagoon grew more and more troubled by the sea that swept across the atoll. Hundreds of leagues of ocean were being backed up by the hurricane, which more than overcame the lowering effect of the ebb tide. Immediately the tide began to rise, the increase in the size of the seas was noticeable. Moon and wind were heaping the South Pacific on Hikihoho atoll.

Captain Warfield returned from one of his periodical trips to the engine room with the word that the engineer lay in a faint.

"Can't let that engine stop!" he concluded helplessly.

"All right!" Grief shouted. "Bring him on deck. I'll spell him."

The hatch to the engine room was battened down, access being gained through a narrow passage from the cabin. The heat and gas fumes were stifling. Grief made one hasty, comprehensive examination of the engine and the fittings of the tiny room, then blew out the oil lamp. After that he worked in darkness, save for the glow from endless cigars that he went into the cabin to light. Even-tempered as he was, he soon began to give evidences of the strain of being pent in with a mechanical monster that toiled and sobbed and slubbered in the shouting dark. Naked to the waist, covered with grease and oil, bruised and skinned from being knocked about by the plunging, jumping vessel, his head swimming from the mixture of gas and air he was compelled to breathe, he labored on hour after hour, by turns petting, blessing, nursing, and cursing the engine and all its parts. The ignition began to go bad. The feed grew worse and, worst of all, the cylinders began to heat. In a consultation held in the cabin the half-caste engineer begged and pleaded to stop the engine for half an hour in order to cool it and to attend to the water circulation.

Captain Warfield was against any stopping. The half-caste swore that the engine would ruin itself and stop anyway, and for good. Grief, with glaring eyes, greasy and battered, yelled and cursed them both down and issued commands. Mulhall, the supercargo, and Hermann were set to work in the cabin at double-straining and triple-straining the gasoline.

A hole was chopped through the engine-room floor and a Kanaka heaved bilge water over the cylinders, while Grief continued to souse the running parts in oil.

"Didn't know you were a gasoline expert," Captain Warfield admired when Grief came into the cabin to catch a breath of little less impure air.

"I bathe in gasoline," he grated savagely through his teeth. "I eat it."

What other uses he might have found for it were never given, for at that moment all the men in the cabin, as well as the gasoline that was being strained, were smashed for'ard against the bulkhead as the *Malahini* took an abrupt, deep dive. For the space of several minutes, unable to gain their feet, they rolled back and forth and pounded and hammered from wall to wall. The schooner, swept by three big seas, creaked and groaned and quivered and, from the weight of water on her decks, behaved loggily. Grief crept to the engine, while Captain Warfield awaited his chance to get through the companionway and out on deck.

It was half an hour before he came back.

"Whaleboat's gone!" he reported. "Galley's gone! Everything gone except the deck and hatches! And if that engine hadn't been going we'd be gone! Keep up the good work!"

By midnight the engineer's lungs and head had been sufficiently cleared of gas fumes to let him relieve Grief, who went on deck to get his own head and lungs clear. He joined the others, who crouched behind the cabin, holding on with their hands and made doubly secure by rope lashings. It was a complicated huddle, for it was the only place of refuge for the Kanakas. Some of them had accepted the skipper's invitation into the cabin, but had been driven out by the fumes. The *Malahini* was being plunged down and swept frequently, and what they breathed was air and spray and water commingled.

"Making heavy weather of it, Mulhall!" Grief yelled to his guest between immersions.

Mulhall, strangling and choking, could only nod. The scuppers could not carry off the burden of water on the schooner's deck. She rolled it out and took it in over one rail and the other; and at times, nose thrown skyward, sitting down on her heel, she avalanched it aft. It surged along the poop gangways, poured over the top of the cabin, submerging and bruising those who clung on, and went out over the stern rail.

Mulhall saw him first and drew Grief's attention. It was Narii Herring, crouching and holding on where the dim binnacle light shone upon him. He was quite naked, save for a belt and a bare-bladed knife thrust between it and the skin.

Captain Warfield untied his lashings and made his way over the bodies of the others. When his face became visible in the light from the binnacle it was working with anger. They could see him shout, but the wind tore the sound away. He would not put his lips to Narii's ear. Instead he pointed over the side. Narii Herring understood. His white teeth showed in an amused and sneering smile, and he stood up—a magnificent figure of a man.

"It's murder!" Mulhall yelled to Grief.

"He'd have murdered old Parlay!" Grief yelled back.

For the moment the poop was clear of water and the *Malahini* on an even keel. Narii made a bravado attempt to walk to the rail, but was flung down by the wind. Thereafter he crawled, disappearing in the darkness, though there was certitude in all of them that he had gone over the side. The *Malahini* dived deep; and when they emerged from the flood that swept aft Grief got Mulhall's ear.

"Can't lose him! He's the Fish Man of Tahiti! He'll cross the lagoon and land on the other rim of the atoll—if there's any atoll left."

Five minutes afterward, in another submergence, a mess of bodies poured down on them over the top of the cabin. These they seized and held till the water cleared, when they carried them below and learned their identity. Old Parlay lay on his back on the floor with closed eyes and without movement. The other two were his Kanaka cousins. All three were naked and bloody. The arm of one Kanaka hung helpless and broken at his side. The other Kanaka bled freely from a hideous scalp wound.

"Narii did that?" Mulhall demanded. Grief shook his head. "No; it's from being smashed along the deck and over the house!"

Something suddenly ceased, leaving them all in dizzying uncertainty. For a moment it was hard to realize there was no wind. With the absolute abruptness of a sword slash the wind had been chopped off. The schooner rolled and plunged, fetching up on her anchors with a crash that for the first time they could hear. Also, for the first time, they could hear the water washing about on deck. The engineer threw off the propeller and eased the engine down.

"We're in the dead center," Grief said. "Now for the shift. It will come as hard as ever." He looked at the barometer.

"Twenty-nine thirty-two," he read.

Not in a moment could he tone down the voice which for hours had shouted against the wind, and so loudly did he speak that, in the quiet, it hurt the others' ears.

"All his ribs are smashed," the supercargo said, feeling along Parlay's side. "He's still breathing; but he's a goner."

Old Parlay groaned, moved one arm impotently, and opened his eyes. In them was the light of recognition.

"My brave gentlemen," he whispered haltingly, "don't forget . . . the auction . . . at ten o'clock . . . in hell!"

His eyes drooped shut and the lower jaw threatened to drop, but he mastered the qualms of dissolution long enough to emit one final, loud, derisive cackle.

Above and below pandemonium broke out. The old familiar roar of the wind was with them. The *Malahini*, caught broadside, was pressed down almost on her beam-ends as she swung the arc compelled by her anchors. They rounded her into the wind, where she jerked to an even keel. The propeller was thrown on and the engine took up its work again.

"Northwest!" Captain Warfield shouted to Grief when he came on deck. "Hauled eight points like a shot!"

"Narii'll never get across the lagoon now!" Grief observed.

"Then he'll blow back to our side—worse luck!"

V

After the passing of the center the barometer began to rise. Equally rapid was the fall of the wind. When it was no more than a howling gale the engine lifted up in the air, parted its bedplates with a last convulsive effort of its

forty horsepower, and lay down on its side. A wash of water
from the bilge sizzled over it and the steam rose in clouds.

The engineer wailed his dismay, but Grief glanced over
the wreck affectionately and went into the cabin to swab
the grease off his chest and arms with bunches of cotton
waste.

The sun was up and the gentlest of summer breezes
blowing when he came on deck, after sewing up the scalp
of one Kanaka and setting the other's arm. The *Malahini*
lay close to the beach. For'ard, Hermann and the crew
were heaving in and straightening out the tangle of anchors.

The *Papara* and the *Tahaa* were gone; and Captain Warfield, through the glasses, was searching the opposite rim
of the atoll.

"Not a stick left of them," he said. "That's what comes
of not having engines. They must have dragged across before the big shift came."

Ashore, where Parlay's house had been, was no vestige of
any house. For the space of three hundred yards, where the
sea had breached, no tree or even stump was left. Here
and there, farther along, stood an occasional palm, and there
were numbers which had been snapped off above the
ground.

In the crown of one surviving palm Tai-Hotauri asserted
he saw something move. There were no boats left to the
Malahini, and they watched him swim ashore and climb
the tree.

When he came back they helped over the rail a young
native girl of Parlay's household. But first she passed up to
them a battered basket. In it was a litter of blind kittens—
all dead save one that feebly mewed and staggered on awkward legs.

"Hello!" said Mulhall. "Who's that?"

Along the beach they saw a man walking. He moved
casually, as if out for a morning stroll. Captain Warfield
gritted his teeth. It was Narii Herring.

"Hello, Skipper," Narii called when he was abreast of
them. "Can I come aboard and get some breakfast?"

Captain Warfield's face and neck began to swell and turn
purple. He tried to speak, but choked.

"For two cents . . . ! For two cents . . . !" was all he
could manage to articulate.